SAM CRESCENT

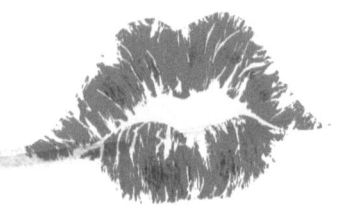

EVERNIGHT PUBLISHING ®

www.evernightpublishing.com

STREET KING

Copyright© 2018

Sam Crescent

Editor: Karyn White

Cover Artist: Jay Aheer

ISBN: 978-1-77339-811-2

ALL RIGHTS RESERVED

SAM CRESCENT

DEDICATION

This is to all the readers that love super possessive, very alpha stalker heroes in their books. I fell in love with West the moment I entered his mind and it has been an amazing ride.

SAM CRESCENT

STREET KING

Sam Crescent

Copyright © 2018

Chapter One

The sound of crunching bones echoed through the warehouse. The sound satisfied West Gallo, as did the scream that followed. Hurting people was something that he enjoyed. Growing up on the worst streets of the city, West had known how to get ahead and to make people follow him.

Fear.

The moment he realized how he could be king of his city, he'd worked tirelessly to get what he wanted. No one stood in his way and got away with it. He ruled this city, and no one stepped out of line. He controlled the MCs, the small gangs, the pimps, the docks, and the cops.

This was his territory, and he made sure his people were properly compensated. Businessmen knew where to invest and how to pay for the right protection. He was, after all, a businessman. The world worked on money. To make money you had to be cruel to be kind. He'd taken down every single person that had stood in his way.

From a young age, he'd made a name for himself in the streets from the fights that were organized. Kids being used to make money. His old man tried to steal the goods from him to buy crack, but he'd soon put an end to that. It wasn't long before his father ended up floating across the river with over twenty knife wounds to his chest.

West had had enough of being anyone's punching bag.

He won every single fight he'd ever fought in. No matter how much he wanted to slam his hand to the ground and beg for them to stop, he'd kept on going until they declared him the winner.

He'd lost count of the number of bones he'd broken. Going from the fighting ring to making his name on the streets hadn't been easy.

Men had thought he was weak.

Had even laughed in his face until they all now bowed to him.

They all did what he said.

He had everything.

Money.

Power.

Women.

Respect.

They all feared him.

"I swear I don't know where he is," the man said between whimpers.

"You're lying to me, and I really hate liars," West said. He sighed and stood up. Removing his jacket, he picked up the sledgehammer, getting a feel for the weight in his hands. It felt good. It would hurt like a fucking bitch the moment it hit someone.

He stared at the man, his target.

The man kept shaking his head.

"You see, Danny—I can call you that, right?" West asked.

Danny nodded his head, looking terrified.

He loved that fear, the knowledge that he was going to get everything he wanted. He released a sigh.

"I trusted Peter to do as I asked, which was to give her a fantastic experience. He's been working with me for years, so he knew the score. He knew what I wanted. You got me? She's smart. Hard-working. You catch where I'm going with this?"

"Please, Mr. Gallo, he didn't mean anything by it."

"He had simple instructions. The experience was what she was after. Workplace experience, and what does she get?" Just thinking about it made him so fucking mad. "He … he pushed her against the fucking wall and made her scream for help. He scared her. No one, and I mean no one, touches her. Do you understand?" His anger increased with every second that passed.

"She wanted it."

That was his first mistake.

Bringing down the sledgehammer, he took out the guy's kneecap.

He waited for the screams to subside and stepped out of the way of the running piss heading toward him. He didn't like it when they pissed or shit. The sight fucking disgusted him.

"Please, please," Danny said.

"She wasn't begging for it, Danny." He tutted. "She was screaming for help, and only when one brave guard decided to break his rule did the bastard stop." West had the tapes.

One of his men had called him that there had been an incident at Hannah Ray's workplace. He'd been a little taken aback to hear that, especially as he'd worked so hard to find the right spot for her in his city.

His men knew what to do. But West discovered that Lawrence Palo had touched her, and not only had he done that, but he'd told all the guards to stay in their places. Only one had reacted to the screams.

It turned out that Lawrence had a thing for young pussy. He liked to prey on them. He made them work late, and when he was one of the last people in the building with them, that was when he made his move.

West had also been informed of the money he paid to the guards. The one that had called him gave the money straight to West, saying he didn't agree with that shit. He couldn't sit back and listen as a woman screamed for help. For that, West had promoted him. Doubled his salary and offered him a job as one of his security men.

There were many things West was capable of. Raping women was not one of them. There had been women that had betrayed him in the past, and killing them was not a pleasure. He'd not tortured them. They'd been handled swiftly.

Growing up, he'd watched his mother constantly take a punch to the face or a beating with the belt. He'd been too young to do anything. All she'd wanted to do was to have the best for them both. Having a crack addict for a husband hadn't been easy, and she'd ended up taking her own life with the shit his father loved so much.

West could even remember the day she killed herself. She'd been in the bathroom, and his father had been moaning about not having any food. The moment they entered that room, he'd watched his father break down. At the time he'd thought his dad had truly loved her. Now with a cynical heart, he wondered if he was mourning the crack she'd used up to kill herself.

"Where is he?" West asked.

"I don't know. You're going to kill me anyway."

"Yes, I am, but you see, tell me now and I'll end it quick, or I can make you live until I find him. Believe me, you're going to want to take the first option."

Danny whimpered. It was a rather pitiful sound.

Stepping away from the man, he waited.

His men had seen this before many times. He liked to play, and it unnerved many of his enemies. Getting other people to do dirty work was great, but he felt there was always a lack of respect from others. That the true power was never inside him, but in his men.

The way he worked, he was the one with all the power.

"Please," Danny said. "I've got kids."

One of his men snorted.

This wasn't the first time West had dealt with men who wanted to use their kids to make some kind of power play.

"You have?" West asked.

Danny nodded.

"Well that just makes all the difference in the world, doesn't it? I mean, I should just let you go and live your life. Completely forget about the betrayal to me? You were there to keep an eye on him, and because he gave you some money and dope, you thought you could do whatever the hell you want."

"She's not worth it."

West grabbed the fucker around the neck.

No one told him who was or wasn't worth his time.

"Where is he?" West asked.

"Fuck you!"

Danny spat in his face, and West released his neck, took out a handkerchief and wiped the spittle away. There was blood mixed in with the spit.

He'd decided on the hard way.

That was fine.

West could work with that.

"It looks like Danny will be with us for some time. Rome, let's make him a bit more comfortable, shall we?"

He watched as Rome and Cage picked Danny up. They moved him toward the cuffs that were hanging from a beam in the warehouse. With Danny's feet broken, he couldn't hold himself up.

This wouldn't have happened if he'd just told him the fucking truth.

"What next?" Rome asked.

"Keep him there. One of you good to keep watch?"

Cage lifted up his phone. "I've got a good book I just started."

Rome shook his head. "He's a badass, remember."

"I got no problem. Make sure he doesn't get away," West said.

Leaving the warehouse, he breathed in the scent of fresh air, closing the door on Danny's screams.

"I want all eyes out looking for Lawrence. Contact the tech guys, the ones at street level. Also put the word out. Anyone protecting him will be met with swift punishment."

"Will do," Rome said. "You want us to grab him the moment there's a sighting or wait for you?"

"I want to know the moment he's been sighted. Get him, take him to the warehouse. You know what to do, but don't kill. That fucker will not get out of here alive. I want to play with him a little."

"Okay."

West moved toward his car.

He didn't have guards riding with him unless he was making certain visits and needed the extra muscle.

"West?" Rome asked.

"What is it?"

Rome had been with him for nearly ten years now. He'd found him at the bottom of a trashcan. Doped up, raped, and beaten. Instead of leaving him to rot, West had taken him home, nursed him back to health, and learned his story. When Rome had gotten over his addictions, together they'd gone out and made every single fucker pay for what they did to him. Rome had been born into a world that only hoped to use him. They'd taken him, abused him, and left him broken.

West had made him whole.

"What is it?"

"I was wondering if I could have next weekend off?" Rome asked.

Next weekend was the anniversary of when West discovered him. The day that Rome considered his birthday.

"Of course. Every year you ask and every year I give you the same answer."

"With Lawrence on the loose, I wanted to make sure I can still take that time." Rome admitted himself into a rehab clinic for two days every year to keep himself on the straight and narrow.

"Even if we don't have Lawrence by next weekend, you can take the time, Rome. You've more than earned it."

With that, he climbed into his car and drove back into the city toward his penthouse suite.

He parked in the secure underground facility and pressed in his code for the top floor. No other apartments were there and he owned the entire building, so he knew what went on at every single level.

Closing the door, he switched on the lights, poured himself a scotch, and stood at the windows overlooking his empire.

Right this second, he was making hundreds of thousands of dollars, and he wasn't even having to lift a finger. This was what he liked more than anything. The hard work he'd put in gave him this life.

Finishing off his scotch, he made his way toward his computer room that one of his tech guys had installed for him.

Firing up the computer, he brought up the evening's events. There she was, sitting behind her desk at six in the evening. She had started at six as well. A twelve-hour day and she looked so fucking tired. Her hair was no longer neatly pulled into a bun but had strands of hair escaping. The suit she wore, so conservative to hide her full figure, was wrinkled.

She looked weary, even to him.

When Lawrence appeared on the screen, West saw her nerves. She bit her lip and looked toward the zone where he knew the elevators were. She didn't want to do whatever Lawrence had said. She wanted to escape.

With gritted teeth, he waited and watched as Lawrence started to attack her in his office.

West had an entire network of security cameras and documents, along with the men and women who knew how to run everything. Nothing got past any of his people. He knew everything that was going down, and with a few codes in his computers he was able to bring up all of his businesses.

Loyalty was something that always had a limit.

Money and greed tended to bring people down. Those were the two things in life that seemed to lure people away. West liked to keep on top of it, constantly prepared for the worst.

Nothing had ever gotten in his way before. He'd always been like this, constantly checking, keeping an eye on everything in his spare time. The women that had been in his life before *she* entered had only been mere distractions. Women were to be played with, not kept. Being wealthy meant he had a lot of women who wanted to try to win him as a prize. He couldn't blame them. Look at his kingdom.

However, one evening with Hannah Ray and no other woman would do. The days after that first meeting, he'd not given her much thought. He'd gone about his day as if he didn't have a care in the world. Trying to take another woman out to dinner though, had changed everything. Something had felt off with another woman opposite him as he took her out to dinner. He'd wanted it to end the moment the date began. It was the last date he ever went on.

Grabbing his cell phone, he dialed Emily's number.

It rang three times before she finally answered.

"Hey," she said.

"How is she?"

"Just a moment. Anna, I got to take this, okay?"

He heard her respond, and the sound of her voice soothed the beast that wanted to snip at Emily for shortening her name. Her name was Hannah, not Anna or Han or any other combination.

Still, he wasn't about to berate her while he could be heard.

The sound of a door closing filled the line and then Emily was back. "What's up?"

"How is she?" He repeated the question.

Emily sighed. "Seriously, West, she's fine. Last night was a bit rough. She had a nightmare, but after we talked it through she was more than fine. You've got to stop worrying. She's stronger than she looks. Give her the benefit of the doubt."

"I want you to be by her side for the next week, understood?"

"I'm already there."

It was what he paid her to do. Not that Emily ever brought up the money or the reason she played Hannah's best friend. He'd found her in the gutter over five years ago. He'd gotten her clean, given her the job, and she was even getting an education out of it, which he provided along with the fake family.

Yes, he wanted Hannah to have all the experiences of a best friend, a life, before he took it all from her.

****

Hannah took a sip of the overly sweet tea that Emily had made her. She wrinkled her nose, hating anything sweet, especially in tea or coffee. She preferred to drink water, but Emily was insistent that a nice brew helped soothe the soul.

Not wanting to upset her best friend, she put up with it, drinking it without gagging.

"Sorry about that," Emily said, coming back into the room.

"It's no biggie." She stared down at the book she'd been reading. Some sappy love story where the hero had been the world's biggest dick and was trying to make it up to the heroine. They were the best kind of romances, but right now she was pissed.

"How are you feeling?" Emily asked.

"Fine, why?"

"You're rubbing your shoulder again."

Hannah glanced at the shoulder that her boss had grabbed. He'd slammed her against the wall and she'd hit the edge of a shelf. The doctors had looked her over and said she'd be fine, more than fine. There was nothing wrong with her. It still hurt though. She hated to think of what would've happened if that guard hadn't come to her screams. She'd been surprised only one person did. Not that it mattered. She hadn't seen Lawrence since. She already had a resignation letter ready to give to the firm.

She hated the whispers that followed her around and everyone knowing her business.

"I'm sorry. I guess I just can't stop thinking about it."

"It's understandable. The guy was a total douche. Do you know what is going to happen?"

"I filed a sexual assault report, and they alerted HR. I can't stay there though. It'll drive me nuts. Everyone will stare at me."

"It can't be that bad."

"It is. It really is. I don't know what to do, but I can't stay there. I'm going to have to find another post that will offer workplace experience." She ran fingers through her hair. Graduating college and getting an experience application with Lawrence Palo had been one of the best things that had ever happened to her. He was a well-known womanizer, but she didn't for a second think something like this would happen. She'd heard horror stories, but it wasn't like she was the most beautiful woman in the building. With long, brown hair, brown eyes, and preferring to spend most of her years with her head in a book, she knew there was no way any guy would fall for her. She was the one nominated to be the world's oldest virgin. Right now, at twenty-three, that was looking like she was right on track.

She'd gone on a few dates in college. They'd been out dancing and having fun. She thought she really connected with a couple of guys only for them to disappear for a couple of minutes and return ... different.

They wouldn't look at her and were constantly checking other women out. They'd gone from being attentive to downright jerks.

"I don't think you should do that. You've wanted to be in the financial sector for a long time and I know Lawrence was a jerk, but they're not going to let him back."

"What if they do? It's my word against his, and I'm just a graduate, Emily. What if I have to work with him?"

Emily held her shoulders. "Listen to me closely. Lawrence isn't coming back. Believe me. I know you're never going to have to see him again."

Tears filled Hannah's eyes. "You're sure?"

"I'm positive." Emily released her. "Let me go and make you some more tea."

She didn't have the heart to tell her friend even after all this time that she hated tea.

Getting to her feet, she picked up the resignation letter and wasn't sure what to do with it. If Lawrence wasn't going to be there then why send it in? She'd give it a couple of weeks and see what happened at work before making a final decision.

Pushing some hair out of her face, she got to her feet. Working in the financial sector wasn't exactly a dream job. She was good with numbers, always had been. They didn't lie to her or annoy her. They were there, plain and simple.

She'd been told to try for teaching, but the thought of teaching any kids filled her with a deep pit of depression. Kids were horrible, at least from what she remembered of them, and it wasn't all that long ago she'd experienced that.

Putting the resignation letter back in her bedroom, she found Emily on her cell phone.

"I've been so selfish. How has your job been?" Hannah asked.

They hadn't seen each other in a few weeks.

"Oh, you know. It's the same. It's been fun to work for West Gallo. He has many ventures, restaurants, nightclubs, casinos, that kind of thing. I help to organize interviews and make stops in each of his endeavors and report back."

"I've never heard of him or any of his companies."

"The nightclubs are the best in town. Be warned though, he does have a few strip clubs as well."

"Oh, well, to each their own. You know my thoughts on that."

Emily burst out laughing. "I don't see there being any male strip clubs any time soon."

This had been a debate in one of their study groups. For some reason strip clubs had been mentioned, and because they'd considered her a goody-two-shoes, they'd made a comment about not offending her delicate sensibilities. That had really pissed her off. She followed the rules because that's what everyone had to do. It didn't for a second make her a prude or lack any sexual desire or even crave something dirty. She'd told them simply that she had no desire to see another woman's tits but she wouldn't mind going to a strip club where men got down and dirty.

That had shocked the entire table.

Being a virgin wasn't by choice.

No.

She'd been on a few dates, and none of them wanted her goods.

So instead of screwing her way through college, she'd read books. Not just the sappy romance kind either that she loved. There were a select few books that she hid in her room that were hers to read in private.

Dark books.

Books that pushed all of her limits. Giving absolute control to a man that may be even dangerous at times. That kind of darkness, the fear, the lure of the unknown called to her. A distant memory in the back of her mind that was still a bit fuzzy. One she tried not to think about or talk about as she didn't know if it was dream or a memory.

"It's a shame, really. It would teach husbands a thing or two of how it feels when they go off and see another woman's tits. I should make a note of that," Hannah said, grabbing her notebook of dreams.

"What note?"

"Being a financial advisor and knowing how to handle money, I'm going to put some aside and look into opening my own male strip club."

"Really?" Emily asked.

"Yes. I think it would be a huge hit. I mean, not to the prudes in our country but certainly to the women that want to have a bit of fun and not see another woman's tits." After making a note, she closed the book and smiled at her friend.

Every now and then she caught Emily staring at her, like she was trying to figure something out. Not for the first time she wondered if Emily was actually her friend or if she was just the easy option in college.

Her previous roommate got expelled for drug use, and before the first semester was out, Emily was in and they were sharing a room. It had been a lot of fun, and she adored her friend. She just wished she knew what she was thinking.

"You know what?" Emily asked, putting a cup in front of her.

"What?"

"I think we should go to one the nightclubs I work for. Get you out on the town and, you know, stop all those bad thoughts about your boss."

She wrinkled her nose. "Last time we went out to party, you abandoned me and no one would dance with me." She was so worried that she stank, she'd poured a whole can of deodorant all over herself to help mask any scent that seemed to be keeping the men away.

"I promise not to abandon you. Come on. It'll be fun. I know you've had a bad experience. All men are jerks. Believe me, I've had all kinds of per—erm, guys that, you know, have tried a thing or two. Don't let them bring you down." Emily touched her arm and smiled.

"You're sure?"

"Hell, yeah, I'm sure. I won't leave your side. We'll have a few drinks, dance together. It'll be fun. You know. Just you and me."

"Count me in."

"Awesome. Now, I'm going to go out and get us some dinner. You want to come for the walk?"

"Nah, it's okay. I'll catch up on a few things here. Clean up a little."

"You're sure?"

"Yeah. I don't want to head out."

"I'll get your usual," Emily said.

She watched her friend leave their apartment. The sound of the lock clicking into place echoed around the room. There were four additional locks on the inside, but she wasn't about to slide them into place, not with Emily needing to come back inside.

Gripping the back of her neck, she released a breath and glanced around the room. Everywhere was spotless. Since coming home after Lawrence's attack, she'd done nothing but clean.

Biting her lip, she walked over to the sofa and

plumped up the pillows for the hundredth time that day. This apartment had been a steal when they'd graduated. Fully furnished with a decent rental agreement. Actually, more than decent. When she saw the space and knew what the rent was, she'd asked to see the landlord or manager because someone was clearly ripping him off.

Of course, Emily told her not to worry about it. That she shouldn't go insulting their potential landlord by offering money advice. She couldn't help it though. She liked to help people, and knowing her parents into their late years hadn't been able to live with ease, she'd vowed to help anyone who wanted it. Money was a pain in the ass as far as she was concerned. People needed it as it made life a hell of a lot easier, but it didn't make for a good life.

Pushing those thoughts aside, she moved around the apartment, putting little pieces of paper back in their place and then checking the pictures. Before she completely lost her mind and started rearranging furniture she made her way into her bedroom. Sitting on the edge of the bed, she ran her hands up and down her thighs.

Something was bothering her, and she didn't know what it was.

Needing to distract herself, she kicked off her shoes and moved up the bed, grabbing the secret book she was currently reading. This was a capture book. A young woman had been taken, and the hero was the girl's captor.

The scenes always became tense as he came down into the cell where he kept her. He fed her but wouldn't allow her to be clothed. She was always open and exposed to him. She hated that before he'd taken her he'd been the guy she'd been lusting after. That was what made it so hard for her.

Her captor turned her on, and she hated that.

So whenever he touched her there was always a conflict.

She didn't want to respond, but in the end, she always did.

Opening up the book to the last page she read, Hannah saw the heroine was still strapped to the bed where he'd kept her. The book was told in the heroine's thoughts, and no one knew why she'd been taken, only that there was no way out for her.

Reading through the next couple of pages, he continued to tease her. To stroke her body, to arouse. No pain had happened as of yet, and that was okay. He liked to bring her to the brink of pleasure before ever letting her fall over the edge.

Hannah waited with bated breath as he spread the heroine's legs. He climbed onto the bed, and there was nowhere for her to go. The heroine didn't want to fight him. She hated this feeling, of being open to him and hating him at the same time. The memory of one of their dates flashed before her eyes, of his charming smile. She couldn't believe that this was the same man that she really had feelings for.

Just as he was about to touch her pussy, to slide his fingers inside, Hannah heard the door open. Putting the bookmark back inside, she placed the book back in her drawer beneath a couple of health magazines.

Pushing some of her hair out of the way, she wondered if she should get it cut. She kept thinking about getting the long length, which was now midway down her back it was so long. She hated going to the stylists though. They never listened to what she wanted.

"Anna, I've got food."

She couldn't get that book out of her mind.

What would it be like to be at a man's mercy? To

have him stroke your body until you couldn't think straight? She'd never been touched, not by a man. There had been one guy in high school she'd kissed, and that was all. Nothing else had happened, especially when they got caught and the boy had been teased about having a thing for a fat girl. She tried not to dwell on all of that though.

The past was going to stay there.

Leaving her bedroom, she found Emily in the kitchen, Chinese food spread out for them to eat.

"Wow, that didn't take long at all."

"I called ahead so they had it ready to go. I walked fast as well." Emily put her cell phone away. "You clear your head?"

"A little, yeah. I feel much better." She grabbed a carton of Chinese food and wondered if such a man was even real for her to find. It seemed too good to even be possible to consider.

It wasn't that she wanted a man who would hurt her. The risk of being tortured and killed didn't exactly turn her on. Those parts of the books didn't appeal to her. She didn't want to get slapped around and fear for her life. Far from it. It was the potential danger of giving herself to a man who could do what he wanted without anyone being there to stop him. Even though she loved to read about it that experience with Lawrence made her feel sick to her stomach.

When she could, she'd throw all of those books out and never look back at them again.

Chapter Two

West looked through the files that were piled high on his desk. Lawrence hadn't been located, and his little minion would soon be dead. There was only so much torture they could do before a man finally gave in. Danny was holding on by a thread, but he clearly didn't have a clue where Lawrence was. West made a note to put the bastard out of his misery later tonight. Lawrence clearly knew when to get the hell out of dodge, but that pissed him off because it meant he had to put extra men onto hunting him down.

There's no way he'd let the fucker leave.

Rubbing at his temples, West tried to clear his head, but he couldn't, not until he had everything under control. Fortunately, Dirty was running smoothly. His latest nightclub was a huge hit, especially as it was connected to celebrities as well as anyone from the local public that was happy to pay the flat fee to enter. He paid handsomely for the latest and best DJs. When it came to his legal businesses he liked to make sure they were a success. It paid him to have money coming in this way. He paid his taxes, which made it hard for law enforcement to pin anything on him. They couldn't find any crime that was linked to him. Nothing that could put him in jail. There would always be rumors, but he would never be caught.

There was a knock at the door, and a second later, Rome entered.

"Sir, Emily's here."

He was getting tired of that woman's attention. She had a job to do, and it didn't involve stalking him.

"And she's with Hannah?"

Putting his pen down, he tapped into the nightclub's security feed and found the exact point she arrived. Ten minutes ago, wearing a small black dress that molded to every single curve and any man with eyes would see just how fucking sexy she looked. He was pissed off.

Following their path, he saw they were at the bar and as he sped up the footage, they remained at the bar. Spinning around, he looked down over his nightclub and there she was. Hannah Ray, sitting at his bar, flirting with the bartender.

"Cage is already heading toward the bartender, West," Rome said.

His closest men knew how important it was to keep Hannah safe, but *only* those closest to him were aware. He put a small security detail on her of two men, besides his own, and they were to keep her safe at all times when he wasn't there. His reach and money were far and great, but there were times when she could come and go without being seen, which was why he had men on it.

Pulling his gaze away from Hannah's fine ass, he checked the club and sure enough, the two men, James and Robert, were there in the nightclub, looking like single men waiting to find a woman. They always played their part well.

They made sure the men who thought they had a chance with Hannah learned their place. Running a hand down his face, he returned his attention to Emily. She was glancing up at the office as she knew where it was. In the past few months, she'd gotten ... clingy. She hadn't made any overt attempts on him, but he saw it in her eyes, the way she looked at him. After these past five years, she was aware of the kind of man he was, the power he held. Like most women, she was addicted to it.

"What would you like me to do?" Rome asked.

"Make sure she has a good time."

He saw Hannah was smiling and her foot was tapping to the beat of the music. She looked relaxed, and as much as he wanted her out of his damn club and away from any danger, he couldn't bring himself to upset her.

"You're sure?"

"Yes."

Returning to his desk, he brought up the camera near the bar and saw her talking with the bartender still. She wasn't flirting at all, just talking.

He couldn't believe she was in one of his clubs or that it wasn't terrifying her.

"I will go and keep watch," Rome said.

"Any news on Lawrence?" West asked.

"Nothing yet, sir. Our contacts believe he's snuck off to a hotel. A flag came up of him trying to get out of the country. Our team was at the airport and the surrounding hotels within the hour, but nothing. He's not out of the country, and we've now got men close to all the airports just in case."

"Does he have anyone who would be willing to help him?"

"No, sir. We've checked all of his contacts. Lawrence wasn't a well-liked man, and seeing as you've put a bounty on his head, unless they don't know who you are, no one is helping him."

"That's what I like to hear." He tapped away on his keyboard, typing in the code to access another camera.

When it came to Hannah he knew everything there was to know about her. Her passions, her loves, everything. From that first meeting all those years ago until now, he'd delved into her life, from the moment she was registered as a newborn through to now. He was a crazy motherfucker; he knew that.

What Hannah didn't know was they had met on

the day she turned eighteen years old. It wasn't a significant meeting by any means. It was what happened a few months after that cemented the obsession he had for her.

Thinking back all those years, he wondered what point it was that he realized that he wanted her. That first meeting, or the one a few months after? Both had stuck with him. Their first meeting he'd not been able to stop thinking about her. She'd been so sweet, so beautiful, so kind, and he'd been so taken aback by her bluntness that he'd not been able to hold back from talking to her.

Pushing those thoughts aside, he finished signing a few employees' paychecks, glanced through some order forms, signed them, and was just finishing up a report when there was a knock on the door.

"Come in," he said.

He knew it wasn't going to be Rome. Unless he gave the order to be left alone, Rome knocked and entered.

Emily walked in, closing the door behind her, hips swaying from side to side, and looking so confident it grated on his nerves.

She'd forgotten her place in the world. The one where she was nothing more than a bug.

"Hey, West," she said.

She sat down in the seat across from him. Her long, fake blonde hair fell around her in waves. She had large tits, a tiny waist, and thick lips that were designed to wrap around a man's dick.

He knew this for a fact seeing as she'd been a whore that worked the streets.

Sitting back in his chair, he looked at her. She'd not touched another drug since she'd been in place with Hannah. She'd done her job well.

He'd also made her aware that nothing would

ever happen between them. He didn't want her. She didn't even matter to him.

If someone was to come and shoot her in the head right now in his office, he'd demand they clean it up and then go and help Hannah home. That's how little this woman meant to him.

She was merely someone he needed at the time. He'd have gotten her killed now.

Killing women didn't sit well with him and he often made sure it didn't happen, but that didn't for a second mean he wouldn't do it.

If Emily continued to push or press or do whatever it was she kept on fucking doing, he would have no choice but to strike out and hurt her.

"What are you doing, Emily?" he asked.

"I brought her here for you. She's more than ready, you know. For whatever you have in store for her." Emily leaned back, crossing her legs.

He wasn't interested in her flirting.

"You know you could have any woman, West. Any woman would be willing to do whatever it is your heart desires."

"Your job is to give her a friend that doesn't abandon her, and you leave her alone in my nightclub, going against my rules." He stood up and moved around his desk. "You think I don't know what is going on here, Emily? You think I don't see past the little games that you play?" He reached out, wrapping his fingers around her neck and tightening his hold. "You need to remember your place in this world. You're nothing but a dirty whore who likes to fuck around with heroin just as much as you love to suck on cock. I remember where you came from. You're not what I want. You'll never be the kind of woman I want." He squeezed her neck, cutting off her air supply.

He saw the flash of fear in her eyes, and he loved that.

Relished it.

She was a fucking bitch.

Nothing more than a whore and he didn't want to put his dick anywhere near her.

"If you put Hannah in danger I will make you pray for death long before you get it. Do you understand me?"

He released her neck long enough for her to speak.

"Yes, sir." Her voice came out on a gasp and a croak.

"Good." He leaned in close. "Remember that."

He let her go, grabbed her arm, and hauled her out of his office. "Now do your fucking job."

Slamming the door closed, he walked back to his desk, brought up the camera, and watched her.

She made her way back toward the dance floor where Hannah was still fucking waiting at the bar.

If Emily said one thing out of place he would fucking end her. He was growing tired of her games. They were not welcome.

She put on her best fake smile as she approached Hannah. He waited as they both started laughing together. They did look like good friends.

There were times he wondered if it was all an act for Emily. If she just had feelings for him, or if it was the power. Emily may like Hannah right now, but that was because he'd not made his move just yet. Once he did and she was in her rightful place at his side, he wondered how Emily's friendship would fare then. When she realized without a doubt that he meant to keep Hannah all to himself.

He already had a plan in mind to get rid of Emily,

if necessary.

She was addicted to money, and as soon as he had Hannah distracted, Emily was out of the picture. Getting rid of Emily right now wouldn't work. Hannah adored her. Emily leaving or disappearing would hurt her.

Everything had to be carefully organized and work exactly how he planned.

Running a hand down his face, he felt that need to go and speak to her. To touch her. To remember that she was real to him. That he'd touched her before, five years ago. When she'd been in his arms, telling him all of her secrets, making his realize just what a sweet woman she was, and how she needed protecting.

Emily pulled Hannah onto the dance floor. Clicking away again, he brought up another camera that showed them having a good time. He saw his men watching, keeping an eye to make sure she was safe.

If anyone ever discovered who she was and what she meant to him, her life would be in danger. It was why he'd been so careful not to let anyone but his closest and most loyal men near her. He trusted them with his own life. Hannah's life was more important than his. It was why he needed to deal with Lawrence. If he decided to reach out to any potential rival—and West did have them—all it would take was her name being mentioned and she'd be used against him.

Emily continued to dance with her, and he was happy once again. He didn't like for Hannah to be alone. With her parents dead, there was no other relative to take care of her or to look out for her.

Finishing up his work, he found himself watching her. This was what he'd struggled with. The amount of time he was just happy to sit back and watch her. She wasn't like other women that he'd met.

She was sweet. Kind. Caring.

Not a nasty bone in her body.

Growing up, she'd do sponsored walks to help charities, and on her weekends, she'd help out at local animal shelters. There had been so many pictures of her in newspapers, not as the main focal piece but someone in the background. Her love of life, animals, and just everything in general fascinated him.

Her need to make a career in finance was also selfless. Her parents had been ill-advised with their money, and so toward their later years—they'd had Hannah late in life—they couldn't afford to send her to college, and with their illnesses, they had mountains of debt.

He'd taken care of all of that.

Hannah's special scholarship was paid out of his own pocket through a shell company. She didn't ask many questions as to why she had been given certain things, and that made it a lot easier.

Staring at the screen, he saw a couple of men were near Hannah and Emily. He didn't have a problem with Emily screwing whomever she wanted. What he had a problem with was when that interfered with Hannah.

Would it really hurt for him to go and spend some time with her? To talk to her? To dance with her?

He'd kept his distance this long, but he was growing tired of waiting. He wanted her.

Was desperate for her.

He ached to be with her.

No other woman would ever do, so he'd not been with anyone else since that second meeting with her.

She was his everything, and she didn't even realize he existed. Getting to his feet, he made a decision. It wouldn't be long now, so bringing forward this introduction wouldn't be a problem.

Everything had gone to plan so far.

He'd waited all this time.

He didn't see a problem with finally taking what belonged to him.

****

Emily tried to hide it, but Hannah saw something was bugging her friend. The music was so loud and the noise so addictive she couldn't help but ignore that niggling feeling that she was being watched.

She tried to distract her friend from whatever had bugged her. Ever since they moved out of their dorm to their new apartment and started their own jobs, Emily had been acting strangely. Whenever she asked her friend what was wrong, she'd tell her the same thing. Nothing was bugging her or wrong.

Her friend was lying to her, and it annoyed her.

Ever since Emily had joined her in the dorms, she'd felt an instant friendship that had blossomed over the years that they'd been together. Study buddies, friends, keepers of each other's secrets. She adored Emily's family as well. She'd gone to stay with them over festive breaks and shared so much with them. Emily was the sister she'd never had.

"Hello, sexy," a man said, moving up behind her.

He wrapped an arm around her waist, and she gasped. His hard cock pressed against her ass, and it startled her a lot. She wasn't used to this kind of attention, or any kind actually.

"I think I'd like to take you home."

She gave his hand a shove. "No, thank you."

No, thank you?

Who said "no, thank you" to a guy that was pawing at her?

"Come on, baby. Don't be like that. Everyone knows women here just want to party."

"Hey, let her go," Emily said, coming forward.

"I'll party with you after I get done with this one."

Emily did no more than grab the man's fingers and yank them back. He dropped to the floor, and Emily let him go.

Within seconds they were back at the bar, and the man wasn't following them.

"Wow, you're going to have to show me your moves," Hannah said, laughing. "I had no idea what to do."

"It's nothing. Just some safety moves I've been taught. Anyone can do them." Emily looked toward the dance floor. "It's all good now. He's gone."

Hannah glanced in the direction, and sure enough, men were moving him off the dance floor. "Wow, that security is tight."

"Yeah. This place doesn't like that kind of thing. You know?"

"Can I get a drink for my friend here?" Hannah said, calling to the bartender.

He gave her a nod and finished serving another couple.

"Are you having fun?" Hannah asked, wanting to find out what was wrong with her friend.

"Yeah, I was having fun. You okay if I go and finish my dance before he finds someone else?"

"Oh, yeah, sure. Go right ahead. I'm so sorry—"

Emily was already gone, so pressing her lips together, Hannah leaned against the bar, watching everything going on around her.

Something was bugging her friend, but what scared her the most was that she actually believed it was herself that was the problem. If Emily didn't want to be friends anymore, then she needed to know what to do to either fix it, or to ask Emily what they ought to do. They lived together.

This was not a complication that she'd foreseen.

Tapping her fingers on the back of the bar, she watched as Emily smiled at the man who wrapped an arm around her, his hand splayed across her stomach.

Not for the first time, she wondered what that would be like. To have a man hold her so possessively as if he couldn't get enough of touching her.

Forcing herself to look away, she stood at the bar and wondered what the hell she was doing here. She could be at home looking for a new job, cleaning, or reading.

She still hadn't gotten rid of those books that she promised herself she would.

Pushing some hair off her face, she wondered if she should get it cut. The long locks were starting to irritate her once again.

"Hey," a guy said, coming to stand beside her.

At first, she didn't think he was talking to her, but then he gave her shoulder a nudge.

Glancing to her right, she saw a man. He was older than she was, but she didn't know by how much.

"Hey," she said. She always found it rude to ignore people.

"You're looking a little lost. You okay?"

She frowned before smiling. "I'm fine. Thank you. I'm just trying to think of a few things."

There was something vaguely familiar about him, but she didn't have a clue. Instead of asking though, she just stood there, wondering what she was going to do about her apartment, about Emily.

There's no way she'd beg her friend to stick around. She'd never begged anyone for anything.

"What can I get you, sir?" the barman asked.

"A scotch, neat, and whatever this young woman

is having?"

"Oh, thank you, you don't have to do that."

"My treat."

"I can pay for it myself." She didn't want him to think she was waiting around for someone to buy her a drink.

"It's my treat. Don't worry. I won't expect anything from you."

That was weird, because she didn't think for a second that he would.

"I'll just take a bottled water."

"You're not drinking?"

"Me and drink don't go together. I can usually handle one glass but after that, nope." She pressed her lips together. Emily told her she was an over-sharer.

"That's rather charming."

In the lights shining around the bar, she noticed he had really light blond hair. The kind that women would love to run their fingers through. It wasn't messy, but she wanted to make it messy. Ignoring the impulse to touch him, she was struck by his intense blue eyes. They were bright and clear, like the ocean. Beautiful and deadly at the same time. She felt a shiver work up her spine and quickly looked away. No man had ever made her feel that way and that quickly in such a short space of time.

Out of the corner of her eye, she watched him reach for the bottled water. He opened the cap and placed it in front of her. The jacket he wore pulled back, revealing some ink around his wrists. She couldn't figure out what it was, but then she realized he was a businessman.

Out of all the men here, there were only a few that wore business suits. Everyone else was in pants or jeans, dressed to party. Not him.

Pushing some hair off her face, she picked up the bottle and took a generous sip. Spinning around, she rested her back against the bar and watched as Emily continued to have her body touched all over right there on the dance floor.

Men couldn't seem to help themselves around her. It was like she wore a neon sign to touch or something like that.

"How do you like the club?" he asked, drawing her attention away from the yearning she felt for her friend.

"I'm sorry?"

"The club? How are you finding it?"

"Oh, it's amazing. Thank you. You?"

He smiled. "I love it, but then, I own it."

"You own this?"

"Yes, I do."

She frowned trying to recall what Emily had said to her. "Wait, you're Emily's boss?"

"Emily?"

"Oh, my friend. She's out on the dance floor." He went to look, but she grabbed his arm. If he didn't like his employees coming to his clubs to party or picking up guys, she didn't want to get her friend in trouble. "I don't know if you know her. She works in one of your offices downtown. She overlooks the…" She came to a complete stop. Emily had never really told her what she did. "She sings your praises a lot. Says how you've worked your way up in the world."

"She talks about me?"

"Yes." Right that second, she couldn't remember his name, and that was starting to bug her. "West."

"That's me. West Gallo." He held his hand out, and she took it.

She went to shake his hand, but he drew hers up

to his lips and pressed a kiss to her wrist.

"I'm at a disadvantage."

Hannah didn't like how much that small kiss affected her. It's not like she hadn't had men kiss her wrist before, but there was something about that kiss that not only seemed familiar but it was like she'd lived it before.

"Disadvantage?"

"You know my name, but I don't know yours."

"Oh, right. I'm so sorry. It's Hannah. Hannah Ray." She tilted her head to the side and smiled. He was her best friend's boss. "So, a nightclub owner."

"I have many other ventures, believe me."

"I know. Emily says you've got nightclubs and a casino, and I'm so sorry. She mentioned a couple of other things, but I can't seem to remember what they were. Would you like me to get her for you?"

"No, that's all right. I'm quite happy to stay here talking with you."

She struggled not to blush, not that she had any control over what her face actually did.

"So, Hannah Ray, do you have a boyfriend lurking around?"

"No. No boyfriend. I came here with my friend."

"And she left you here?"

"She wanted to dance. I'm happy to be here." She didn't want Emily to get in trouble, which seemed ridiculous. She wasn't being paid to babysit her or anything.

She took a sip of her water, and she wished talking to guys came naturally to her. When they were at work, she could talk all day long and it was not a problem. Right now, though, she didn't have the first clue what to say.

Turning back to face the bar, she glanced at him

in the mirror across the bar behind all the bottles of drinks.

He was looking at her, and when she turned her head toward him, sure enough, his gaze was on her.

When she stared into his eyes, she couldn't look away. Trapped within his gaze, she felt her entire body heat up.

She'd never known a heat like this or the feelings that were filling her up. Her tits felt heavy and her pussy slick.

No man had ever looked at her like this, as if he could really *see* her. It was somewhat hypnotic.

This gaze her a taste of what it would be like to have a man want her.

To be hungry just for her.

"Excuse me, handsome," a woman said, tapping West on the shoulder.

Their gazes broke, and as Hannah pulled away just a little, she was able to give herself a shake. She didn't know what the hell was going on, just that she didn't want to pull away.

Get a grip, Hannah.

"I was wondering if you'd like to buy me a drink," the woman said.

"I find you incredibly rude. Leave."

She looked up to see the shock on the woman's face. Whoever she was, she clearly didn't expect to be treated like that.

"Are you kidding me right now? Seriously? I come over here after you've been eye-fucking me and this is what I get?"

"Miss, we're going to have to ask you to leave." A security guard came up to the bar.

Hannah couldn't believe what she was seeing.

"This is horseshit. I can't believe this is

happening. Do you know who I am?"

"This is my club, and I don't take kindly to being spoken to that way. Get her out of here," West said.

Hannah watched as the two men, the security guards patrolling the building, removed the woman from the building.

"I have to apologize for that. Sometimes people don't know any respect."

"No, it's fine. If you wanted to go and dance with her or something, I wouldn't have minded."

"Hannah, I'm trying to get *you* onto the dance floor. Not that woman."

"You are?"

"Yes. I don't know how to ask, but would you like to dance with me?" He held his hand out to her, and she couldn't help but think of the devil as he did. It was so stupid to think of such a thing.

Every single part of her mind was screaming at her not to take this man's hand. That it was dangerous but she didn't know why. Nothing made any sense to her. Her body lit up like a Christmas tree when he looked at her. The intense need that consumed her frightened her a little.

Against all those warnings going off inside her head, she took his hand and followed him onto the dance floor.

One look around and a couple of people seemed a little taken aback. Did they all know him? She'd never heard of him until Emily mentioned him.

Just as they got onto the floor, the DJ changed the song, telling people this was for lovers.

Something wasn't right. She didn't know what it was, but it was there as he wrapped his arms around her back, pulling her close. He took her arms, placing them around the back of his neck.

His rock-hard body was hard for her to ignore as it rubbed against her.

She felt open, exposed, and in so much need it was unreal.

The scent of something musky, spicy, and incredibly arousing clung to him. This man, so large, six feet if not a few inches taller, wanted to dance with her. This never happened in her world.

It seemed almost too good to be true.

One song led into another, and she didn't want the dancing to stop. West didn't run his hands down her body, grip her ass, or make any lewd comments, and yet she was turned on.

"You're good at this," she said, needing some sound other than the slow beat of the romantic music that was playing.

Only a few couples remained on the dance floor, and she noticed Emily wasn't one of the couples.

Resting her head against his chest, she closed her eyes and felt weird. This was all strange to her, but she wasn't about to tell him how she felt.

"I've had a lot of practice. You're an easy dance partner."

"Your toes are all intact?"

"Every single one of them. So, tell me, Hannah, how would you feel if I asked you out on a date?"

"I'd be a little confused because you don't know me," she said.

"That's very true. I don't know you. We've only just met."

She couldn't help but smile. "Erm, I don't know. I'm not very good at this. I'm not used to dancing with handsome men."

"You think I'm handsome?"

"You know you are. A lot of women would love

to be where I am."

His grip tightened around her waist. "No one would replace you."

How could she not swoon at that?

She was loving this. A little more than she should.

Chapter Three

Finally, West had her in his arms and it felt fucking fantastic. Hannah was so sensual as she swayed to the beat of the music. He wondered if she knew she was turned on. Her tight nipples pressed against the front of her black cocktail dress, giving away her need. He happened to notice that every now and then, her legs would press together almost as if she was trying to stop her own arousal.

Did she feel this connection with him still?

Something had been happening before their rude interruption, and he was still fucking pissed about that. Fortunately, Rome and Cage had seen what was happening and they'd taken care of it.

He'd also given the DJ instructions before coming here. The moment he went onto the dance floor with a woman, he was to change the music to that for lovers. He'd gotten a few curious looks, but no one dared to speak out against him.

This was his fucking club, and right now he had the woman that he'd been taking care of in some way for the past five years. There was no way he was going to miss such an opportunity.

After all of his careful planning this wasn't how he imagined their first meeting to take place. He'd wanted it to be more random, but seeing her alone at the bar, looking so damn lost, he couldn't help himself. Walking away hadn't been an option.

"Is there, like, an internet link or something for those lines?"

He smiled. She thought he was using some line for how he felt. "No. These are all my own."

"They're kind of awesome."

He adored her smile. She had a dimple in each

cheek when she smiled, and she really was so beautiful.

"You think my pickup lines are awesome?" he asked.

"Yes. Come on, you can work on them some more."

"How about we go out to dinner and we'll see which ones are good and bad?"

"Dinner?"

"Yes."

"I could eat now," she said. She threw her head back and burst out laughing. "I can't believe this, but I am starving. How about we go out now?"

"You're sure?"

"Yes. I've just got to speak to Emily."

He didn't want her to speak to Emily, but he followed her off the dance floor. He gave the signal to the DJ to continue with the fast beat music as they made their way to the bar. Emily was downing a shot as they approached. He would have to get Rome to look into her and to make sure she wasn't taking anything.

"Hey, honey," Emily said.

The smile she wore was forced, and he wanted to pull her up on it but couldn't in their current situation.

"Hey, so, you won't believe this. This is West Gallo. West, this is my best friend and roommate, Emily."

"You're the one that works for me?" he asked.

She knew to play her part. "Yep. I work damn hard for you, sir."

"Where was that guy you were dancing with?" Hannah asked.

"He wanted to head out, and as I followed him, I heard him making excuses to his wife. Not going to happen. There's no way I'm ever going to be the kind of woman that breaks up a home."

"Damn, what a piece of work," Hannah said.

He was now bored and wanted to move on.

Emily was not behaving appropriately.

Pulling out his cell phone, he sent a quick message to Rome that after he left, he was to search Emily and give her a drug test. He knew it would test positive for alcohol, but he wanted to see what else she was on, if anything.

Only the best people worked for him, and if Emily couldn't get her head in the game, he didn't have a place for her.

"West and I are going to get something to eat. Would you like to come?" Of course Hannah would invite her.

He turned his head from side to side letting Emily know the answer she had to say.

"I'm quite tired, actually. I'm going to call it a night." She got up and hugged Hannah. "You have fun. I'll make sure not to lock the door for you."

"You're sure?"

"I'm positive."

"If it makes you feel any better, I'll get one of my men to drive her home." He nodded toward Rome and Cage, who came near.

They knew their part, and when it came to Hannah, he had warned them to always wait for his instruction as to what to do.

"Could you please see that Emily makes it home safely?"

"Will do, boss," Cage said.

"Excellent. If that's all." He placed a hand at Hannah's back and they made their way out of the club. A couple of people recognized him.

His reputation always preceded him, but they had to know of his past as well as who he was.

No one would ever accuse him of anything, nor would they bring up what he'd done for fear of that happening to them.

He didn't take bullshit lightly, and with Hannah, who didn't have a clue about him, he was being extra cautious.

The valet was already there with his car.

"Here you go, sir." The man got out of the car, and as he went to open Hannah's door, West dismissed him.

"I've got it from here, thank you."

He'd never picked a woman up in a bar. Besides Cage, Rome, and Emily, along with a few others in security, no one knew about his obsession with this woman.

Helping Hannah into his car, he leaned in, strapping her into place. As the back of his hand rubbed against her breast, he heard her sudden intake of breath, almost like shock that he'd touched her.

He didn't give her any sign that he heard it or that he even noticed. Closing her door, he rounded the car, and climbed in behind the wheel. Strapping in, he turned the ignition over, and pulled away from the curb.

"This is a really nice car," she said.

"I love the best."

She chuckled. Her hand ran across the chair, and she looked impressed. "I can tell. I don't know the first thing about cars, but this is a pretty good one."

"I can afford it if that is what you're asking."

"Oh, no, I don't mean like that. I didn't even think of the money. Wow, do I sound like a gold-digger or something?"

"No, you're perfectly fine."

The pill he'd slipped into her drink would be working soon. It was a concoction his lab had come up that was designed to make the person who took it relaxed. To let go of their inhibitions, but not too much.

Hannah's body was already starting to look more relaxed than when they'd been at the bar.

"This is amazing," she said.

He watched as she pressed the button for the window to wind down, and she stuck her head out. There was no oncoming traffic, so he watched her.

She let out a little squeal, and he found her reaction sweet.

There was no way she would have done this without the little pill to help her loosen up. He felt a spark of guilt that he'd done that; that he'd given her something to help the start of their relationship.

He'd been torn from the moment he was given the vial of pills that he asked for. Hannah was just so … closed off. She fought at every single turn, and conversation wasn't easy for her. She always got nervous, and he didn't want her to experience that with him. So, he'd given her a little something to help.

Now though, he felt a little guilty.

"Oh, wow, I cannot believe I just did that. I've always wanted to do it. Is that crazy? I saw it in a movie once, and it looked like so much fun. I remember telling my dad about it, and he totally freaked at me. Told me I'd get myself killed." She scrunched up her face. "There was a lot he said would get me killed. I always had to be a good girl. A nice girl. You know." She slapped a hand across her mouth. "There I go again. I can't seem to be quiet." She chuckled. "This is so much fun. So, tell me, West, how is Emily?"

The sudden change of topic took him by surprise. "What do you mean?"

"I don't know. I get the sense that she isn't happy with me? I don't think she likes hanging out with me. I saw the way she looked at you, West. I think she likes you. Do you like her?"

He couldn't fucking believe this.

Gripping the steering wheel tightly, he counted to ten.

"If I liked her, she'd be here in this car and you wouldn't."

"You like me?" she asked.

"Yes."

"Wow, that is so cool." She released a laugh. "I can't believe I'm saying these things. Honestly, I'm not childish at all. Wait? How can you like me? You don't even know me." she asked.

"I want to get to know you, Hannah."

"From meeting each other once?"

"How do you think couples get along their entire lives? It starts with one meeting."

"Oh. yeah. Sorry. My bad. I just can't seem to think straight, and I know I'm not myself right now. Something is confusing to me."

He took her hand, locking their fingers together. "It's fine."

Even with the effects of the pill, he didn't mind her rambling or her nerves. It was wonderful to hear her talk, and he felt like a fucking pussy because he was content to sit and listen to her just say words.

Parking up outside of the city, he turned toward her, and he saw her eyes seemed to sparkle. Her stomach growled.

"I am hungry."

"Me too. Are you okay?"

"Yeah. My head's a little fuzzy right now."

"Come on, let's get you some food." The pill would last a couple of hours. Long enough for them to have some food before he had to take her home.

As he climbed out of the car Hannah did the same, but the heels she wore were not cooperating with her.

When he picked her up in his arms, she let out a laugh.

"You can't carry me."

"Oh, yes, I can." He carried her toward the diner, and when they were just outside the door, he put her on her feet, banding an arm around her back.

"Everything smells amazing," she said.

Opening the door, he entered the diner and nodded at the man working. This was one of the few diners he frequented, and they knew the drill. Not to ask questions. Not to stare. To leave him be whenever he was here.

This was the first time he'd brought a woman with him. He wondered what they were all thinking.

Taking a booth in the back, she sat down and pushed some of her hair off her face. He loved the length of her long locks, the way they cascaded around her and would look damn good spread out across his pillow every single night.

The dress she wore molded to all of her voluptuous curves. She wasn't a slender woman, not by any means. She had nice, big tits, a sizeable ass, and a rounded stomach. She would make an amazing mother, and the thought of her being swollen and heavily pregnant with his kid made his dick harden.

"I feel the need for something greasy and really unhealthy. What about you?"

"The same."

The waiter came to their table.

"What can I get you folks?" he asked.

"I'll have the double decker cheeseburger, fries slathered with cheese, and a large chocolate shake. Is that okay?" she asked. "You're not ready for closing?"

"It's certainly fine. We're open all day."

"Awesome. It all smells amazing."

"I'll have what she is having. Include some onion rings for me."

"Oh, can I have some of those? They sound so good," Hannah said.

The waiter took their order and left them alone.

"This place is making me so hungry," Hannah said. She tilted her head to one side. "You know, I'm sure I've seen you before somewhere. I don't know where, but it's the little things."

"You've seen me?" he asked. Of course he knew the answer to that. They'd met each other once before, twice before in fact.

"Yes. It's the little things that you do. Like when you held my hand." She put her hand across the table, and he took it. "And you kissed it."

He pressed a kiss to her hand.

"Yeah, exactly like that. I don't know why I recognize it, but I do. Have you done that before?"

"I'm sure if we'd met you'd remember." No, she wouldn't. He'd made sure of it.

"It's just so strange. I feel excited and equally terrified of you at the same time. I don't even know you but I feel I want to know you. That I can trust you." She once again shoved some hair off her face and let out a frustrated moan. "I really need to get this cut." She lifted up some of her hair, and he shook his head.

"Don't cut your hair."

"Why not? It's really irritating."

"Because I think it looks stunning, and one day I want it spread out across my pillow before I fuck you."

This caused her to lower her hair. "You mean that?"

She wasn't running away out of fear, so that was a plus.

"One day, Hannah, you will realize there I don't say anything that I don't mean."

Their food came, and he watched as Hannah picked up her huge burger and tried to take a bite. He did the same, and he found himself having a lot of fun. It was stupid and goofy, but it was just the two of them. No one was watching them, and he could be open with her. Share this moment where he'd not been able to share all that many.

He stole a couple of her fries as she stole a few onion rings from him, and they talked about absolutely nothing of any importance.

Hannah giggled through some of his questions, and he loved how she came alive around him. He didn't like that she was nervous around him or terrified. He'd work on that.

By the time he got her in the car and he drove her toward her apartment, the pill would start to wear off. It would make her sleepy, almost as if she was in a dream.

Pulling up outside of her building, he turned the ignition off, and she sighed. "I'm home."

"Yeah."

"I really had a lot of fun tonight. So much fun," she said.

She unstrapped her seatbelt, but rather than climb out, she shocked him as she moved to straddle him in his chair.

"I feel like I'm in a dream right now and nothing makes any sense. I couldn't do this awake, so I'm going to do it now."

Before he could stop her, she cupped his face and her lips pressed against his.

She was inexperienced, but he didn't mind that.

In time, he'd show her exactly how to kiss.

Running his hands down her back, he gripped her ass, and she moaned, rubbing herself against him as she did.

She ran her tongue across his lips and then slumped in his arms. She passed out, and there in his car, he held her for a few seconds. Stroking her hair, he allowed himself to let go before he opened the door and carried her up to her room.

****

Hannah's mouth felt incredibly dry. Her head was pounding, and as she rolled over, she realized the pounding she heard wasn't in her head. No, that was the front door. She lifted her head and opened her eyes.

She was in her bedroom.

Her bed was empty.

She hadn't brushed her teeth before bed. Her mouth tasted so horrible. She needed to use the bathroom and brush her teeth.

Running a hand across her face, she realized she wasn't wearing the dress she wore last night. She wore a shirt.

She rolled back over so that she was on her back and sat up. One look in the mirror and she moaned. She looked like a monster had attacked her.

Her long, brown locks were all matted, and she'd not showered from the night before.

"Don't cut your hair."

She'd been out last night with a man. Shit, everything was confusing to her.

Climbing out of bed, she ran toward the shared bathroom that connected her and Emily's bedroom.

She stared at the mirror and Emily's door wasn't open, so she lifted up the nightshirt. There was no soreness so she was still a virgin. Her memories were vague.

West.

That had been his name.

Emily's boss.

She'd met him last night.

They had danced, and after that, she couldn't really remember what was happening.

She sat on the toilet, relieving herself before flushing and washing her hands. Throwing water onto her face, she washed away the signs of the makeup she'd worn the night before, feeling a little refreshed but not a whole lot. Brushing her teeth helped, but she wouldn't tackle her hair until she had a shower.

There had been knocking at the door?

Leaving the bathroom, she walked the few steps to the kitchen. There on their little table was a huge vase filled with wildflowers. They were so shocking, beautiful, stunning, and breathtaking.

Emily leaned against one of the counters. "You look like death."

"Thanks to you as well. A new admirer?"

"I wish. They're for you."

Emily held out the small card.

Taking it from her friend, she opened it up.

"Thank you for a wonderful night, West." She didn't add that there was a kiss on the end.

"I take it you two had a good time," Emily said.

Hannah didn't know what to say. "I don't know."

"How could you not know?"

"It's all a little fuzzy. I think we had a good time. Flowers? Is this a good thing?"

"I wouldn't object to West Gallo sending me flowers."

She heard something in Emily's voice. There was a hardness there. "Is this okay?" She pointed at the flowers. "Do you have feelings for him?"

"No, of course not. I meant that he's a good-looking guy. He's also loaded, and just, wow, I mean he oozes sex appeal."

"Oh, well, I think we had a good time. I mean, we must have for him to send me flowers." She rubbed at her temples, feeling a headache start.

"How much did you have to drink last night?"

"I don't know. Not a lot. I mean, I had one drink with you and then water. You don't think I was drugged, do you?"

"No, I bet you weren't. I've got to head out. You're okay?"

"Yeah, yeah, I'm fine. I'm going job hunting."

"What have I told you? Don't let that loser ruin your love of your job."

"I know, but it's no hardship to look, you know? I may just go to the library."

"Call me if you need anything." Emily was already out of the apartment.

Taking a seat at the table, Hannah stared at the flowers and the card. She didn't know what the hell to do.

Did this mean anything at all?

Would he want to go on a date?

"Ugh! I've never been on a date."

She may have even babbled most of the night away.

She moved her head from side to side to try to work the kinks out of her shoulders and neck.

When that didn't work, she got up, made herself a quick coffee, and left the flowers on the table. They were really beautiful with all the different varieties of flowers and colors. Such a contrast to each other and even in a vase they looked so wild.

Ignoring them, she sipped at her coffee while running a bath. She really needed to shake off this horrible groggy feeling.

Once the bath was full, she stripped down and paused as she looked in the mirror. Her lips were the same, her body as well.

No sex had happened last night.

Not even a little inkling of a feel.

She ran a hand over her ass, and a flash of male hands gripping her butt as she kissed West.

Did she kiss him last night?

This was so embarrassing.

The thought of West with his hands all over her, not being able to get enough of her, set her pulse on fire.

Climbing into the tub, she leaned back in the water and grabbed her cup, taking generous sips of the dark coffee.

She'd met West before. She was sure of it.

The problem she had was she couldn't remember exactly where.

Why did he seem so familiar?

Wait? He'd brought her back home?

Did he even ask where she lived?

How did he know where she lived? She couldn't remember telling him her address.

No, her paranoia was getting the better of her.

There's no way that she wouldn't have told him. He was giving her a ride home.

She pushed her nagging suspicions to one side and finished her coffee. She'd probably never see him again so it wasn't like it was any hardship.

The time they shared dancing and having a meal had been fun.

With her cup empty, she placed it on the floor and then took the time to bathe. Dipping her head under the water, she lifted up. Soaping her body first, she rid herself of the night before, clearing her mind as she did. Once her body was clean, she shampooed her hair before putting conditioner on.

Once that was all done, she was ready to start her day.

She pulled the plug, stepped out, and wrapped herself in a towel. She was putting her bathrobe on when she heard a knock at the door.

There was no time to wrap her hair up as the knocking wouldn't stop.

"I'm coming. I'm coming." She stood up against the door, looking through the peephole but couldn't make out who stood there. "Who is it?"

"It's West Gallo."

This made her step back and her heart speed up.

"What's wrong?"

"I came to see if you were all right. I called, but you didn't answer."

"You have my number?"

"Do you really want to talk with your neighbors listening?"

She didn't think of that.

Opening the door just a little, she left one of the locks on that allowed her to peep outside. "I'm not appropriately dressed. How did you get my number?"

"Emily gave it to me."

"Just like that?"

"Yes."

"Oh. Well, she shouldn't have."

"You didn't have a nice time last night?"

"I did. I think I did."

He chuckled. "You don't sound so sure."

"Usually when I have a good time I remember it all."

"Ah," he said. "I see."

"Did I do or say something … that would…?" She blew out a breath, not really sure what she wanted to say or do.

"No. You passed out in my car, and I carried you up to bed."

"I wasn't in my dress," she said.

"Emily took care of all that."

"She didn't say anything."

"I can't speak for her. I promise I'm not going to hurt you."

"Isn't that what all people say before they attack?" She leaned back around the door so he wouldn't see and hit her head against it.

Get some damn sense.

What is wrong with you?

"I was wondering if you'd like to go out today?" he asked.

"Today?"

"Yes."

She nibbled her bottom lip.

"You want to go out today?" she asked.

He chuckled. "Am I making you nervous?"

"A little bit."

She heard a door close and knew she didn't want to talk about this for everyone else to hear or whatever couple had decided to come out of their apartment. Closing the door, she slid the lock out and then opened it wide enough for him to step inside.

He took the door from her and closed it.

Locking her fingers together, she stared at him waiting for something, anything.

"I can't remember everything that happened last night." She spoke slowly.

"We had a good time. That's all you need to

know."

She frowned at that.

"Thank you for the flowers. They're really beautiful. Erm, I was going to go and look for another job today."

"Another job?"

"Yeah, something happened at the job I'm currently in." Just thinking about what Lawrence had done to her, not that he'd done anything, but it unnerved her. She'd wanted to go home early that day and she'd even told him she wished to leave, but he'd told her he needed her. So, after everyone had left, she'd gotten a little uneasy. When he came out to her and said there was something he wanted to discuss in his office, it had made her even more nervous.

No one was around, and she'd noticed the way all the women seemed to avoid him.

She pushed the thoughts and memories of how he'd shoved her against the bookshelves, of the things he'd said to her.

"I don't want to go back there. I'd rather just find my own way. I know this job came through my graduation as part of my scholarship agreement, but I'm hoping to arrange a meeting with them so that I can talk about moving. You know, I want to start fresh." She saw how good he looked in a suit. Last night's had been black with a crisp white shirt.

The shirt was still crisp white, but the suit was grey and it spread out over his body. She glanced down at his wrists, and sure enough, she saw the ink that decorated his skin. She wanted to do nothing more than push the shirt back, to look at him, and to see what he was hiding.

"You okay in there?" he asked.

"I'm sorry. Zoned out."

"You do that a lot?"

"Recently it seems I do. I don't know if I'm going to be good company."

He placed his hands on his hips and smiled.

He had large hands. Big. She wondered if his fingers would be rough or if that was all in her imagination, which was once again running wild. She couldn't focus at all.

"How about we talk about your job opportunities over breakfast?"

"Breakfast?"

"I own a waffle house a couple blocks from here. I've got my car waiting."

"Exactly how much do you own?" she asked.

"The entire city, pretty much."

"The entire city? Wow, you must be really important."

"I do all right."

She chuckled. "I'm going to go get dressed. You're okay to stay here and, you know, not snoop?"

"Nah, I gotta snoop."

She laughed and left him alone in the sitting room.

The apartment wasn't that big, and rushing into her bedroom, she closed the door and quickly changed into a matching pair of white lace panties and bra before tugging on a pair of jeans and a large flower print shirt, one side gathered at the hip so it helped to give her some figure; a little at least.

Dressed, she ran a brush through her wet hair to clean out some of the knots. When it was smooth, she rubbed her hair with a towel to help dry it out. With her hair nearly dry, she brushed it again, and was all done.

No makeup.

A pair of slip-on shoes and she was good to go.

Oh, a spray of perfume.

She left the bedroom and found him looking at the few pictures she had of herself, Emily, and Emily's family, along with pictures of her parents.

"You're close with Emily?"

"Yeah. We've known each other since college. She's been a real rock. Especially when my parents passed. I don't know what I'd have done without her, you know?" She stepped up beside him.

"Are you ready to go?" he asked.

She was as ready as she'd ever be.

She turned off the coffee machine, grabbed her cell, and sent a text to Emily to say she was heading out.

On the way to the door, she was hit by nerves. What if this was a mistake?

"What is it?" West asked.

"I'm not used to this," she said.

"Used to this?"

"Going out. Hanging out with men. It's all brand new to me, and I'm going to make a fool of myself. I need you to promise me not to hurt Emily."

"Why would I hurt Emily?"

"I don't mean physically or anything. I mean, you know, I don't want you to fire her. She loves her job."

"So long as Emily knows what she is doing and knows her place, she will have a job."

"Okay, good. That's good."

Closing the door, she clicked the locks into place.

Following him down the flights of stairs, she didn't have time to analyze that nervous, excited, and terrified feeling that he always seemed to inspire. He'd done nothing to hurt her or for her to even fear.

Get a grip, Hannah.

It's going to be okay.

On the bottom floor, he took her hand, and she

followed him outside to where his car was waiting. He held the door open, and once again another flash in her mind of another door opening flooded her senses.

The memory or dream plagued her.

Pushing it aside, she took his hand, climbing inside.

No matter what, she was safe with West. That's how she felt, and again, it terrified her that she knew that.

Chapter Four

West knew he should stay away. Being near her right now was dangerous, and she wasn't ready. Last night had proven that to him. One taste of her sweet lips and he wanted more. Lawrence was still out there, and it pissed him off. He needed to keep cool rather than make a mistake. This was the only curse of being at the top. There was always someone intent on bringing you down.

Danny was gone, though.

His body would never be discovered.

His death hadn't been easy.

There were not many ways of drawing Lawrence out. Danny had told them before he died that Lawrence was a selfish prick. If he thought it would help his cause, he'd hand over his wife and anyone that was close to him. There was no heart in the man.

It wasn't news to West.

He'd discovered all about Lawrence's little secret activities. West had known there were parts of Lawrence's life that were not his problem, but he'd been the best at what he did, and since he was also paying the son of a bitch a good sum of money, he truly believed Hannah would have been safe.

This was his mistake.

A big mistake.

One he would never make again.

He'd put Hannah with a monster.

Just thinking about what he'd uncovered—the brothels Lawrence frequented that gave him women to beat up before fucking them—it would seem Lawrence had a rape fantasy and he paid women to let him play it out.

Well, now he was going to find out what happened when you tried to rape another man's woman.

Glancing over at Hannah, he saw she was staring out of the window. Silence filled the car, but it wasn't uncomfortable.

Some women loved making noise just for the sake of it. Most women knew who he was, but Hannah didn't have a clue. He'd made sure she didn't know who he was or had heard of him.

For the past five years he'd manipulated her life in some way, bringing her to this point they were at now.

Last night had been his breaking point.

He couldn't stay away from her.

Watching her from afar no longer held any appeal, not when he could have her.

Emily had been home last night, but he'd sent her to the bed so that he could handle her. He'd stripped Hannah naked before putting her in her shirt.

He'd not done the gentlemanly thing and closed his eyes.

West had looked and known that there was no turning back.

Five years he'd waited.

Some would think he was a pervert.

At forty years old, he was seventeen years her senior.

She was unlike any other woman he'd ever known.

He couldn't let her go.

A sick fuck he may be, but he only had it bad for her.

No one else would ever do.

Five years he'd been celibate, waiting for her.

After he'd made sure that she was okay and comfortable, he'd looked around her room. The effects of the pill would keep her asleep and dead to the world for a few hours. He'd discovered her sexy lingerie along with her secret supply of books.

He'd watched her reading them many times.

Her face would flush, and every time she put them down, there was always a longing within her eyes.

Holding the books in his hands, he'd known his woman had a desire. The need for the forbidden, the temptation. She just had no one to trust with this knowledge.

He had cameras in her apartment. Emily's bedroom was clear as he had no interest in watching her.

Before Hannah moved in, he'd installed cameras around the sitting room, kitchen, on the outside of their main door, inside. With a few placed cameras he saw the entire apartment. The only places that were safe were Emily's room and the bathroom, but he did have sound.

He got to hear everything.

The drive was silent, and as he pulled into the waffle house parking lot, he saw Rome and Cage were not far behind. He gave them a nod but climbed out of the car.

Hannah was already out of the car by the time he made it around to her. He grabbed her arm and placed her up against the vehicle.

"Next time wait for me to help you out."

"Why?"

"I like to be a gentleman."

"That's so sweet. I really don't mind."

Anyone could take her out with a bullet. She was an easy target, but he didn't say that.

"It's what I like to do." He pressed a kiss to her cheek and took her hand, leading the way into the waffle house.

The scents of bacon, chicken, and maple syrup flooded his senses. He couldn't help but have his mouth water. Waffles were one of his favorite breakfast foods.

Taking Hannah to the back where his own private booth was, he waited for her to sit before taking a seat himself.

"It's about time you showed your face here," the waitress on duty said, coming into the room. She wore an apron smeared with waffle batter.

"Hey, Aunt Martha." He gave the older woman a hug. "I'd like you to meet someone. Martha, this is Hannah. Hannah, Martha. She was my mom's friend growing up. She makes the best waffles in the world."

"I certainly do. Sweet, savory, spicy, you name it, it can go on a waffle. You do like waffles?" Martha asked.

Hannah nodded.

"I'll bring you out the house best. You know I've got you covered." Martha patted his stomach and left.

"She seems really nice."

"She is."

"Where are your parents now?" she asked.

"Both dead."

"I'm so sorry." He saw the smile on her lips fall. "That was so wrong of me to ask."

"It's fine."

"My parents are gone now as well," she said. "It sucks."

He couldn't relate to her love of her parents. His parents' deaths were very different.

"So, your work dilemma. I've got a job opening up working close with me at one of my nightclubs."

"Dirty?"

"No. Not Dirty. Sin, it's called."

"Emily said you had more than one nightclub."

"It's a little farther out than your apartment. I can arrange for transportation. It's within my financial department, and you'll be able to acquire the skills you need for whatever you hope to become."

"I want to help struggling families with their finances. My parents were given really bad advice, and I don't want anyone else to have that happen to them."

"That is very ... noble."

"It bugged me when I went through their belongings. They kept a record of the advice and then of course of their money being badly invested. It ... annoyed me."

He had yet to hear her swear. Even on camera she never said "piss," "fuck," "shit." It was always "ouch," "sugar," "damn.' This was just another part of her he found so refreshing.

"What would I have to do?" she asked.

"You'd oversee the profit and loss. See where the money is best invested, where I need to make changes. I'm starting small at the nightclub to help you gain experience. The further up the chain you go, the more detail you'll get."

He saw she was tempted, and he wasn't surprised. This was the deal of a lifetime. A rare experience opportunity that he'd not been able to put in place after she graduated but could now have her as close to him as he wanted.

Sin was his main base. The nightclub was his first real investment when he got out of the fighting ring. He'd made a name for himself, and he'd put all of his energy into Sin. Then the first pimp came along. Malone was the pimp's name. He'd come into his club without an invite and started to make demands. He wanted over fifty percent of the club's profit and a place for his girls to take customers. That had been the only time Malone entered his property. He'd never left it.

Killing Malone hadn't given West any kind of pleasure. If anything, it had started an all-out war within the city. One he'd been determined to win, which was why he was where he was now.

He gave a rundown of the list of benefits she'd receive working with him. From health care to free dental and of course a staff discount at any of his properties.

"You're driving a hard bargain."

"I don't understand why you feel the need to think about it? It's a pretty good offer."

"It's not just pretty good. It's the best offer. I don't get it though. I tend to believe if it's too good to be true, it often is."

"You don't like my job offer?"

"What's the catch, West?" she said. "I'm not an idiot. I'm young, I know, but I'm not a fool. Tell me what's going on here."

He liked that she had reservations and a clear instinct that something wasn't right.

I've been watching you for five years and you're mine. I've declared you're mine, and one night soon you're going to be in my bed, riding my cock.

"Can't you just believe that I like you?" he asked. He held his hands out in surrender. "Not all of us guys are bad."

He was just plain lying now.

He wanted her any way he could have her.

"Fine. You're right. I shouldn't doubt you at all. You've been really sweet and considerate. I'd love to take the job. I've got a week's notice to submit at my old place."

"You're sure they can't overlook that, you know, considering?"

"Considering what?" she asked.

Shit.

"Considering that you've only just graduated and

it wasn't a perfect fit? You mentioned that something had happened in your previous job."

"There's a lot I've got to do. I've got to hand in my notice and also speak to the people in charge of my placement," she said. "I know it sounds complicated, but this was part of the scholarship agreement."

"How about you give me the phone number? I'll call them. Make the arrangements and you won't have to worry about any of that."

"You're sure?"

"Positive."

He pulled out a pen and a card from inside his jacket pocket.

What she didn't know was that he *was* the scholarship. Through a shell company, he'd put everything in place that also included that little catch for her to work where he placed her. He'd thought it was a rather good idea on his part at the time.

"I don't know if they'll accept this from you."

"You won't know until you try."

"You're really making this easy for me," she said, laughing.

"You only live once. Clearly, working at the other place wasn't doing anything for you."

"You're right. You're so right. I hated it, and after everything I really just want a fresh, clean break." She took the card and wrote down the number, not that he needed it.

He took the card, stared at the number and smiled. "I'm sure everything will be easy to arrange."

"Will I be working with Emily?"

"No, she is based in another part of my company."

"Oh."

"Is that a problem?"

"No, of course not. It's your business, and you can do what you like with whomever you like." She tucked some hair behind her ears again.

The wild length was driving her crazy, but he wouldn't have her cutting it. He wanted to live out a few fantasies with that hair.

Martha came back out carrying two plates of breakfast waffles. "Enjoy." She gave his arm a squeeze. Martha was the only person from his past as a boy that was still living. After he made a name for himself, he'd gone back to the apartments that had once been his home and been so fucking horrified. The building was a crumbling mess, but no one would move the people who lived there.

He'd taken Martha, who'd been fighting illness, housed her, and together they'd opened up this waffle shop. It hadn't been easy in the beginning, but between the two of them, they'd been able to make it work.

Watching Hannah dive into her waffles, he would make sure it worked with her as well.

****

One week later

Hannah couldn't believe how quickly her life had changed in the past couple of days. Not only were her scholarship people happy for the change, they welcomed it. The company she'd been working for prior to Lawrence's attack were accepting of her termination immediately.

Then of course working at Sin proved to be really enjoyable. There was always a car waiting for her to take her to work, and if West wasn't available, someone would be there to take her home. She didn't have to worry about catching a cab or the bus or waiting for Emily. Her colleagues were amazing. Sin was on the main floor while on the three floors above it were offices.

From what she understood on her first day, West Gallo had many different businesses, and this was his first-ever club. The one that started it all and since then, he'd expanded but kept his base within one building. She worked on the top floor with West and six other employees. Two of them were in finance, another two were investment, and another two in insurance. The second floor was HR, and the first floor was something else that she couldn't remember.

She'd been so completely floored by his operation that she'd missed some of the introduction. The first floor hadn't needed her though so that wasn't a huge deal. She'd been included in HR as well as finance because her skill set went in two directions because she wanted to help people.

HR provided her that element.

Finance helped her within the company, but it wasn't exactly what she wanted to do. Helping a businessman in this way wasn't how she imagined her life would be.

Still, the pay and health benefits were a plus, especially just after graduation. She could get the experience she needed from a working standpoint, and when the time was right, either use West's company to help her grow or leave and start her own financial consulting firm. That was where her true dream was.

At the end of her first week, she actually felt good, positive even about the progress she'd made. The work was challenging and not boring. The hours were manageable without feeling tedious either.

The only problem was West.

Not that he was any problem; far from it.

Everyone who worked in the building, including the nightclub staff, were constantly voicing their praise of him. She saw clearly that he was well-loved as an employer. Emily spoke of him often as well. Thinking about her best friend wasn't easy. The past week they'd not spent much time together, and when they passed, Emily wasn't happy.

"How are you doing?" West asked, coming out of his office to stand with her at the copy machine.

They were alone as everyone else had gone out to lunch. She liked to bring her own and had already been snacking on it.

"I'm doing great." Glancing over at him, she couldn't help but check out the way he looked in a sexy hot suit. This was a black one, and she couldn't make her mind up if she preferred him in black or grey. They both looked so good on him. "Everyone here is really nice."

She didn't have the first clue what to say to him.

This was the only problem she had.

Conversations with men were not easy for her.

"How have you been?" she asked.

Her cheeks were on fire so she had to be blushing.

"Busy as always. Taking care of business is never easy."

"Can I ask you a personal question?" She hated doing this, but thinking about Emily helped her to not think about her own attraction to the man before her.

"Sure."

"Have you and Emily dated?"

"Your friend Emily?"

"Yes."

"No." His voice was firm, direct.

"Oh, I just … I think she has a bit of a crush on you." She inwardly cringed, hoping that she hadn't just gotten her best friend into trouble.

"I have never nor will I ever have any romantic feelings for her. I don't see her that way."

"Of course. I mean, this is just me. I'm so sorry. Please don't say anything." She turned toward him, her hands out in surrender.

"Did she give you any reason to believe anything is going on?"

"No, no, of course not."

"I don't like this, Hannah."

"I swear. She never has. I just thought, you know, that you both might have had a thing." Now she was wishing more than anything that she'd kept her mouth shut. This was why she didn't do well around men. Especially not men that were making her so damn horny and she still hadn't thrown those blasted books out that didn't help the situation. One look at his rough hands and it made her ache in ways she'd never experienced before.

Biting her lip, she avoided looking at his hands and instead stared into his intense blue eyes. So bright, so beautiful, so clear.

"Please, don't say anything."

He stepped up close to her, the scent of his musky cologne invading her senses. Her nipples tightened, and her pussy went slick. She wanted nothing more than to have him take her over. To have his way, to show her what it meant to be taken by a man. Being a virgin was a complete and total drag. She'd love nothing more than to have him take it from her.

"There's only one woman I want, and I'm looking right at her."

Time froze as she stared at him. They barely knew each other. He held her captive in his gaze, and she didn't have a clue what to do or what to say.

One week they'd known each other, and it wasn't like they'd spent any real time together.

"I … erm, I…" She hated it when she couldn't think what to say. She was a grown woman, for Christ's sake. "I don't know what to say."

"How about you go on a date with me tonight?"

"Is that allowed?"

"Why wouldn't it be allowed?"

"You know?" He shook his head. "Dating in the office? Isn't that wrong?"

"I'm the boss, Hannah. For you I can make an exception."

She tucked some hair behind her ear just for something to do. Anything other than this feeling that was currently consuming her.

She wanted to say yes so badly, but part of her held back and she didn't understand it. West had been nothing but nice to her. This job, the transport, even the company, it had all been wonderful. He made her laugh, and his jokes were goofy.

"What's wrong?" he asked, stepping a little closer.

Hannah didn't even realize that he could get closer. They were already standing right in front of each other.

"Nothing. I'd love to go on a date with you." She ignored that screaming need to not go with him. "When would you like to pick me up tonight?"

"I'll pick you up at eight."

"I want to warn you that I've not been on many successful dates. The few I've been on something weird happened."

He leaned against the copier, arms folded.

She wondered if she'd ever see all of his ink.

"What happened?"

"It would all start out well, and I think I must have done something wrong."

"Why would anything have to be weird about you?" he asked.

73

"It happened on all the dates. I'm not kidding, nor am I crazy." She held her hands up in surrender. "I couldn't even tell you what I did wrong. Only that they were fine, happy, and we were having a lot of fun, then boom, they change. They were real jerks as well." She shrugged. "It's one of the reasons I stopped going on dates. The sudden hot and cold was like whiplash, and believe me, I know what that feels like." She pressed her lips together, knowing she was talking way too much. "What I'm trying to say is if you find me boring please tell me. I really like this job. A whole lot more than my last one."

He chuckled. "I doubt you could ever bore me."

"You'd be really surprised." She clasped her hands together, needing something to do.

Why are you still talking?

Get a grip already.

You're going on a date, and you need to learn to shut your mouth.

"Relax, Hannah. We're going to have a good time." He leaned in close and his lips brushed against her ear. "I promise."

Just as the elevator door pinged, letting them know they were not alone, West pulled away and made his way back to his office.

She watched him go, somewhat taken aback by his sheer magnetism. What made him so different? She felt drawn to him.

Even now she wanted to follow him, and that was crazy.

Get your head out of your ass and get back to work.

Taking the sheets of paper she'd copied, she sat at her desk and tried to focus on work, but it was no good. She found herself looking toward his office. West was either on the phone, pacing back and forth in his office, or sitting behind his desk.

He filled all the spaces with his presence, commanded respect, and she saw his employees were loyal to him.

The rest of the day went by without event. When it was time to leave, West didn't come out of his office, and Rome was there to take her home.

She grabbed her bag and jacket, leaving with his driver.

West told her that he didn't always use Rome and Cage, but they were loyal, hard-working men and didn't mind taking her home.

"Did you have a good day?" Rome asked.

"Yes. It was good."

Staring at numbers all day she found rather relaxing. She loved it when some number didn't add up. There was nothing more she loved that getting a pad of notepaper and scrawling all over it to find out what was missing.

"Good."

"Erm, I'm going on a date with West tonight." Her cheeks were flaming as she said this.

Rome nodded.

The elevator opened, and they stepped out into the parking lot. Rome opened the car door. She was never allowed to ride up front with him, always in the back, which she hated. According to Rome it was the way it was done. She had to sit in the back or bring it up with West.

So far, she's just done what she'd been told rather than bring it up with him.

Buckling her seatbelt, she waited for Rome to climb inside.

"Are you looking forward to going on this date?"

"Yes and no."

He chuckled.

"That's not very comforting."

"Women normally love to be wined and dined."

"Well, I'm not most women."

She heard him mumble under his breath. It sounded like he said, "clearly," but she wasn't sure.

"Anyway, I'm a disaster with men. I struggle to talk to them."

"You're doing pretty fine right now."

"I do something that messes up."

"Like what?" he asked.

They were already out of the parking lot and on the way back to her apartment.

"I don't know. Whenever I'm with a guy it's always going great. I wonder if I pick the wrong places to eat."

"Why?"

"They always go to the bathroom. Maybe that's it? They always go to the bathroom, and when they come back, they're never the same again. Always saying horrible things. Do you think it could be the food?" she asked.

Rome chuckled. "It could be. Not everyone likes Italian or Chinese. Or you're really overthinking it and by the time they've got to the bathroom, they've realized you're not going to put out."

"You mean have sex?" She wanted to make sure they were on the same page.

"Yeah, fucking. It's all the same. You've got to understand that a lot of guys are only interested in the pussy."

She had gotten semi-used to Rome's blunt language. He made no apology for the way he talked. This past week, she'd found him oddly refreshing.

"Is that all West is interested in? Sex?"

Rome paused. "West … is different."

"How?"

"He just is. He's not after sex. I mean, he could be. I'm just the driver, you know."

"You're a very good driver," she said, not wanting him to seem less than what he was.

He laughed. "Don't worry, Hannah. I know my place here."

"What topics do you think I should talk about?"

"You're wanting me to coach you in your date?"

"No." She paused. "Yes."

"Just be yourself, Hannah. You'd be surprised how well that will turn out."

"I'm not sexy or alluring. I read books in my free time, and I've even started to look for animal shelters so I can volunteer on the weekends." She leaned forward, wrapping her arms around the headrest of the seat in front.

"Sit back," Rome said. He didn't take his eyes off the road. "Don't ever put yourself in danger on my watch."

She rolled her eyes but did as he asked.

He was always being careful with her.

Folding her arms, she wondered if she'd made a mistake.

"Does he date a whole lot?" Hannah asked.

"No. You'll be the first woman he's dated in a very long time."

"How long?"

"You really like to ask detailed questions."

"I'm sorry. I can't seem to help it."

"Five years."

She stared at Rome, and in her mind, she saw something flash. She wasn't entirely sure what, but it seemed to be there. Waiting. All she had to do was focus on it and she'd know what it was.

Instead, Rome pulled up outside of her apartment building and whatever she'd been thinking about vanished.

"Thanks for the ride."

She climbed out and gave him a wave, heading inside.

As she was walking upstairs to her apartment, she stopped.

Not once had she told Rome that she'd been inside an Italian and Chinese restaurant when it happened. They weren't the only places.

Strange.

Pushing those thoughts aside, she went to face her roommate.

Chapter Five

Glancing down at the time, West was fast losing patience with the whore they'd picked up off the street. Rome slapped her face, trying to bring her around. They had a nice large bag of crack for all of her worries.

This woman came to them in Sin claiming to know Lawrence's location. She'd taken something, and they'd not been able to find out what secrets she was holding, which pissed him off.

He was running out of time.

There was no way he'd be late for this bitch.

Tapping his fingers against his leg, he waited, wondering what the fuck was going to happen.

The woman moaned and opened her eyes.

They were glazed over and fucked up.

"Oh, no," she said.

Her body was bruised, but his men had not laid a finger on her.

West moved forward, crouching down to look at her. She let out a little moan. "It's all a dream."

He grabbed her chin, hard.

She cried out but didn't fight him as he pulled her forward.

"Do you know who I am?" he asked.

"Yes. You're *him*. The king. The one that brings death to those that disobey him." She whimpered. "I've not been bad."

"I need to know what information you have for me. You've seen Lawrence."

The woman hesitated and nodded her head.

"You better not be lying to me." He reached out, taking the bag of crack from Cage. "You see this? Play your cards right and all of this will be yours. All of it. You can get high for as long as you want."

Her eyes went from dull to full of promise. She licked her cracked lips. This woman disgusted him, but she was a means to an end. He wanted to put that piece of shit in the ground, and the only way to do that was to find out what this woman knew.

"He was at a hotel. He paid me fifty bucks to suck his dick and listen to him. All he wanted was a piece of West's woman. He said he didn't get it. Didn't understand the lure of the girl. He kept on rambling about how there were prettier women. Much better women. Women he knew could suck dick like a pro." Her brow creased. "He was being mean. Told me I wasn't worth the fifty bucks and tried to take the money off me. His dick tasted funny, and he wanted his money back." She sniffled. "Then he hit me. He kept on hitting me. Told me that he was going to get her. Anna. He was going to get her and fuck her, and take that sweet cherry. Then he was going to ruin her. To make her hate all men's touch so that you'd never be able to touch her again."

West released her face.

"The name of the hotel."

She told him. "I don't know if he's still there. When he said your name, I had to come. I had to warn you. I don't want to be a bad girl. West Gallo kills bad girls." She licked her lips again, looking at the crack. "Please."

He handed her the bag. "Rome will take you wherever you need to go."

Rome already had a bag over her head and was escorting her out of their secret location.

"You okay, boss?" Cage asked when they were alone.

Hannah wasn't the sexiest, most beautiful woman in the world. She didn't make women yearn to be her or to wish they could take her place. To most men, she was probably even considered a little plain, boring even. He didn't see it though.

Beautiful women were all fine and great, but they didn't call to him. Some of them had been sweet, charming, but they didn't hold a special place in his heart. He'd also known some women that were cruel. They believed because of their looks they didn't need to be nice. That people should fall all over them just because they were pretty.

Hannah was nothing like that.

She had this smile that lit up her entire face.

Even when there wasn't anything to be happy about, she'd always try to make others around her feel so. She was hard-working, caring, kind, sweet. Everything that he'd always taken as weaknesses, she held inside her. It was a secret strength that drew people to her.

The men he'd threatened to stay away from her hadn't even tried to put up a fight. The moment they knew he was willing to kill them they had all done as they were told.

She belonged to him and had for the past five years.

He'd been the one pulling the strings.

Bringing her closer into his web without her even realizing it. The scholarship, the job, the best friend, the best friend's family. He controlled everything. Now it was time for him to collect, and he couldn't wait to have her at his mercy, begging him.

If he got his wish, she'd never know the truth about who he was.

He wasn't delusional.

There was no way that she'd always be in the dark.

What he hoped was for her to be so in love with

him or bound to him there wasn't a way for her to leave.

"Lawrence is a threat," he said. "I want extra men around Hannah at all times." His first mistake with Hannah's safety was proving to be his biggest. What he couldn't risk was Hannah being hurt.

"We'll find him."

"So far, we've failed to do that, and now he poses a threat and I don't like it. I want you to check all the available hotels. Look through his records. Try to find anything that could give away a possible safe house. I don't want him to be able to shit without me knowing about it. Got it?"

"Got it."

He stared down at the ground.

Many lives had been taken here.

One day soon, Lawrence would join them.

He'd underestimated the man, and he wouldn't do that again.

"Did you find anything in Emily's room?" he asked.

"Nothing. She's not using again. If she is, she's hiding it."

"I want another man following her. Someone she's never seen before. I want to know everything she's doing."

"You're sure?"

"Yes. Don't question me."

"Emily's been loyal to you for a long time."

"Yeah, and she better know what will happen if she thinks she can betray me." He wouldn't have Emily believing she had any power here.

She was there to do his bidding, nothing more.

With Cage's orders finished, he left the warehouse, climbed into his car, and headed toward Hannah's apartment.

So far with Hannah everything was going smoothly. Even on the work front, his businesses were all working on his side, not creating any hiccups. His Aunt Martha liked her from that one visit to the waffle house.

Parking in the only available space outside her apartment, he pressed the buzzer.

"Who is it?" Emily asked.

"West."

The door buzzed, and he let himself in. Taking the stairs two at a time, he came to a stop outside their apartment where Emily was leaning against the doorframe eating an apple. She wore a pair of shorts and a crop top. The strap was hanging down her arm, showing that she wasn't wearing a bra.

"Where's Hannah?"

"Finishing getting dressed." She closed the door after he entered. He watched her move toward Hannah's bedroom door and give it a knock. Her voice softened. "Hannah, your date's here."

"I'll be right out."

Emily spun to face him with a smile. "You heard her. You got a hot date planned for tonight?"

"Yes."

"Should I expect her back?" Emily asked.

"This game you think you're playing ends now."

She walked up to him, her hips swaying. Her hair was bound on top of her head. "What game? I'm not playing any games." She went to place a hand on him, and he caught her wrist.

"No." His voice was firm.

Emily was crossing a line.

"You know she's a virgin, right? At twenty-three years old no cock has ever been inside her. She would never be able to handle a guy like you."

"And you think you can?"

"I know what to do with a man like you. How to suck your cock. How to take it to the back of my throat so I don't gag on it. I know what to do to get you off, West. You can fuck my mouth, my pussy, my ass. I can take whatever you want and make you beg for more."

Wrapping his fingers around her neck, he slammed her against the wall. "Let's get one thing straight. You're here to do a job. You think because you're Hannah's friend I won't find a way to kill you? I can end you any time that I want. I've got a whole crew of men that would be just as happy to fuck your body and break you. You think I don't know what you are. You're a whore, Emily. I gave you a second chance, and for a few years you've done really well. You've done everything I needed you to do. You fuck up, I can end you any chance I want." He squeezed just a little harder to see the fear flash in her eyes. Leaning close, he made sure she could hear him. "You think I can't make Hannah do everything you can. She's a virgin. Untouched by anyone else. I can get her to do exactly what I want and she will do it with a smile and not expect payment at the end of the night. Hannah's not a whore. She's a good woman, a kind woman, and she would never try to steal your boyfriend from you. That's what makes her worth everything I've ever done."

The door opened, and he let Emily go. They'd both been whispering quietly so Hannah wouldn't hear.

She had to muffle the sound of her gasp as the other woman came out.

"Is everything okay?" Hannah asked.

She wore a red dress that molded to her curves and flared out over her hips. Her tits were pressed up, enhancing her cleavage, and she paired the dress with a pair of flat shoes. He'd spent an hour watching her try to train herself to walk in high heels. There had been a moment where he thought she was going to hurt herself.

Whenever she was alone, she'd try to walk in them, but it never worked.

"Yeah, everything is fine." He gave Emily a pat on the back. "She was choking on a piece of apple."

Worry filled Hannah's eyes. "You're okay?" She rushed over, running her hands over Emily's back, tapping her.

"Yeah, yeah, I'm fine. I was being silly. Clearly taking too big a bite."

"Are you going to be okay?"

"Yeah, of course. I'm fine. Really. I'm going to enjoy a couple of movies. I'll see you when you get back." Emily hugged her, and he raised a brow.

She played nice, she lived.

It was as simple as that. She wanted to fuck with him, then he was also happy to play that game as well.

"Call me if you need anything."

"Have fun."

He placed a hand at Hannah's back, and they left their apartment.

"I think she wants to move out," Hannah said as they were walking downstairs.

"You think that?"

"She's not been the same since we graduated. It's almost as if she's bored or something. I don't know. I shouldn't be unloading on you like this."

"You're not unloading. I'm sure it's all just a little overwhelming for her. You know, graduating, a job. You guys have a nice apartment."

"Thanks. I love it so much. It was such a great place, and the rent is a steal."

He smiled.

The apartment belonged to him, and the money she paid for the rent, he was putting into a small bank account for their children's education.

He was a man that was prepared for everything.

Opening the door for her, he helped her inside.

"I can do that."

He strapped her in, ignoring her protests. "I like to make sure you're safe."

With her inside the car, strapped in, he rounded his car, climbed in, and drove out of the city.

It was a Friday night. She didn't have anywhere else to be, and he intended to be her only concern for the next two days.

"Where are we going?"

"It's a surprise."

He knew her parents had met on a rare date in a cute little bistro not far from where they lived. The same bistro was still open and had extended into a restaurant for couples. He'd booked them a private table and even made sure the chef cooked the exact same thing that had been available the night her parents met.

There was not a part of Hannah's life that he didn't know.

His obsession for her knew no bounds.

He'd discovered so much about her, even through her medical records. At the age of nine, she'd fallen off her bike onto a shard of glass and required seventeen stitches down one leg.

She still had the scar, even though it had faded.

There had been a police report as she got beaten up on her first day of high school. The girls were removed from the school as it hadn't been their first offense.

She went to prom and sat all night watching everyone else dance because no one had taken her.

So much knowledge and she didn't even know that he was there.

The day they met had been … interesting.
She didn't remember it, but he did.

****

Five and a half years ago

West was bleeding, and he was pissed off. He wanted to kill every single person within the fucking fast food chain. The burgers were disgusting and the service crap. When Rome finally picked him up, heads were going to roll.

War was about to break out on his turf, and he'd just spent the entire night negotiating with a fucking MC Prez about staying out of his city. The conversation had ended in bloodshed. The club was now burning to the ground with the Prez's head on a spike. He didn't get why people thought numbers would take him down.

He was used to fighting his way to freedom.

Gripping the coffee, he took a sip of the acrid liquid, wanting nothing more than the smooth Italian blend he loved so much.

This was the last time he took a job on his own.

While he'd been in a meeting with the Prez, his crew had destroyed his car.

Now he was stuck in a fucking town that was something out of a fifties movie, or at least felt like it.

There was so much politeness around him, it pissed him off.

"You okay?"

It took him a second to realize the voice was coming from his left and was actually talking to him.

Turning his head, he saw a young woman who couldn't be much older than eighteen.

"Yeah, I'm fine."

She looked kind of mousy and was on the plump side as well.

He took another sip of the coffee and had to give

it up.

"You should have ordered the tea. No one drinks the coffee here. My dad says it's like tar."

"You shouldn't be talking to strangers," he said.

"I know. I'm bored, and you look really aggressive." She shrugged. "I guess we're both in for a bad day."

He noticed she was sitting in a large section that was labeled "party." He glanced down and saw she sat on the other side of the chain.

"You're at a party all by yourself?" he asked. Who had fucking parties at burger joints? There's no way she was younger than eighteen.

"Pretty much." She looked across the space to the far corner.

He saw two people who looked old enough to be her grandparents on the phone and arguing.

"It's a long story," she said.

"I'm not going anywhere." If Rome took any longer he'd bleed to death.

"Okay. Today is my birthday. My parents—"

"They're not your parents."

She chuckled. "They are. They had me really late in life."

Clearly a midnight fuck that had resulted in a kid.

"That must be interesting."

"It has been. They're amazing though, even if they are nearing sixty now."

That would mean her mother was forty-two when she had her.

"Did they forget to hand out the invitations?"

"No. They think they did. What they don't realize is that Amanda, one of the most popular girls in school, is having a party at her house, complete with a pool and stuff like that. Clearly, this is not anyone's idea of a good time."

"You're spending your eighteenth birthday alone?" he asked.

"Yeah. It's not so bad. I get to, like, look like a loser to all of the other diners. That's a plus."

He couldn't help but laugh.

"There you go. See. It's really easy to laugh."

"Yeah, it is." He tried to ignore the pain, but he was going to bleed to death any minute. "So, eighteen. That's a pretty big deal."

"Yeah and no. It's just another number. Sure, I'm legal now to do a couple of things, but in some states I have to wait." She shrugged. "They're really upset. This was supposed to be a nice surprise. I don't think they grasp that teenagers don't eat at burger joints with clowns."

"You don't like clowns?"

"Hate them. They're scary. They tried, and that's all that counts."

Hannah didn't seem pissed off, or annoyed. She accepted that her parents had fucked up but didn't say anything.

"Why are you alone?" she asked.

"I had a really long night."

He saw Rome pull up outside the diner.

A few minutes ago, he'd have been so happy to see that fucker. Right now, he didn't want to leave this young woman alone.

"My ride is here," he said.

"Have a nice day." She ran her hands down her pants and stared out across the diner.

"It will all get better for you one day," he said.

She chuckled. "Yeah, one day I'll be queen and I can make people come to my party."

"You never know, Hannah. You know what they

say."

"What do they say?"

"Stranger things have happened at sea."

****

Present

That one chance meeting had stayed with West for a long time after. He'd gone on the dates with women that threw themselves at him. Work had taken over, and he'd lived his life until their next encounter.

Hannah didn't remember either one, and that was okay.

"Oh, my," she said as he pulled up outside of the restaurant where her parents had first met. He remembered the story he'd listened to, and Emily had told him about it.

"What is it?" he asked. "Would you like to go someplace else?"

"No, no. This is…" She covered her mouth with her hand. "I can't even believe it. This is the place where my parents first met."

"It is?"

"Yeah. I mean, wow. They were, erm, they weren't even looking for each other, and friends had put them together on a date." She chuckled. "Both Mom and Dad said they were going to tell the other that they weren't looking for anything long-term. One day led into two, then three, and within the year they were married."

"I had no idea." The lie spilled easily off his tongue.

"This is amazing. I had no idea it was still open."

"I saw it online. It had amazing reviews. Would you like me to go someplace else?"

"No. I'd love to go inside."

He parked the car. There was no valet parking so customers could come and go as they pleased. The reviews online were amazing. There were even some with couples claiming to have still been together after a date.

With his hand on the base of her back, they entered the restaurant. There was light music, murmurs all around them.

Such a romantic setting.

The maître d' asked for his name, and once he gave it, led the way to their table. It was the first time he'd entered an establishment and hadn't been noticed.

He grabbed the man's hand when he pulled out Hannah's chair. That was what he wanted to do, no one else. Helping her into her seat, he thanked the maître d' and took his own seat.

"Before we do this I need you to promise me something," she said.

"What?"

"Don't go to the bathroom until the end?"

He laughed. "Are you being serious?"

"Yes. I have this horrible feeling that all bathroom breaks on dates for me are cursed."

They were not cursed. He simply had a man who scared the shit out of all the men who dared to date her.

"I promise. If it will make you feel any better."

"Yes. Yes. It would."

Her eyes held a sparkle that he found utterly enchanting. She kept looking around her, and he saw the glow from deep within her.

Taking her hand, he ran his thumb across her knuckles. "Tonight is about you having a good time."

"You've been amazing, West. My job and helping with the scholarship. I was so worried they'd tell you no."

"The key is knowing what you want and not waiting around for someone to tell you that you can't have it. Take it."

The waiter came to their table, handing them each a menu.

"I'm Daniel. I'll be your waiter for the evening."

"Thank you, Daniel," she said.

"Order whatever you like," West said. He didn't like the sudden need to smash that fucker's face in. He was only a waiter, but he didn't want anyone near his woman.

Again, another element of his obsession with Hannah.

He'd never in all of his years felt this possessive toward anyone. Hannah was the first, the only.

He was used to being the one with all the power. Of having women throwing themselves at him and him being the one to pick and choose which one he wanted. Hannah wasn't throwing herself at his feet.

She wasn't doing anything other than being her sweet self.

Daniel had left them alone.

"I'm not much of a drinker. That one I had at your club last week really did a number on me. I'll have a sparkling water."

The pill he'd slipped into her drink without her seeing was what caused her to feel the way she did. It loosened her up, but the effects only lasted so long before it exhausted the taker and put them into a deep sleep.

Glancing down the menu, he heard her gasp and knew she'd found the same meal that her parents had shared.

"Can we share the steak meal with all the trimmings? It serves two with the garlic herbed butter?" she asked.

"It sounds wonderful."

He nodded toward the waiter and placed their

order.

****

Everything was so perfect. Even better than Hannah could have imagined. With West it was like they had their own little world. They finished their meal, and throughout dinner he asked her constant questions about herself, her family, where she saw her life in five years. She did the same, asking about his life and she noticed he didn't like talking about his family and would often change the subject or at least talk about Martha.

She could understand.

She got the sense he didn't have as good a childhood as she did.

Her parents had been old, but they'd wanted her. They'd gone against doctor's order about the possible stress and illness her mother could have from having a child at an older age. Her mother had told the doctor it was all poppycock. Forty-two wasn't old.

She loved her parents, and being in the restaurant where they met, she felt a connection to them. Like in some weird strange way they approved of West.

It was pure crazy, and she was lost in the magic and fairy tale of dreaming. She knew they were gone and there was no way of knowing what they'd think of him.

"Let's go for a walk," he said, taking her hand.

There was a small nature park a few feet away. It was probably why the restaurant had survived all this time, the nature park bringing in tourists and families.

There was a small walkway that entered the main park that was lit up, looking like a magical starry night.

She held onto West's arm as they walked. Neither of them spoke, and she didn't believe words were necessary.

This felt incredible.

"I could stay here forever," she said.

They came to a stop beneath a lamppost.

It was night out, but she didn't feel in a rush to bring their night to a close.

"We can. I'm sure I can arrange a hotel. We could do this every single day."

She shook her head. "It's so tempting, but we need to go back to work. People count on us. Well, they count on you."

He took her hand, pulling her close, and she gripped his shoulders, feeling their strength. "Nothing wrong in dreaming."

"This has been a wonderful date."

"Wonderful. I can live with that."

She chuckled. "I never know what to say to you, and I seem to just spill out whatever comes into my head without thinking."

"You don't have to think or have a filter. I like hearing what's going on in that head of yours."

He stroked down her back going to the base, grazing the top of her butt. That first night, the one that was fuzzy, he'd grabbed her ass as she kissed him.

Thinking about his lips, she couldn't help but glance down, and they looked so tempting. Were they as good as she remembered? Was the kiss a dream? Did it really happen?

"You want to kiss me right now," he said.

Heat flooded her cheeks.

"I want to ask you a question."

"Then ask. I'll answer."

"Have we ever kissed?" she asked.

"Why don't you kiss me and find out?"

That wasn't an answer.

She wanted his kiss.

Stepping closer, she lifted up onto the tips of her toes, keeping hold of his shoulders to help her with balance, and pressed her lips against his.

That first tender touch ignited a fire deep inside her. She ran her hands up to his hair, sinking her fingers into the short length. His hold tightened around her, and those hands gripped her ass exactly how she imagined they would.

His tongue pressed against her lips, wanting inside, and she didn't want to stop him. As she opened up on a moan, he plunged inside, and she touched his tongue with hers. Within seconds he had her pressed up against the lamppost, his body surrounding her. He released her ass and took her hands, holding them behind her body, keeping her locked in place.

There was nowhere else she wanted to go, and when his cock pressed against her stomach, she couldn't help but whimper. She'd not seen him, but from the feel of him against her, she knew he wasn't small. This man was big in all departments, and she craved him.

He nudged her leg open and pressed his thigh between hers. He lifted his leg up until he was touching her pussy. She let out a gasp, shocked by the sudden need that flooded her body. This wasn't what she expected, and yet it was perfect. It was everything. She didn't want him to stop but to keep on going. To touch her, to take her, to rid her of that pesky virginity that she wanted gone.

"Are you wet for me, Hannah?"

She whimpered as his lips grazed her neck. Closing her eyes, she forgot where they were as his hands moved over her body, touching her breasts, moving down to her ass then back up.

"Get a room," someone said as they walked by, and the spell she'd been under was gone.

They were in a nature reserve where anyone could see them, and she'd been ready for West to have sex with her.

"You make me lose my mind. Come on before I do something we both regret."

Chapter Six

West took her home, and she didn't hear from him Saturday or Sunday. Hannah kept her cell phone on her, much to Emily's annoyance, but she didn't care. Attempting to go to sleep after their perfect date had been hard. She'd eventually fallen asleep in the early hours of the morning only to wake up hot, needy, desperate, and in need of a cold shower. The books she loved so much still in her possession didn't even help. Nor did the internet and porn.

She wanted West.

He'd become like an addiction. After only two dates she wanted to give him her body, everything, just to feel what she did pressed up against that lamppost.

She expected to see him in work the following week, but much to her surprise, he was absent.

Everyone else at the office didn't find it odd. West kept odd hours, and Sin wasn't the only place of work. His business was all over the city, and he had to make random visits to make sure everything was running smoothly.

Lunch breaks she ate by herself, staring at his office door. Night was the worst or being driven home by Rome or Cage. Neither said anything about him, and she was too embarrassed to ask.

Each night she'd go asleep alone only to wake up partway through the night, slick with sweat and horny. Touching herself didn't help. The orgasms she created were lackluster and only left her feeling bored and sad.

By Friday night, she was more than happy to have a girls' night with Emily.

A chick flick was playing, but she'd not been following the story line. It held no appeal to her, but Emily loved these kinds of films. Hannah was more of an action person. Big car explosions, lots of gunfire, and fighting was her deal.

"What's it like to have sex?" she asked, blurting the question out.

"It's sex. You know. Cock goes into the pussy, lots of jumping around, and job done."

She frowned. "No, I mean, is it nice?"

Emily glanced over at her. "You've never asked me about sex before."

"It's stupid."

"You do know what happens? That you need to have condoms and practice safe sex. That you have to actually have physical contact?"

"Yes, yes. I know. My parents were very much aware of sex." They'd made sure she was aware of everything to do with sex, from condoms to safe sex to saying no if she didn't want it.

"Okay, what would you like to know?"

"How does it feel? I mean, does it really hurt?"

"My first time did. It was painful, but after a few seconds it felt okay."

"Do you think it'll hurt with any man or someone with a smaller … penis?"

Emily chuckled. "You can call it 'dick' or 'cock.' I won't be offended. It doesn't matter who it's with. I guess if we're going with romance then you should be doing something for love, but it's not always like that. Sometimes you just need to get your rocks off, you know?"

Hannah shrugged. "I don't know."

"Is this because of West?"

She tucked some hair behind her ears. "You know I've never had sex before."

"Yep, you're still the mighty virgin."

"I'm not proud of it. I've just not found that

someone I want to be with."

"Do you think you've even tried?" Emily asked.

"It's beside the point. I can't stop thinking about West. How he makes me feel. I want to be with him. Intimately. I think about him all the time. The way his hands are and I want them all over me."

"Then you've got to tell him."

"What if he laughs?"

"West won't laugh."

"Why?"

"He's crazy about you."

"He is?"

"Anyone can see it. He's totally smitten. I'm sure if you asked him to walk over broken glass and lava he'd do it for you."

Emily sat back, her gaze on the television.

Hannah had noticed this lack of interest in talking. They didn't really speak unless they had to.

"Em, I don't know what's going on between us right now. I think I've done something wrong, but I don't know what. I will understand if you don't want us living together anymore or if you just want to live separate lives. Just tell me. Don't make me try and guess that you wish we'd not moved in together."

Rather than sticking around, she left the living room, closing her bedroom door.

She lay down on her bed and grabbed her pillow, hugging it tight. She was so confused. Sleep wouldn't help. All she did was think about West and the fact she'd not seen him all week.

Why did her life have to get so complicated?

Her bedroom door opened and closed. She heard Emily climb onto the bed and her friend was behind her, hugging her.

"I'm sorry I've been a bitch lately. It's not you at

all. I promise you that."

Tears filled her eyes, and she hated how sad she felt. Emily was the only real family she had left. Without her, she had nothing.

"I don't want to push you away. I miss you, Emily. What did I do wrong?"

"You've done nothing wrong. You're a fantastic friend. I'm the one with the problem. I'm here for you, and I'm not going anywhere. I promise."

They lay together for several minutes, and it reminded Hannah of all the times she'd been sad in college, especially when it came to her parents.

"Sex is something that can be amazing and addictive. I've seen the books you try to hide, Hannah. You've got to be careful. Men out there will hurt you for what they want. They're not good. Like that loser Lawrence. He was a fucking weirdo, and you need to be careful. I don't want anything to happen to you."

She hugged her friend close.

"Thank you, Emily."

"Anytime."

****

The following Monday, West sat in his office watching the elevator doors for when Hannah would arrive. The past week his other work and details of Lawrence's hideout had kept him away from her.

He had to be careful about where he took her and who saw them. Enemies were always around, and he wouldn't put her in danger again. Keeping his distance, he had to be content with watching her. He had cameras in his office so that wasn't hard, but at night, he got to sit at home and listen to her.

The space he was giving her helped his cause. She wanted him. He'd felt it on their last date. The way she rode his leg. How she gave herself over to his touch.

There was a passion and fire burning within Hannah, unused and ready to be taken, to be nurtured.

All he had to do was be careful how he nurtured her. The wrong kind of handling and he'd destroy what was building between them. Her security detail kept him updated on her whereabouts at all times. Rome and Cage continued to drive her to and from work.

No one had figured out that the woman he was obsessed with, his one true weakness, was so close to him. When he finally took her and the world knew who she belonged to, he'd have no choice but to take this life away from her.

She'd have to be protected and kept safe.

There's no way he'd risk her safety.

He'd listened to her conversation with Emily, even when Hannah had laid her cards on the table. Just as he'd been about to call Emily to order her what to do, he'd watched her go into Hannah's room and make up. Emily's actions had saved her in that moment. He wouldn't hurt her so long as she was doing her job.

The elevator doors opened, and he watched as Hannah was the first to arrive. He'd already closed all the blinds in his office, giving him privacy.

She walked over to her desk, and the moment she looked toward him, he saw the frown. She put her bag down and stood in the doorway.

"You're back."

"I'm back. Come in. Close the door."

Hannah didn't even hesitate. She entered his office. The lamb coming to the slaughter. She had no idea he was the big, bad wolf. He'd worked tirelessly to make sure she never knew the truth. That his identity was kept from her.

She didn't know that he'd killed people. Where she'd had a mother who baked and tucked her into bed, he'd fought his way to the top.

She stepped up to the chair opposite his desk. She wore a pencil skirt that ended at her knees, a white blouse, and small jacket.

The bra she wore wasn't padded as he saw the outline of her large nipples pressing against the shirt. He'd watched her dress this morning, her fingers stroking over her body. She'd struggled to sleep each night, and soon he'd put her out of her misery.

Their first meeting hadn't gone to plan, but he always intended to get beneath her skin. To become an addiction she couldn't shake. His touch. His mouth. His cock. He wanted her to worship him the way he did her.

"How have you been?" she asked.

"I've been well. You?"

"Great."

"Come here." He'd been treating her with kid gloves. That ended now.

She stepped closer toward him. She stopped at the edge of his desk, and he pointed where he wanted her to stand. Right in front of him with the desk at her back.

Standing up, she tilted her head back to see him.

"Did you miss me?" he asked.

"Yes."

She didn't even hesitate.

All of his carefully organized plans were staring him right in the face. "I missed you, too. Lean your ass on my desk."

"What?"

"Do it."

She leaned back, her hands going to either side of her. Cupping her face, he pushed some of her locks out of the way. She'd not cut it, and he was damn happy about that. Running his thumb across her bottom lip, he pressed against her mouth and she opened up, sucking on him.

Pulling his thumb out, he wet her lips. "I've been thinking about these lips of yours." He pressed his to hers, kissing her. She moaned, and he stroked his hands down her body, grazing across her nipples as he did. "Do you know what I think about?"

"No."

"I think about how good it would be to have them wrapped around my cock." His lips were pressed against her ear.

She gasped again, her body seeming to jerk as she understood what he was saying. Cupping her tits, he kept her in place. Nowhere to run. "Have you thought about me touching you, Hannah? My mouth on your tits, sucking those big nipples?"

"West?" She cried out his name as he pinched her nipple. The sound echoed around the room.

No one was outside yet, not that they'd comment. It wasn't their place to say shit. They knew their jobs and were doing them well. If they tried to interfere or make Hannah uncomfortable, he'd deal with them. They all knew who he was and what he was capable of doing to them.

Each of them had secrets they wanted to keep hidden.

So long as they did what was required of them, he didn't have a problem. Any of them stepped out of line, he'd step on them. Simple as that.

Running his hand down her body, he went to the edge of her skirt and started to lift it up. She didn't fight him.

She wanted this.

He'd listened to her need, watched her stroke her pussy to orgasm only to be unsatisfied. He'd gotten so hard watching her play with herself. She'd worn her nightshirt with no panties, and lifted it up, exposing that sexy cunt that he wanted so much.

Today, he was going to give her the orgasm she'd been craving and that would blow her mind.

With her skirt around her waist, he cupped her pussy.

Her panties were already soaking wet, and as he tore them from her, she let out a squeak of protest.

"I don't have another pair."

"Then you're going to have to go without." He touched her naked pussy. She had a small smattering of curls over the lips of her pussy. He didn't mind those. He'd never seen the appeal of a completely shaved or waxed pussy. When the pubic hair grew back, it always felt and looked wrong to him. A personal preference on his part.

As he slid a finger between her slit, her mouth opened on another gasp.

He couldn't penetrate her today. When he took her hymen, she'd be spread across his bed, legs wide open so he could watch her take him.

Damn, the thought alone made him want to blow his load right now.

Teasing around her clit, going in circles then back again, he slid down to her entrance only to pull right back up so he wasn't tempted to thrust inside her with his fingers.

"Open your shirt. Show me those tits."

Her hands shook as she followed his instructions. The bra she wore had a small catch in the front, which she flicked open. Those full tits spilled forward, and he took one between his teeth, sucking on the flesh.

"Lean back," he said.

There was enough light coming behind for him to see her.

She leaned back until she was flat on the desk.

"Put your legs on the desk."

"What?"

"Do it."

She didn't argue with him, putting her legs on the desk.

Gazing down her body, he looked into her eyes and moved down to her tits, which shook with each of her indrawn breaths. Down he went to her pussy. The skirt was bunched up around her waist.

The lips of her pussy were plump, open, and he watched his fingers as he teased her clit.

She was so wet.

The only reason she was still a virgin was because of him.

The dates she'd been on ended at his will.

She'd been his for a long time, and that was never going to change. Pulling his chair closer to him, he sat down and stared at her pussy.

"What are you doing?"

"I'm going to play." He gripped her hips and moved her so that she was at the edge of the table. Her legs splayed open as he put her feet on the arms of the chair.

Spreading her pussy lips, he leaned down and stroked his tongue across her clit. She cried out his name, and he loved hearing that sound. He'd gladly listen to it all day long. He wanted nothing more than to lose himself in her touch.

Sucking her bud into his mouth, he ran his hands up her body, cupping her tits. She arched up into his hands.

"You like my tongue on your clit?"

"Yes."

"You want me to fuck you, Hannah? To show

you what I really want to do to you?"

"Yes, please, yes."

He flicked his tongue across, over, and around her clit, drawing out her pleasure. He watched her body, seeing her getting closer to the peak. He held her there, captured, not letting her go until he knew she couldn't handle anything else. The moment she was ready, he thrust her over the edge and listened to her pleasure as it spilled from her lips.

She shuddered, pushing her cunt up to his mouth.

"I can't take anymore," she said after just a few seconds of his prolonged teasing.

He placed a kiss to her clit and stood, pushing the chair out of the way. Opening his belt buckle, he stared into her eyes.

For a split second, he saw the worry staring back at him, but within one blink it was gone, replaced by excitement. She was so easy to read, and he loved watching her. He got off on it.

Pulling his dick out, he ran his fingers up and down the hard length. Pre-cum oozed out of the tip, and he massaged it into his flesh.

"I'm not going to fuck you yet. You can relax. When I do take you it's not going to be in my office. Not the first time."

"Oh."

She looked a little disappointed, but he'd make it up to her soon.

Spreading the lips of her pussy open, he placed his cock against her. She was so wet that he didn't need to find any extra lube. Up and down, he rubbed his cock all in her cream. Each time he bumped her clit, she gasped.

It would be so easy to put his cock to her entrance and slide in deep, but he didn't want to spoil her first time. When he took her, he wanted her to feel every inch of him, to be able to take his time, loving her body, showing her how good it could be between them.

He wasn't interested in a quick fuck.

With his cock between her slit, he leaned over her, slowly moving up and down, careful not to slip inside her. Taking possession of her lips, he kissed her. Her hands sank into his hair, holding him close as he slowly worked his cock.

Kissing down her body to her neck, he sucked on her pulse, licking down to take one of her nipples into his mouth. He bit down on the flesh and soothed it out with his tongue.

He wanted inside her. His orgasm was so close, but he stayed in control.

Once he'd given her other breast attention, he pulled back, grabbed his cock, and started to work it. Staring at her body, knowing she belonged to him, he brought himself close to the edge and finally, looking into her brown eyes, he came, spilling his seed across her pussy and stomach. His orgasm seemed to go on forever. When he finished, he sat back in this chair, staring at her.

Drops of his cum spilled between her lips, falling to the desk.

He wondered if a drop of cum fell inside her, if that was enough to make her pregnant. His next plan was to have her bound to him in such a way that she couldn't disappear.

Opening his drawer, he took out some tissues and cleaned her up. After he'd wiped his cum from her body, he did the same with his cock, putting himself away. The air was heavy with the scent of sex.

She didn't speak, and he wasn't surprised. She looked taken aback by what happened. Helping her with the skirt then with her shirt, he put her back in order. Her hair was fine. She often left the unruly locks untamed.

"I don't know what any of this means," she said, finally speaking.

He kissed her lips. "It means you're mine."

"How?"

"You belong to me. Whatever you want, I'll do what I can to make sure you have it. Whenever you need me, come to me."

"You mean for sex?"

"And other things. I'm not leaving you alone tonight," he said. "After work, you're coming home with me."

"You don't have to do that."

"You're coming home with me." He tilted her head back with his thumb underneath her chin. "What are you thinking right now?"

"I don't think this was a good idea. What if you get bored with me? I like my job."

"You will never have to worry about your job, and I won't ever get bored with you."

"You don't know that."

"Do you trust me?"

"Yes."

That was her biggest mistake. He wasn't a man to be trusted.

"Then know I will do everything in my power to keep you happy." He kissed her again. "Now, you're going to need to get some work done. I've got a few things to do. For the rest of the day, I want you to think about me. About me being inside you, taking that sweet pussy. You got me?"

"Yes." She released a sigh.

"Good."

He kissed her again and took a step back. He had to let her go otherwise he was taking her back to his apartment to claim her.

"Get to work."

West watched her go.

Another part of his plan was complete. She'd be his before the end of the week.

Pulling out his cell phone, he saw a missed call from Rome and dialed him.

"Let me hear it," he said.

"We've had an interesting development," Rome said.

He listened as Rome gave him the details.

Tonight wouldn't be good for him and Hannah as he had to deal with her roommate.

Chapter Seven

"What was Lawrence doing at the same coffee shop as you?" West asked.

"I don't know. I told you, I was just there to get a cup of coffee. I was thirsty, and I hate the coffee available." Emily was sitting in a chair, her hands tied together.

West sat opposite her.

He wasn't interested in her excuses.

"I was the one that put the call in that I'd seen him."

"Why didn't you call one of my guys?"

"I was at a table. He forced me to keep my hands flat on the surface like this." She placed her hands out as well as she could with them tied, trying to show him what happened. "Then he started to ask me a bunch of questions. I wanted to grab my cell. To call you. To warn you. I couldn't."

West glanced over her shoulder at Rome, who nodded.

Since Emily had been difficult, he'd put a few extra men on her to keep watch. He didn't trust her, not even a little bit.

"He wants her," Emily said. "You need to make sure there's more security. I don't know. He kept asking questions about my place in her life. What I had to do with you. That he'd been looking into my background and he'd discovered I wasn't who I said I was. He scared me, West."

He stared at Emily.

The cover he'd given her was bare minimum. There'd be no reason for Hannah to look too deeply into who her friend was.

"I want my men at her apartment, outside her

door. Double the protection," he said, looking at Rome.

"Done."

Looking at Emily, he waited.

"I didn't tell him anything."

"You're lying to me, Emily. We know you tested positive for heroin. Just tell me what the fuck happened."

He watched as tears welled in her eyes.

"He knew, West. He knew. When he told me to put my hands on the table, he stabbed me with a syringe and injected me with it. I didn't take it willingly. I promise."

"I'll deal with it." He looked toward Cage. "Get her back into rehab. Major detox. I don't want her outside for a month."

"Please, West. I can do this. I promise."

"I don't care what you think you can do. I know what you can do, and you're not coming out until you're clean. You don't want that shit now, but it'll fester inside you until you're desperate for more." He snapped his fingers and walked away.

Heading outside of the warehouse, he looked up at the night sky, aware Rome had followed him.

He'd underestimated Lawrence.

"He's going to attack Hannah. It's only a matter of time before he loses patience and does so," Rome said.

"That will never happen." He'd never put his woman at risk, not when he was so close to having her.

"You ever thought about using her as bait? It'll draw him out."

"And then what? Have her look at me like a fucking monster as I tear him apart limb from fucking limb? You know what I demand. Hannah knows nothing."

"With all due respect, sir. You know it's only going to be a matter of time before she finds out who you are."

"She'll never find out."

He heard Rome snort.

"You can't protect her forever. You know I'm right, otherwise I'd be dead already."

He wanted to attack Rome, to silence him, but there was truth in what he'd said. He'd gotten this long without Hannah finding out who he was or what he'd done. But it wouldn't be long before someone spilled all of his secrets. Especially Lawrence.

"Put extra men on her. I'm not going to allow Lawrence to touch her. To draw him out, we're going to need to find another way."

"The only other way is to bring a lot of men, scour the entire city. Flush him out so he doesn't have anywhere to run or to turn."

"Give the order. I want Lawrence alive."

He climbed into his car and didn't give any further instruction. It wasn't needed. He didn't go to his apartment.

Driving straight to Hannah's place, he parked in the only available space and climbed out.

There was a chance that in time she'd find out exactly who he was. What he did. How he lived his life. When that time came, he intended to already be so deep in her soul she couldn't let him go.

He buzzed Hannah's number and waited.

"Hello."

"It's me, West."

"Oh." She buzzed him in, and he didn't stop to think or to change his mind. He just needed to know that she was safe. That she was waiting for him.

At her door, he saw it wasn't open and gave it a knock. Within seconds, she opened the door. She looked a little nervous.

In her mouth was a spoon and in her hand a large tub of ice cream.

"West?"

Stepping into her apartment, he closed the door and flicked the lock into place. Taking the tub and then the spoon, he placed it on the small coffee table. He grabbed her hand, pulled her close to him, and slammed his lips down over hers as she gasped.

Sinking his fingers into her hair, he kissed her lips and pressed her against the wall.

Her hands covered his before gripping his arms.

She only wore a pair of pajama shorts and a crop shirt. Running his hands down her back, he gripped her ass. He couldn't get enough of her lush curves. She was so fucking precious to him.

Breaking from the kiss, he trailed his lips down her neck, sucking on her pulse.

"What are you doing here?" she asked.

"You know why." He bit down on her tender flesh before sucking out the burn. There was only one person he trusted with her safety and that was himself. He wasn't going to allow anything to happen to her.

There's no way he'd be able to survive if something did.

Lifting her up, he held her against his body and the wall.

She wrapped her arms around his neck, and it wasn't enough. He needed to be closer to her.

"Where's your bedroom?" he asked.

He was already moving across her apartment as she pointed out her room. He couldn't walk straight over there, otherwise he'd let on that he knew where she stayed. There had been one time he'd been inside her apartment. He didn't want her to freak out. It wasn't normal for men to remember these things, was it?

Kicking open her bedroom door, he placed her on the bed and stood back, staring at her. She wasn't wearing a bra, and her erect nipples pressed against her nightshirt.

He held her hand, pulling her to her feet, and gripped the edge of her shirt. Staring into her eyes, he lifted the fabric over her head and tossed it to the floor.

When she made to cover up, he took her hands, holding them out.

"Don't ever hide from me. I want to see all of you."

Slowly, she pulled her hands away from his, and they landed on his chest. She paused, and he waited to see what she'd do next. She slid them beneath his shirt and pushed his jacket off.

Lowering his jacket to the floor so it didn't make a sound of the weapons he had hidden, he wrapped his fingers around her wrist, kissing each pulse on the inside.

Placing her hands back on his chest, he waited as she took her time undoing the buttons that held his shirt in place. When that was off, he saw her gaze back on his body. Her fingers lightly traced over the ink he'd gotten over the years, her touch setting him on fire. He wanted nothing more than to slam her to the bed and fuck her hard. The ink wasn't anything special. Most of it was black tribal ink that caught his attention—sharp edges and smooth curves. It had taken hours for the artist to create as he wanted it to be perfect. The only splash of color was the single rose on his inner wrist.

He held himself in check, and taking hold of her hand, he placed it over his heart. That's where she'd been for five years, and not a moment went by that he didn't crave more. She was a lot stronger than people thought.

Wrapping his arms around her, he moved her back to the bed, taking her shorts down in the process.

When she was lying naked on the edge, her legs spread, he stepped between them. Her eyes were on him as he removed his belt and lowered his pants. Next, he removed his boxer briefs, kicking off his shoes and pushing both the items of clothing out of the way.

Leaning over her, he stroked the tips of his fingers up one thigh going to the apex and cupping her pussy.

She arched up against her, spreading wide, and as he teased her clit, he found her already so slick and wet.

He wanted her more than anything else.

Moving her up the bed, he stared into her eyes.

"You look nervous," he said.

"I am. I mean, I want to be good at this."

"You're going to be amazing. You've got nothing to worry about."

"It's going to hurt?" she asked.

"I'll do everything I can to make the pain go away." Pressing a kiss to her lips, he continued to stroke her clit, drawing out her pleasure, setting her on fire as he felt his own need curling deep inside him. His cock was already so hard and the tip leaking copious amounts of pre-cum.

Stroking her to the edge of orgasm, he saw she was so close, and as he did he pulled away, grabbing his cock and placing it at her entrance.

"Wait. Wait." She put a hand on his chest. "A condom. We need a condom. I'm not protected."

He gritted his teeth.

He'd hoped she'd be too far gone to demand something like that.

It annoyed him that she'd want anything between them, but he had to remember, she'd not been waiting five long years for this. Besides, there would be more than enough time to get her pregnant, to have her the way he wanted.

Plans didn't always go the way he intended, but he always got what he wanted in the end.

Always.

"I don't have any with me. I'll pull out."

"That's not safe."

"I'll never do anything that will not keep you safe." Of course, that didn't mean having unprotected sex.

Thinking about Hannah heavily pregnant, with bigger tits and waiting to have his child, turned him on, but he wasn't about to tell her that when she clearly didn't want to have children just yet.

Time.

He'd give her time.

"Trust me, Hannah. I've not done anything to prove to you otherwise that I'd hurt you."

She nodded.

Gripping his cock, which hadn't lost any of his arousal, he ran the tip up and down her slit.

Pulling out wasn't a form of contraception.

Far from it.

He wasn't about to tell her that though.

Hitting her clit with the tip of his cock, he watched her cry out. Her body was sensitive as he'd brought her to the edge of orgasm but not let her topple over that cliff.

"You want this, Hannah? You want my cock?"

"Yes."

Slowly, he eased the head against her entrance. Staring into her eyes, he knew this would hurt her. That pushing past that hymen, making her his, he'd hear her cry of pain. Still, with one hard thrust, he tore past that cherry, seating to the hilt as her scream rang out in the air.

He captured her flailing hands, keeping them locked beside her head, trapping her to the bed so she didn't have anywhere to go.

"It's fine. I've got you."

Her pussy was so tight, so slick, and so hot wrapped around his dick. Tears leaked out of her eyes, and he hated that he'd hurt her.

It was the last thing he wanted to do, to cause her pain.

He licked away her tears before taking possession of her mouth. Her cunt contracted around him, and he had to concentrate not to blow his load there and then. She was so incredibly tight, more so than he imagined.

Running his hand down her thigh to cup her ass, he lifted her leg up.

The action opened her up a little more, and he sank inside her, moaning as he did.

"So perfect," he said. "Does it still hurt?"

"No."

Slowly, he stared to rock inside her, pulling out until only the tip of his dick stayed inside her and then thrusting in deep. Her cunt started to go slick and he was able to thrust inside her with ease.

Her nails bit into the flesh of his arms as he continued to take her, to get a little deeper with each thrust.

After a few minutes, she didn't just lie there but started to thrust up against him, driving her pussy onto his dick, clearly knowing what she wanted.

"That's it, baby. Ride my cock. Fuck, yeah, that's what I want. Harder." Reaching between them, he found her clit, slowing down his thrusts, letting her do all the work as he teased her clit.

He closed his eyes, counting to ten to gain control. All he wanted to do was come so hard, to flood her tight cunt with his cream.

She screamed his name as she came.

Each pulse squeezed his cock until he couldn't help it anymore. He fucked her hard, the headboard hitting the wall with each of his thrusts. She wrapped her arms around him as he took her lips once again.

Filling her pussy with his cock, he felt his balls tighten. The first stirrings of his orgasm, and when he came, he did so with a groan and at the last minute remembered. Pulling out of her wet hole, he ran his hand up and down the length, coating her pussy with his spunk.

It wasn't the ending he'd wanted, but it was going to have to do.

When he finished, he saw his cum was mixed with her virgin blood, his cock smeared with it.

He'd taken her.

Now she belonged to him, and there was no going back.

****

"Emily could come home at any minute," Hannah said.

"I don't care." West wrapped his arms around her waist, pulling her back against him. She'd be lying if she said she didn't love how attentive and possessive he was. Not only had he taken her virginity but immediately after, he'd run her a bath, and that's what they were doing now.

West was way too big to be inside this small contraption, but he held her close. His hands stroked her, building up a flame that only he could put out.

She was no longer a virgin.

He'd taken her cherry.

It had hurt so badly.

When he pushed his cock inside her, the burn had

startled her, and then as he went to the hilt, she'd been overwhelmed by just how big he was.

West wasn't a small man in any sense of the word. Every single part of him was big, ready for anything.

Leaning her head back against his chest, she felt safe, secure, content. Happy even.

"We have to share this bathroom, and I don't want her seeing you."

"This is a jealousy thing? You don't like other women looking at me?"

She nibbled her lip, suddenly nervous. "Is that okay?"

He chuckled. "I love it. No other woman could ever compare to you, but if you're nervous and want to mark your territory, go right ahead. I'm not going to stop you."

"That's ridiculous. I'm not going to do that." She didn't like the thought of other women wanting him. "Are you seeing other women?"

"You think I'd string you along like that?"

"No." She couldn't help it. "I don't know much about you."

"You know a lot. There's no other woman but you, Hannah. I've not got a dozen mistresses lying around waiting to service me. I've been alone for a long time. Waiting for you."

She snorted. "You've not been waiting for me."

"I've been waiting for the right woman, and that happens to be you." He nibbled her neck and she closed her eyes, trying not to moan but it was impossible.

When it came to West, she couldn't seem to get any of her senses under control.

When she'd heard the buzzer of the apartment, she just figured Emily had forgotten her key. Hearing his voice had done things to her body. Made her ache. Her pussy had been slick with arousal, and need had flooded her. Seeing him outside her door, she'd known she wanted him. That if he touched her, she'd give him everything.

That kiss he'd given her had been filled with hunger.

She'd been so desperate for him.

So in need of him taking her.

"Did you get all of your work done?" she asked.

She'd been so disappointed when he'd told her he'd have to cancel their evening. It's why seeing him tonight felt so right for her.

She'd not been saving her virginity for a special occasion or anything.

Being with West, it felt right.

"Most of it. I didn't stay for everything though. I wanted to come and see you."

She leaned back, smiling up at him. "I like that. I like that you came here."

"There's nowhere else I'd ever want to go."

She pulled out of his arms and moved so that she was facing him. She missed his touch, but she wanted to be able to look him in the eye as she spoke.

"Come back here."

"No. I want us to talk. That is allowed right, to talk?"

"We can do whatever the hell you want." He leaned his head on his fingers, smiling at her. The ink on his wrist drew her attention. All of his ink was black and white, no color whatsoever.

The rose though looked vaguely familiar.

"Is that a regular tattoo?" she asked.

"I don't know. Why?"

"I just … I thought I'd seen it before."

Silence fell between them for a few seconds, and she tried to think where she'd seen that ink before.

Nothing came to mind. Not where she'd seen it or on who. It was like there was a giant hole of feeling something, but it was out of her grasp.

"You've been in a tattoo parlor?"

"What?" She pulled out of her confusing thoughts and looked at him. "Sorry, I completely zoned out. What did you say?"

"Have you ever been inside a tattoo parlor? I've seen your body and there's not a piece of ink on you."

"Oh, no. I've never gotten inked or anything like that. I'm afraid of needles. I can't stand them. I had thought of getting a tattoo. Like a dolphin or a Chinese symbol but it's never come to pass." She rubbed at her temple, feeling a headache coming on. "Do they hurt?"

"Some of them did. I liked it though. Being under, having something come to life on my body."

"It sounds awesome. Not the actual drill though. I've seen some of the television shows where celebrities get tattoos. The sound reminds me so much of the dentist." She wrinkled her nose. "I don't like going to the dentist. Not even a little bit."

He burst out laughing. "It's not like going to the dentist. It pinches the skin some. I've got a very high pain threshold."

"You see, minimal. I get a paper cut, I cry."

"I'm sure you've got a higher pain threshold than that."

She shook her head. "Not really."

"Come here."

She felt her cheeks heat with the look he was giving her. "What are you going to do?"

"You'll see." He winked at her, and he looked so sinful but also so welcoming that she couldn't say no.

Lifting up, she crawled toward him, aware of her tits hanging in front of her. She didn't cover up though.

West caught her hips and moved her so that she was straddling his legs. Hers were wide open as her knees slid down the sides of the bath. He ran his hands over her ass, up her back, in her hair.

He tugged her head down and their lips met.

She moaned, cupping his face as she opened up and he slid his tongue inside. There was nothing else she'd rather be doing in that moment than kissing him.

Down his hand went, going to her ass. He tightened his hold on her butt, squeezing the flesh. He spread the cheeks of her ass wide before letting her go. His hands were once again in her hair, only this time he tugged on the strands.

With the way he pulled, she arched her chest up. It was like an offering to him, giving him what he wanted as he held her captive.

"Now these tits are so pretty. I've been wanting nothing more than to have them in front of me like this. To tease. To lick. To suck." He stroked a hand down her chest, across each nipple, before holding still in the center, between the valley of her tits.

Her pussy was already wet. It didn't matter that they'd not long ago had sex. She wanted him again.

She didn't want him to stop.

"You look like a sexy little offering for me and only me." He moaned. "Now, let's see how much pain you can take."

She tensed up, expecting something painful and brutal. His lips covered her left nipple and she relaxed, all tension leaving her body.

Only, the suction on her breast tightened. It became almost unbearable, and she cried out as he used his teeth, biting down.

She couldn't pull away, not that she wanted to.

He soothed out the pain with his tongue before sliding between her breasts to give some attention to her other nipple. He started licking then sucking, and his teeth grazed her bud before biting down.

She cried out, but the pain was addictive.

With each pull on her tit, she wanted more.

She didn't want him to stop.

Her pussy was on fire with need. She wished he'd touch her there, to stroke out the need that consumed her.

"I can see you like a little pain."

His hold eased up on her hair, and she looked at him.

"See, there are some pains that you can handle."

She looked down at her chest as he placed his hand on her tit. He cupped her flesh, his thumb running back and forth over her nipple. Biting her lip, she watched as he pinched her tightly before letting her go.

Her breasts looked heavy. The buds were red from his torture, but it felt good.

"Are you wet for me?" he asked.

"Yes."

"Let me have a feel."

He cupped her pussy, his finger sliding inside her, making her gasp from the pleasure. He added a second finger, stretching her out. His thumb caressed over her clit as his fingers plunged inside her.

"I want you. I've got to have you again." He pulled his fingers from her pussy, and before she knew what was happening, he lifted her up and lowered her onto his stiff length.

There was no way she wasn't going to be sore tomorrow.

She gripped his shoulders as he filled her to the hilt once again. She couldn't believe she was having sex twice in one night.

His cock hit deep inside her as she lifted up and rocked onto his dick.

West held her hips, guiding her over his cock, making her take all of it.

She did so willingly.

She didn't want him to stop.

"Do you like that, Hannah? You like my dick inside you?"

"Yes." She loved it when he talked dirty to her.

"I love fucking you. I love your tight cunt wrapped around my dick. I've been thinking about nothing else since we met. Now that you belong to me, I'm going to take you every single chance I get. I'm going to own this pussy, baby."

It was like something out of her books.

His brand of possession aroused her.

"Please, West."

"What do you want?" he asked.

"I want you to fuck me."

He pulled her off his dick, and she was startled as he had her in his arms, carrying her through to the bedroom. Within seconds, she was on the bed, spread open, and he was between her thighs, pounding in deep.

He fucked her hard, and she loved every second of it.

"Watch me, baby. Watch me take your pussy."

She looked down at where his cock was filling her. His dick was slick with arousal as he continued to pound in deep.

She couldn't look away, not that she wanted to. It was such a beautiful sight.

This was dirty.

This was what she'd secretly yearned for.

Not just to have her virginity taken.

But to be used, to be given pleasure, to be pushed. The way West held her, his words, all of him, he was the person she'd been waiting for, and she didn't want to let him go.

Chapter Eight

The last thing Hannah wanted to do the following morning was go to work. She stared down at the sheets with the smear of blood on them. She remembered reading a book where a virgin's sheets were hung out the window for all to see the claiming.

She was so pleased that it was a very old, outdated custom. Pouring powder into the washing machine, she set the sheets to wash. She'd come down in an hour to place them in the dryer.

It was already seven in the morning, and she made her way back up to her apartment. She was no longer a virgin.

Far from it.

West had fucked her hard last night. They had sex twice, and her body was feeling it today. Her pussy was so sore from the rough sex last night.

She'd loved every second of it, and even as she took a step, she didn't mind the memory it kept awakening.

Entering her apartment, she saw West waiting for her. He was on his cell phone, and he held a finger to his lips.

She smiled at him and went straight into the kitchen to prepare them some coffee.

"Okay. I see. Yeah, I don't like this." There was a long pause. "Option two it is. Thanks." He hung up his cell phone.

Glancing over at him, she felt a shiver run down her spine. He didn't look happy. In fact, he looked ready to murder whoever stood in front of him.

"Everything okay?" she asked.

She didn't know what the morning-after routine called for.

Pushing some hair behind her ear, she left the kitchen, offering him a cup of coffee.

"It's fine for now. Not the best, but I can deal with it." He took the cup from her. "Where were you?"

"I put the sheets in to wash. There's a laundry room in the basement."

"Don't leave the apartment without my permission."

She frowned. "West, you're not my dad."

He stared at her. "I'm sorry. I was worried."

"There's nothing to be worried about. I'm completely safe." She stepped into his arms, hating that feeling that was once again building inside her.

Something was going on inside of West's head. She didn't know what it was or even what he was thinking. He didn't say anything, but that didn't mean he wasn't thinking something or keeping something from her.

Tilting her head back, she smiled at him. "We've got to get ready for work."

"Yeah, about that. You're coming out with me today."

"I am."

"Yes. You're going to see a couple of my other businesses."

"That should be fun," she said.

He ran a hand down her back. "I'd take you away to keep you for myself for the next couple of weeks. I don't want to share you."

"Like a vacation?"

"Yes. Exactly like that. You, me, a hotel room. No one from the outside world looking in."

"That sounds really nice. It's been a long time since I've been on a vacation."

"You'd come with me?" he asked.

"I don't know if I can. I'd have to ask my boss if he'd let me go on vacation. I've not been with him very long. He may not want me to go so soon after just hiring me."

"Maybe you can do something to convince the boss to give you time off."

"Like what?" she asked.

He was teasing her, and she'd never seen this side of him. She loved it.

"Maybe offer him something he couldn't refuse."

"Like what?"

"Something tempting. A promise to do whatever he wants to you."

"Like a slave?"

"Not like a slave. He doesn't want you to not have a choice."

"What does he want?" she asked. She was getting so aroused at the thought of being at his mercy. Of him taking the choice away.

Maybe there was something wrong with her?

"To give you pleasure and for you to trust him that he'd never do anything to hurt you, but if he wants you to try something that he knows you'll enjoy, you do so. No hesitation."

"And for that I can go on vacation with you?" she asked.

"Yes."

She couldn't help but smile. "I've never done anything like this. Reckless. Wild."

"You think this is wild?"

"Isn't it?"

"It's certainly something, but it's not wild. Not yet." He leaned in close so that his lips were against her ear. "I can show you wild though. Would you like that?"

"Yes." She spoke the word on a whimper.

Her nipples were so incredibly tight.

"We better get going. I'll arrange the necessary details for you to be on vacation with me as soon as possible."

She nodded.

He took a sip of his coffee, and she glanced around the apartment. There was no sign of Emily.

Leaving the kitchen, she made her way to Emily's door. "Emily, are you here?"

"What's wrong?" West asked.

"Did you hear Emily come in last night?"

"No."

She opened Emily's door. The bed was pristine, no sign of anyone having slept in it.

"That's strange."

"What is?"

"That Emily wouldn't be here. She's normally here before I head into work."

"Maybe she met someone."

"I don't know." She shrugged. "I'll call her."

She grabbed her cell phone, dialing Emily's number only to be told she wasn't available.

"Should I call the police?" she asked. Worry filled her.

"Why don't we leave it for the day? She may call you?" he asked.

"You're sure. I don't want to leave it too long and risk her being hurt." She worried. "What if I call her parents? Or her brothers?"

"Why don't you stop worrying. Your friend is probably having a one-night stand or something." West cupped her face. "Relax, okay? She'll call you."

She took a deep breath. "Yes, relax. I can do that."

"You're sure."

"Yes."

"Good. Let's go."

She grabbed her bag and followed him out of the apartment. She still wasn't happy that she'd not seen Emily since the day before. They were having a few difficulties within their friendship, but that didn't mean she wanted anything bad to happen.

She didn't like that sick feeling that twisted her gut.

Once again, West opened the door for her and buckled her seatbelt. When he first did it, she'd hated it, but now though, she found it rather charming of him.

Sitting back in his chair, she felt different.

Alive.

Her body ached from a night of sex.

The man who'd taken her to heaven sat beside her, pulling away from the curb.

Everything was coming together in her head.

If only her parents were here to see him. She wondered what her father would think. Would he hate him?

West was a commanding presence.

The first stop was the nightclub where she first met him. He asked her to wait in the bar. Several people were working and she took a seat, feeling out of place as he went about his business.

She didn't get how she was going to learn anything if he didn't have her near.

It wasn't her place to say anything though, so she stayed silent, waiting for him to return.

"How are you doing?" one of the men said. He'd been cleaning glasses. She didn't see a nametag anywhere on his shirt.

"Hi," she said. "You work here?"

"Have been for a long time now. The name's

Chase." He held his hand out, and she shook it.

"Hannah."

"Well as you can see, I'm the bartender in this place. Are you joining as the wait staff?"

"Oh, erm, no, I'm not."

"Oh, why did boss man bring you?"

He seemed really nice, and he put her at ease.

Hannah smiled. "I'm kind of with West."

"You are?"

"Yes."

"Wow, you didn't strike me as the kind to, you know?"

She frowned. "What?"

"Oh, it's nothing. You just seem so ... sweet."

"That doesn't sound like a compliment."

"It is, believe me, it is, but you know all things considered you're not cut out for this life."

Chase was clearly talking about something else, and she was in the dark.

"I don't follow." She felt so out of place. Did she stick out like a sore thumb?

"It's a surprise he's brought such a pretty, sweet lady along with him. With his line of work, I didn't think it would be appropriate." Chase winced after he finished speaking. "I really need to not talk."

She frowned. "His line of work?"

"I shouldn't say anything," he said.

"It's fine. We're good here, Chase."

"You know. The stuff that West Gallo is known for. His reputation precedes him. You do realize the kind of guy you're involved with."

She didn't have a clue what to do or say. Something was going on, and she glanced around the nightclub. No one was there as it was closed during the day.

"I'm sorry. I clearly don't," she said.

"Chase, you're needed 'round back."

She turned to see Rome standing behind her. She'd not even heard him approach.

"Sure thing." Chase was gone.

"Don't listen to everything you hear."

"What did he mean about the kind of work West is involved in?" she asked, turning toward Rome, who took a seat beside her.

They rarely talked when he drove her home, but she felt comfortable with him. He'd never given her a reason to be alarmed.

"Nothing for you to concern yourself with. He wanted you to know that he'd be out in a minute. Just having to make a few private calls."

"Oh."

She hated that she was being lied to. Pressing her lips together, she searched around the nightclub, but she didn't see any sign of Chase.

"Can I use the bathroom?" she asked.

"Sure. You know where it is?"

"Yeah, I do." She got to her feet and headed in that direction. Glancing behind her, she saw no one was following her and took a quick detour around the back near where "Staff" was marked on the door. Entering the room, she saw it opened up into a large storage room.

She didn't know where Chase would be. He just got called away, and she wanted to talk to him.

To find out what he was going to say.

Just as she was rounding a corner, her cell phone started to ring.

Checking the screen, she saw it wasn't a number she recognized.

"Hello," she said, not really sure who it could be.

"Hey, Hannah, it's me, Emily."

"Emily, thank God. I was so worried. I checked your room this morning."

"Yeah, something came up. It's work-related."

"Work-related?" If it was work-related why didn't West tell her all about it? Rubbing at her temple, she started to feel a headache start. "Where are you?"

"It's not important. Some sales stuff. He's wanting to buy a new club, and I'm checking out the details."

"When will you be back?"

"A couple of weeks. West wants me to do a thorough check. Are you going to be okay by yourself?"

"I'll be more than fine. I can handle being alone." What she didn't like was the feeling that she was being lied to, either by Emily or by West.

"I'll call as often as I can. I didn't mean to worry you," Emily said.

"It's fine. You know me. I worry about everything." She wanted to say so much more but instead kept her thoughts to herself.

"I better go. I've got a few things to do. Take care, Hannah."

Emily was gone before she got the chance to say goodbye. She stared at her cell phone. This wasn't like her friend to just vanish like this, but then, since moving to the city, nothing had been the same.

Biting her lip, she didn't like the unsettled feeling she was getting.

"Did you get lost?" Rome asked, startling her.

"You scared me." She pressed a hand to her chest. "Yeah, I missed the damn bathroom, and I wasn't watching where I was going. I got a call from my friend."

"Everything okay?"

"Yeah, everything is fine."

"You shouldn't be back here."

"It's just storage."

"That's true, but accidents happen all over a workplace. You've got to be extra careful, and you've not been trained to lug beer around."

She didn't argue with Rome.

"How long have you been working for West?" she asked, needing answers desperately.

"A long time now."

"Ah, do you like it?"

"Is this for an employment form or something?"

"I'm just curious. Making conversation seeing as I seem to be useless right now." She didn't like standing around doing nothing.

Right now, her mind was going off in all different directions, and she wasn't sure which way was up or down.

"West is a damn good man. Fearless. He goes after what he wants, and people either have to move aside, or risk getting hurt in the process."

"He's a lethal businessman?"

"He's lethal all right. He adores you, Hannah. I've never seen him care about another woman like he does you."

"He barely knows me."

Rome smiled. "Sometimes all it takes is a moment to realize someone is worth that time."

They had walked back to the main bar. Chase was nowhere to be seen. West, however, stood waiting.

"Found her. She'd gotten lost in the storage room."

"Is everything okay?" West asked.

"I got a call from Emily. I was distracted and rather than go to the bathroom, I went into the storage room." She shrugged. "Can I use the bathroom before we go?"

"Yes, of course."

She nodded, quickly making her escape, only this time she did go to the bathroom. She had to be imagining everything.

****

West watched the sway of her hips as she walked away. He'd never get tired of staring at her ass. It was so fucking sexy, full, ripe, and curvy. Last night she'd awakened in his arms, and he intended to explore that.

"Did he get the chance to talk to her?"

"The last I heard was he mentioned your reputation. She doesn't know anything, but she's curious."

"You can tell?"

"She started to ask questions about you, West. She's ... I don't know what she is, but she has a hunch something's not right."

"Get rid of Chase. I don't want him to show his face again. Put him in the fighting rings. He wins the first twenty fights, he'll get his job back. Train him if you have to. Either way, I want to make some money on him, and give him a talk. Tell him to mind his tongue and that I've killed people for less." He'd overheard Chase telling Hannah all about who he really was. He wasn't ready for Hannah to know anything. His reputation always preceded him, and Chase had been trying to get his attention for years to do more for him. He didn't think for a second that he'd been talking to Hannah to get his attention, but now he fucking had it. He'd liked Chase. He was a good kid for the most part, but he needed to stop running his mouth.

"Will do."

"What's the news on Emily?"

"The clinic said she had a good night, all things considered. No ill effects from the drugs, but she looks nervous."

"Fine."

"You got her to call Hannah?"

"I had no choice." It was why he didn't think Hannah was snooping. He needed a couple of minutes alone to get hold of Emily to ask her to call.

He should have thought about it last night before he visited her, but alas, it was the last thing on his mind. "I want you to arrange my beach house just off the coast."

"You're taking her away?" Rome asked.

"Until I have Lawrence, I want her to be far away from the danger."

"West, with all due respect, Lawrence is not your only concern. I've heard of an uprising of the cartels. They want to make a deal for distribution of their product. Cage got the call last night."

West gritted his teeth. The cartels were a fucking pain in the ass. He'd negotiated with them years ago. They stayed out of his city, and he let them live. Using his docks, that would require a huge fee. Not only that, he'd have to pay a lot more to the law enforcement to look the other way. To not sit down and negotiate would mean a street war.

He'd survived one before. They were bloody, publicly fought, and privately won. It's how he got out on top.

He toppled the last Street King to be where he was now. No one had stood a chance against him.

"Get me a meeting with Enrique for this Friday. You and Cage are the only two I trust with her safety."

"We need to be by your side."

"You'll be taking care of Hannah. It's as simple as that. Do you understand?" he asked.

"With all due respect, you're going to need me by

your side. The cartels are raging, boss. They will not accept any kind of 'no deal.' You know this."

"Rome, I've dealt with Enrique before. I'll deal with him again. He knows what is good for business and what is not. I won't have anyone coming into my city, poisoning my streets without knowing first, what I'm getting out of it."

The door closed, and he watched Hannah approach. He wanted her naked.

Stripped bare, spread open, so that he could fuck her hard.

"You're ready to go?"

"You've finished all of your work?"

"Here, yes. Come." He wrapped an arm around her waist. "Organize the meet."

He led Hannah out of the building.

"I feel I should be back at the office."

"And why would you feel like that?" he asked, helping her into the car. He loved buckling her in.

"Because I'm supposed to be helping, and right now I feel like I'm hindering. You don't have to worry about me."

"No need to worry."

He climbed behind the wheel, and joined the traffic.

"Can I ask you a question?" She turned toward him.

"You can ask me anything."

"Chase, the bartender back at Dirty, he was saying some things."

He gripped the steering wheel tighter. "What kinds of things?"

"He said something about your reputation, and it made me wonder. Have I missed something? You have a reputation? What for? I didn't get it."

"Before I became a businessman, I didn't come from very good people. My mom, she tried, don't get me wrong. My dad was a deadbeat. An addict. He didn't have time for the woman he married or the brat he helped to conceive."

"Oh, I'm so sorry."

"Don't be. Before I was even a teenager, I'd get into a lot of fights. I had a lot of anger. I was entered into fights. To win meant money. As I got older, I started to earn a lot of money. In time, that money helped me set up what you see now."

"You won every single fight?"

"Yes. You see, Hannah, I don't lose. I never allow myself to doubt for even a second that I'll lose. I win, it's as simple as that."

"And if you do lose?"

"I don't lose. I don't have time to lose."

He navigated the streets, growing increasingly impatient with other drivers who constantly stopped and started or didn't have a fucking clue where they were going.

"So, your reputation is that of being a fighter?"

"A winning fighter." It wasn't lies. It was just part of the truth. Part of the legacy he'd created. If people didn't know who he was now, the Street King, they knew of his undefeated reputation.

"Did you love fighting?"

"It helped to calm the rage inside me. I wanted to hurt people, and fighting gave me somewhere to fight, to hurt. It's what I needed."

"Do you still fight?" she asked.

"No." It wasn't a total lie. He didn't fight within a ring. The only beatings he dished out were to those who deserved them.

There was never any innocence within the ring.

That was taken long before anyone entered.

"Do you miss it?"

He had to think about her question. Before each fight, he'd feel the monster building within him. He'd remember the sight of his mother, dead from an overdose even though she wasn't an addict. He'd see his father, and the hatred he felt for that son of a bitch, knew no limits. He'd attack his opponents, but the real person he'd been fighting was his father.

"No. I don't miss it. It was another time."

Killing his father hadn't helped ease the monster within. If anything, it had made him hungry. His old man got away too lightly, and it had pissed him off that he had no restraint. It took him a lot longer to finally ease the pain that he'd experienced.

Meeting Hannah had filled him with a new sense of purpose.

She had no idea that he was in love with her and had been for a long time. She was the first person that made him believe in love, in happiness, in the good of others.

Even when she'd been alone and all those fuckers at school hadn't turned up for her birthday, she'd accepted it, and instead talked with him. A stranger who the night before had massacred an entire MC.

"At least now you know that you're someone to aspire to. You started off fighting and worked your way up to be a well-respected businessman." She reached over, taking his hand.

She didn't know the truth. That he was about to force Chase, the bartender who nearly told her the truth, into a fighting ring. How he was going to make him fight his way to survival. Or that he was hunting Lawrence and when he finally got his hands on the man, he intended to put all of his skills into practice to make sure he lived long enough to feel all the pain and wish for death.

He wasn't a good man.

Never claimed to be.

His lies were all to help Hannah adapt.

Pulling up into the spot outside of Sin, he turned off the ignition. He'd never doubted his decisions before.

When he started this, he only saw one goal, Hannah as his wife. No, that was too basic. Hannah belonging to him, completely devoted. He'd not considered anything else.

He worked hard to make sure she had an easy life while he let her live out her college dream. Manipulating her life behind the scenes where she didn't even know him.

Now though, what if she found out?

He shook his head. He wouldn't let that happen.

"I can't go on a vacation," he said.

She smiled, tilting her head back. He cupped her cheek, running his thumb across her flesh.

"You're a busy, hard-working man."

"I've got a late-night meeting Friday. Rome is going to keep you company," he said.

"I can stay home alone, you know. I'm not going to do anything crazy." She frowned.

"What is it?" he asked.

"Why didn't you tell me you'd sent Emily out to buy another building or to look at potential buildings for investment or another nightclub? She said one of those things, but I can't remember which one."

When he called Emily, he'd ordered her to tell Hannah something, whatever was required to stop her worrying. It wasn't like she could have told her that she was in rehab because her ex-boss had drugged her.

Your lies are going to push her away.

"It completely slipped my mind. I organized this

weeks ago, and seeing as Emily was the only one available, it seemed like a pretty good deal."

"She's not been working for you that long."

"Her work has impressed me so far. I'm all about helping my employees advance and not to keep them contained unless absolutely necessary."

She sighed.

He wanted to know what was going on inside her head.

"I better go in." She opened the car door, and he grabbed her hand, pulling her in close. He kissed her lips, letting her know without a shadow of a doubt who she belonged to.

That sigh she had on her lips seconds ago was soon replaced with a moan. At the start of the kiss, she'd been cold toward him. As he licked across her lips and she opened up, he'd felt her soften.

"Think about me all day."

"You're not coming up?" she asked.

"I'll be up in a minute."

He watched her go into the safety of his office.

Climbing out of his car, he released a whistle. He didn't go into his building, and he rounded the back, moving slowly.

He caught sight of the guy with the camera just before he kissed Hannah. There was no way he'd reject her or push her aside.

Kissing her had been a mistake, especially out in public.

The man he was sneaking up on was staring down at his camera.

West heard the small beep as he turned to a new picture. Whoever had hired this guy had used a fucking amateur.

When he was close, he grabbed the man and

slammed him up against the brick wall. Before he could react, he had a hand around the man's throat, the camera on the ground as he squeezed tightly.

"I don't take kindly to having my privacy invaded." He pulled him off the wall only to slam him again. The brick and his body stopped the man's escape. The man's head hit it with a thud but he didn't care. "Who do you work for?" He released his hold to give the man time to speak.

"I don't know."

"Wrong answer."

He rammed his fist into the guy's gut. While he was on the ground panting for breath, he picked up the camera and saw the photos of Hannah and himself. He didn't like the look on his face. Anyone who looked at them would see that he was in love with her. This picture in the wrong hands could prove his undoing.

Taking Hannah away from him would be a big mistake.

"Who ordered this?" he asked.

"Please. I don't know. I just got the call. I was asked to follow her."

This was going to take a lot more than a morning interrogation.

Annoyed, he slammed his first into the man's face, knocking him clean out.

Pulling out his cell phone, he dialed Cage.

"I need you to come and collect a body for me. While you're at it, see if you can find out who sent the order to follow me."

Chapter Nine

That night, West was waiting for Hannah to finish work. He leaned against the car, and Hannah stared at the vehicle, seeing it was a different one than this morning.

"You like changing cars often?"

"I've got a few I like to make an impression with."

He'd not come back into work, and while she knew it wasn't her place to ask, her curiosity was getting the better of her. West was fast becoming a mystery. Between his rearranging dates and vacations to his disappearances and just everything in between.

"What's going on?"

"I'm taking you somewhere."

"I'm not going home."

"No. I think it's time I showed you my apartment." He held the door of his car open.

Everything was moving so fast for her. One moment he was just a guy in a bar. Now he was … what? Her boyfriend? Lover?

She didn't know what any of this meant anymore, let alone what her place was in the scheme of things.

Being alone at work, going through numbers and figures, gave her time to think. Between graduation, Lawrence, the new job, sex, and everything in between, she didn't know what the hell to do.

Just this morning it had been a whirlwind of emotions and now she found herself grounded.

"I think I should go home," she said.

"Please, Hannah. Don't withdraw from me now. I know it's not easy dating me. I've got a lot of commitments. I don't want to keep letting you down."

"You're not letting me down. Honestly, you're not. I just, I need some time. That's all. We're going really fast, and there are times I don't even think I know you. We barely know each other."

"The best way to do this is to find out by being around each other. I promised to show you my place. Let me do this, and if you're not happy, I'll take you back home."

She tilted her head to the side, watching him.

She hated feeling like a bitch to him, but what else was she supposed to do? In all seriousness right now.

He blew hot all the time.

The cold wasn't even there. Whenever she was with him, she felt surrounded by him.

"Fine." She climbed into the car, and he buckled in her seatbelt. "How come you didn't come in for work?"

"Something came up. Cage hit a snag, and I had to deal with a few problems. It's nothing I couldn't handle."

"Are you used to constantly being dragged away from what you wanted to do for the day?" she asked.

"That's life, right?"

"Yeah, it is."

She pushed some hair off her face and stared out of the window.

That nervous feeling had returned, and she didn't get it.

How could being with one man make her feel so happy and so scared at the same time?

"You know. The stuff that West Gallo is known for. His reputation precedes him. You do realize the kind of guy you're involved with?"

Chase's words rang in her head.

She couldn't shake them.

They were there, like a constant reminder that she

was missing something.

Staring out of the window, she tried to make sense of what she actually knew about West Gallo.

He owned several businesses that included a waffle house and at least two nightclubs that she'd seen with her own two eyes. He was a businessman. He came from a family with fucked up parents. One died of an overdose, and the other she wasn't sure of. He'd been one hell of a fighter. No losses throughout his career. The money he earned from fighting had helped to fund his current business ventures. She loved the way he kissed. The touch of his hands all over her body. Stroking her in ways that brought her pleasure at every turn. The feel of his cock. The taste of the forbidden.

Pressing her thighs together at the memories, she looked over at him.

He was staring straight ahead, not paying any attention to her.

She knew quite a bit about him, but again, not anything deep or meaningful.

What was she hoping to find?

The drive to his apartment seemed to go so slow. Rubbing at her head, she tried to think of a million and one different reasons as to why she shouldn't be anywhere near West Gallo.

There were none.

He'd not given her any reason to think that she was in danger.

The complete opposite, actually.

When he pulled into the private parking for his building, and he climbed out of the car, she was relieved to finally be doing something other than thinking.

Her mind was driving her crazy, thinking of all the endless possibilities about West. She needed to think of the reality. She was a woman he met in the bar, and he was also her boss.

Simple as that.

"I know you're not happy with me right now, and I hope to make it up to you."

"You don't have to worry about anything," she said. "I'm sorry for sniping at you earlier. I'm just … I'm going crazy with all the changes. I'm good. Honestly. Ignore me."

He pulled her into his arms and smiled. "You're not going crazy or anything." He pressed a kiss to her lips. "We had sex last night. How are you feeling?"

"Do you mean sore?"

"Yes."

"I'm a little sore." She looked around the parking lot. "I would really prefer it if we didn't have this conversation here."

She already felt her cheeks heating at the thought of someone overhearing them.

"Come on."

He took her hand, leading her out of the parking lot to his apartment block. He gave a nod at the man behind the main desk, and she blew out a breath.

She was actually going to a guy's apartment.

How weird that she was twenty-three years old and hadn't been inside a guy's place before.

During college she'd been so busy with school work that spending prolonged time with men didn't appeal. Besides, the dates she went on didn't exactly go to plan.

Far from it.

The doors opened up and they stepped inside, enclosing them within the small confines of the elevator.

Staring at his reflection, she couldn't help but admire the sheer maleness of him. The jacket he wore was open, spread out across his chest.

To her, it looked like nothing could keep him at bay. Everything stood at attention, demanding respect.

The doors opened, and she followed him to his door. He released her hand, typing in the keycode, and then she was inside his space.

He flicked on the light, and she licked her dry lips.

His apartment was huge.

"Not bad for a kid that had nothing growing up."

She stepped into his apartment, aware of her small heels clicking across the floor, echoing around the room.

Everywhere she looked spoke of luxury, wealth, hard work.

Spinning around to look at him, she smiled. "You must be very proud."

"It feels a lot better like this." He put his keys into a small dish.

She watched as he removed his jacket, the expanse of his shoulders catching her eye. He was so much larger than her size eighteen frame.

"Have you ever gone for something you knew you couldn't have?" she asked.

"No."

"Why?"

"Because there's nothing in this world that doesn't have a price. That I can't get by some means or another."

He stepped closer to her, and she held onto her bag. Her nipples grew tight as she watched him. What was it about this man that called to her?

Less than an hour ago, she felt she needed space, and now she wanted nothing more than to be in his arms.

"Take off your clothes," he said.

He began to open the buttons of his shirt,

revealing his inked chest and large, muscular arms.

The shirt fell to the floor, and she watched it go.

She wanted to reach out and touch him.

Only, she put her hand to the button of her jacket.

Opening it up, she stared into his eyes as she removed her clothes. Piece by piece, they dropped to the floor.

West stood before her naked first. His cock was already hard as he wrapped his fingers around the length. As he ran his hands up and down, she watched him play with himself, tease his cock.

She liked to watch.

Even as she was naked, her hands clenched into fists at her side, she kept her gaze on him.

Biting her bottom lip, she stared up his body, wondering for the first time if he'd experienced many broken bones in his time.

With her gaze on his, the blue of his eyes captured her once again like they did that first time.

"Come here."

Like a lost little lamb, she moved toward her wolf.

She took each step slowly, torturing them both, prolonging that pleasure she knew would explode between them.

She stopped when his cock grazed her stomach, leaving a small patch of pre-cum where he touched.

"Am I close enough?" she asked, looking up at him.

West cupped her face, one of his thumbs running across her bottom lip. "I found your secret stash of books, Hannah."

Her eyes grew wide.

"The dark ones. I read a few pages of them, and it made me wonder, do you read them because you want the same? Or do you read them because they disgust you?"

"They were private," she said.

He leaned in close, his lips going to her ear. "When you let me inside your pussy, you left all privacy behind. There's nothing about you, Hannah, that I don't want to know." He nipped at her ear before doing the same to her pulse. Little bites down her body until he reached her tits. "Are you going to tell me the truth or lie to me?"

They were her secret.

She should have gotten rid of them when she had the chance, but she'd kept them.

They were a temptation that she couldn't deny. Not anymore.

"I like them," she said.

The moment she spoke aloud, she felt lighter. Like a dark secret had been trapped within her, making her feel all wrong. West knew, and he hadn't run away.

Opening her eyes, which had closed of her own accord, she returned his gaze once again.

"I don't want to be hurt or sold or used by other men. I have no desire for that."

"What do you want?"

"I don't know. To explore. To push boundaries, I think. I don't ... I've never done this. I lost my virginity twenty-four hours ago. I've not really had time to think about what I really want."

"You've had those books a lot longer, Hannah. Tell me the truth."

She stared at him. He wasn't going to back down, and she had no idea what to say.

The truth?

What was the truth?

The books had stuck with her, and in the middle

of the night when she was alone, they helped her to deal with … everything. Apart from when West came into her life, nothing had satisfied her other than the pleasure of his touch.

He held her in place, not letting her escape. With his gaze on her, she didn't know what to do or say.

"What do you want from me?" she asked in a whisper.

"Only the truth."

She licked her dry lips.

What would it hurt to tell him the truth? To finally spill her secrets that she'd been keeping to herself?

"To be wanted. To be craved. For someone to look at me and not be able to look at another woman. To be at the mercy of the man who owns my heart. To be taken. To be used but to know at the end of it, he won't look at me any differently. He'll look at me like the men in the books."

"Which is?"

"The key to his happiness. The person he's been searching for all along and only just found." She wanted a fairytale mixed with total erotic.

****

"You've got it," West said.

He ran his thumb across her lower lip. He'd already known the answer. She wanted the excitement and danger. The fairytale. Only the prince didn't kiss her hand but fucked her until she couldn't walk straight.

Pressing his lips to hers, he slid his tongue across her mouth and relished the sound of her gasp. She opened up, and he took what he wanted, plunging inside, tasting her. As he kissed her, he moved her back until the wall stopped her. Grabbing her hands, he placed them above her head, trapping them in one of his.

He stepped close to her so that his body was right next to hers, touching her. Enjoying her. She was so soft in all the right places, a temptation every time he saw her.

The past five years he'd showed incredible restraint, and it hadn't been easy. Far from it. There were times he'd look at pictures, see her sad face and know he'd be able to make her happy if he was given the chance. Only, his plan kept him away.

It wasn't like he even stuck to it after she'd been at the nightclub. He'd not been able to hold back in the end. His control was completely lost on him.

Breaking from her lips, he trailed them down her neck, sucking on her pulse so he'd leave a mark. Other men would know she belonged to someone. That someone was him. Damn, when it came to this woman, he couldn't seem to help himself. He wanted the world to know that she was his but also knew he had to be careful.

There was still so much to do.

"I need you to trust me, Hannah," he said.

"I do."

"Good."

He let go of her hands, capturing her hips as he once again moved her. This time, he had her near the sofa, bent over it.

Running a hand down her spine, he stood directly behind her.

Spreading the cheeks of her ass, he stared down at her slick pussy and tight little asshole. Cupping her mound, he felt how wet she was.

"So slick. You want my cock?"

"Yes."

"You'll get it when I'm ready. I'm so fucking hot. So ready to fuck you." He wrapped his fingers around his dick, working the length. Pre-cum leaked out of the tip and he rubbed it into his shaft.

As he went to his knees behind her, Hannah jerked up.

"What are you doing?"

Landing a slap to her ass, he glared at her. "Bend back over. I didn't give you permission to stand up."

She slowly got back into position.

Sliding a finger inside her heat, he smiled, unable to help himself.

He moved her legs so that she was wide open. The angle was an odd one, but he didn't care. Pressing his face against her pussy, he licked her hole, stroking around then pushing inside. Tongue-fucking her in slow strokes, he heard her moan.

Running his hands up her thighs, he drew them in close to her pussy and stroked across her lips. Wetting his fingers, he moved them back, watching as he played with her asshole.

She tensed up.

"Don't fucking move," he said.

Hannah stayed perfectly still.

"You ever thought about anyone fucking your ass?"

She whimpered. "Yes."

"I'm going to, Hannah. I'm going to take your body and wipe away all trace of innocence you possess. You'll never be a virgin again." He had so many plans for her body. So much he wanted to do and he was going to make her ache, beg, and yearn for the pleasure of his touch.

Circling her asshole, he continued to stroke her pussy with his tongue. Flicking the hard bud of her clit, he moved down to tease her entrance before fucking inside her.

With one finger, he pushed against her puckered

anus. The tight muscles kept him out, but he worked on her pussy, turning her on. When he entered her ass with the tip of his finger, she cried out his name, the sounds echoing in the room.

He loved hearing her pleasure as it went straight to his dick.

With his free hand, he worked his cock. Starting at his balls, he moved up to the head, then back down again.

All he wanted was to be inside her tight pussy.

With the tip of his finger still in her ass, he took his time, thrusting inside her, going a little deeper with every passing second.

He pulled away from her pussy and watched as he took her ass.

Hannah thrust back.

"You want my mouth here?" he asked.

"Yes, please, yes."

"You're going to be my good girl?"

"Yes."

"You're going to trust me when I try new things?"

"Yes."

"I'm going to fuck your ass one day, and soon. You're going to let me?"

"Yes."

He loved hearing her say yes.

"I'm going to make every single one of your fantasies come true, Hannah. You're going to look at those books and see they pale in comparison to what I can do to you." All of his finger was inside her ass, and he started to move it in and out of her.

She tensed up, and he sucked on her clit, the action clearly taking her by surprise. His face was full of her pussy, and her cream soaked his mouth.

Tasting her, he knew he was going to flood her cunt with his spunk. His mission was to knock her up. To take her. To make her beg and scream for more.

She'd belong to him in every single sense of the word.

Once she was rocking onto his face and taking one finger with ease, he added a second finger, stretching her out.

She cried out, her moans turning him on.

She was so close.

He sucked her clit between his teeth, creating a small bite of pain before he soothed it out with his tongue, stroking over her repeatedly.

"I'm going to come, West. I'm going to come."

He didn't stop.

The moment she came, he licked her clean, driving her toward a second orgasm as he fucked her ass with his fingers and took her to a completely different level of pleasure.

When she was near a second orgasm, he didn't let her go over the edge.

Moving from her pussy, he stood up behind her, his fingers still in her ass. He gripped his cock, running the tip over her slit, getting himself all nice and wet with her orgasm.

He stood poised at her entrance, seeing that tiny pussy hole. It looked almost too small to take him, but he knew better.

Slowly, inch by glorious fucking inch, he sank inside her, and watched as her hole opened up.

She was still so incredibly tight that he knew it was going to take a lot of good, hard fucking for her to loosen up.

With only a couple of inches of himself inside her, he grabbed her hips and slammed to the hilt.

They both moaned, their sounds combining and echoing off the walls.

"You feel so amazing," he said.

Her pussy tightened around him, squeezing him with every single pulse. Her ass was doing the same to his fingers. He couldn't wait to fuck her hot little ass. He made a note to go to a sex shop and to purchase some little goodies that would help her first time.

West held himself still, waiting for her to get accustomed to his length. He didn't want to hurt her.

That first time, she'd experienced pain, and he'd also taken her while she was sore.

The more he fucked her and filled her with his cum, the better chance he'd have of keeping her all to himself. Running his hands over the curves of her ass, he couldn't think of anything better to have than this woman.

The only thing missing right now for him was a mirror so that he could see everything. He wanted to memorize the look on her face the first time he took her ass.

Running one hand over her back, he started to wriggle his fingers, going in deep and pulling out only to thrust back inside.

After a few seconds of teasing her, she stared to move, pressing against him. West allowed Hannah to set the pace. She started to slide off his cock only to push against him so that he hit the hilt inside her.

She moaned and whimpered.

"Tell me what you want, baby?" he asked.

"I want you to fuck me. Please, West."

He held her hip with one hand, keeping the fingers of his other in her ass. He stared down at her pussy, pulling out of her until only the tip remained, and he looked at his dick, already slick with her orgasm.

Tightening his grip on her hip to the point that he knew she'd feel pain, he slammed in deep. She cried out, and he didn't give her the chance to recover. This time, he repeatedly fucked her, taking her hard.

The sounds echoing around the room were those of their pleasure and the slapping of bodies.

"This what you want, Hannah? You want to belong to me. Because you do. I'm never letting you go. You're all mine. No other man is ever going to know just how perfect your pussy is."

No other man would ever touch what belonged to him. Running a hand up her back, he gathered her hair into his fist, wrapping the length around his hand. He held her hair, using it as leverage, and her pussy went even more wet as he did so.

Pounding away inside her, he wished her had a mirror just so he could see how perfect she looked. Sexy, at his mercy, ready to take his cock.

Her moans and gasps kept filling the air, and he couldn't look away from his cock as her pussy opened up around him. He rocked his fingers into her ass at the same time.

He was so close to coming.

Her pussy tightened around him as her orgasm hit.

Closing his eyes, he gripped her hip as his release hit. Plunging as deep as he could go, he growled as each spurt of his orgasm flooded her waiting womb.

Fucking take.
That's it.
Fill that cunt.
Get her pregnant.
Make her mine.

Seconds passed as his climax started to subside. Opening his eyes, he saw stars. He'd never experienced a more intense release in all of his years.

He pulled his fingers from her ass and leaned over her back. Letting go of her hair, he pressed a kiss to her neck. "You're so fucking perfect, Hannah."

"That was amazing."

"You want to do it again?"

"Yes."

He chuckled. "Soon. We'll do it again soon. I promise." He just needed to have a few minutes to regain his composure. He'd never been so driven to claim a woman. From that moment five years ago when he'd had her in his arms, he'd known she'd mean something to him and that he wouldn't be able to let her go.

Just thinking about it right now, the fact he'd been able to wait five years to him seemed like some kind of a miracle. He didn't know how he managed it.

Always watching from afar, manipulating behind the scenes.

"I never thought it could be like this."

"Not even with all those books?"

"They're fiction, West. Not fact."

"We're only just getting started."

"It can get better?"

"Lots better. You just got to give me a chance to show you everything."

"And if I'm afraid?"

"A little fear never hurt anyone. I'll be there, and you must know by now I'll never let anything happen to you." *Be careful, she doesn't know the whole truth.*

"I do." She turned her head and he saw her cheeks were a nice shade of red. "I want this with you, West. I know we've only been together a short time, but I want it all."

To Hannah, it had been a couple of weeks, but not to him.

He felt like he'd waited a lifetime, and now he intended to make up for lost time.

Chapter Ten

After dropping Hannah off the following day, West drove to the warehouse where the amateur photographer was waiting. The camera had already been destroyed. Rome and Cage got the information about his address, and went there to clear all memory of him out of the place.

No one was looking for him.

West had hoped to return last night, but seeing Hannah, watching her, he'd been unable to hold back. Fucking her was an addiction he couldn't shake.

Five years of suffering blue balls would do that to a guy.

He'd even put himself through the torture of watching her touch herself, to bring herself to an orgasm that always left her unsatisfied. Sitting back and not doing anything about that had been hard for him, especially as he knew what she needed.

Last night, he'd fucked her and shared a bath with her before going to bed. Sneaking out wouldn't work, so he'd sent a message to Rome to let him know he wouldn't be back that night.

Now, he was, and he stared at the bruised face of the photographer. He didn't look impressed now with what he'd found.

"What's his name again?" West asked.

"Charles Freeman," Rome said.

He nodded.

Charles Freeman. A nature photographer and wife investigator. He helped husbands get proof of cheating wives so they could divorce them. Some of the men paid a good sum as well. Charles was not hurting for cash.

So it raised the question, why risk his life hunting him down?

"Please, let me go. I didn't do anything wrong. I was just taking pictures."

"You're taking pictures of West Gallo. I want to know why. I'm neither a nature attraction, nor am I a cheating wife." Thinking about a wife though, his ring would look really pretty on Hannah's finger.

He already had the perfect one picked out. It was in his vault back in his apartment.

"West Gallo?"

"Yes. That's me."

The man whimpered.

"Ah, I see my name does ring a little bell inside that head." He pulled the man's head back. "What else you got for me?"

"I didn't … I was told to look for a woman. Hannah … ugh, Hannah someone. I can't think. The guy claimed to be her fiancé and that he thought she was cheating on him. I got a picture of her, and I found her. That's all. I swear. I didn't know who she was or why. I was just on an assignment. Please."

"We checked your bag, and there's no items that would link you to her."

"It's in my email."

Rome was already opening up the laptop. "Password."

"If you pass it to me I can open it."

"Just tell me your password," Rome said.

Seconds passed, and West reached into his jacket, pulling out his little knife. He flicked the blade up, having no intention of using it on him.

It did the trick.

"Fucking hot stuff with a big dick. It's all capitals."

West smirked. "You got a big dick?"

"Fuck you," Charles said.

West laughed. Considering this man had already pissed himself three times, he had to give him kudos for trying to look tough. The piss around him gave it all away though.

"I don't swing that way, but I know a couple of guys that would love to make you their bitch."

He closed his pocket knife. He'd never use that on anyone. It was what he used to cut up apples. There's no way he'd risk human blood mixing with his food.

Disgusting.

There were many things he was capable of.

Cannibalism was not one of them.

He watched as Rome opened up the email, bringing up Hannah's picture.

"It's true," Rome said. "It's Lawrence. He sent the email and claimed she was his fiancée. Dirty fucker even used her graduation photo."

Getting to his feet, West walked toward the desk where the laptop was. Sure enough, there was Hannah, smiling at the camera with Emily's arm around her shoulders, but the image had been cut.

He'd been at Hannah's graduation.

Staying at the back, he'd watched her, sitting, waiting. When her name was called, he'd clapped along with the crowd.

He'd been so damn happy for her and proud.

Of course he'd also known it was one step closer to her belonging to him.

"What do you want to do?" Rome asked.

"Get my tech team on this. Trace it back to an account and find out where Lawrence is."

He didn't like the feeling he was getting.

Between business with the cartels later this week, a random photographer, and a hunch, it was sure to be a trying one for him.

Standing in front of Charles, he shook his head. "Please, I'll do anything."

"The problem is, I can't trust you, and anyone I can't trust I have to get rid of. It's nothing personal to you."

With that, he grabbed a piece of rope. Stepping behind Charles, he tightened the strings, and waited as he fought. It was only a matter of minutes before he died, and afterward, he released him.

"What's wrong, boss?" Cage asked.

His men knew the score. They'd taken out many of their threats and enemies without batting an eye.

"I have a feeling Lawrence was getting her identity and using pictures of her with me in the hope of selling them."

"That seems rather … resourceful."

"He knows what she means to me. That knowledge in the wrong hands could get her killed."

"They'd certainly use her as bait. You're thinking the cartels," Rome said.

West looked at his men and nodded. "It would make sense. If Lawrence has reached out to them, promising them something in return for his safety, it would explain their sudden need for a meeting."

"Why arrange a meeting without their leverage?" Rome asked. "That makes no sense."

"It would seem they were getting cocky and thought taking Hannah wouldn't be so hard."

"We're going to have to be careful now. If the cartels have sent men in to extract her, they're going to blend in," Cage said.

"I know." He ran a hand down his face.

"And going on vacation now will look suspicious," Rome said.

"I know."

All along they'd been playing chess, and he'd been so focused on Hannah he'd not even noticed the rules had changed. They had pushed him into a checkmate, and that pissed him the fuck off.

The fact they still didn't have Lawrence was a clear indication of that.

He couldn't give Hannah up.

Not now.

Stepping back, that wouldn't work.

He was trapped with only one way out—to fight.

"You could work this to your advantage," Cage said. "Well, we know they're here. We know they're coming for her."

"I can pretend to be Charles," Rome said. "I can even send some pictures. Lure them out. You find out what they knew, and when Enrique comes to town, you'll be ready."

He was already starting to see a positive.

Stepping up to Rome, West stared down at the computer.

"This will draw him out."

"Send him an email. Tell him you've got the pictures but you can only give them to him in person."

"No can do, boss. This has already been negotiated. Over email only," Rome said, glancing through the other correspondence.

"Fine." West stepped back from the computer, giving himself a couple of minutes to think. His men gave him the time.

He was already pissed that he'd been pushed into this fucking corner as it was.

"Send the email," he said. "Tell him you'll get the picture to him shortly." He looked at Rome and Cage. "One of you will be taking a picture later this evening. Then I want one of you near Hannah at all times. You're the only two people I trust."

They were the ones who knew how important she was to him.

He wouldn't have anything happen to her.

Not due to his mistakes.

Rome started to type.

West called his team to come and take care of the body.

The moment he saw everything was taken care of, he got in his car and made his way back to Sin.

Entering his office, he watched Hannah as she worked. She was on the phone, making notes. She'd not caught sight of him yet, and that was okay. Leaving her to work, he made his way into his office. As he passed her desk, she looked up and smiled. That smile would stay with him forever.

He winked at her as he entered his office, closing the door.

Pulling out his cell phone, he dialed the rehab clinic, getting an update on Emily's progress. It would be a lot easier to kill her, but seeing as Hannah was attached to her and he didn't like killing women unless he had to, he made the extra effort to check.

Once he was happy that she'd not gone into a sudden state of panic and need, or withdrawal, he focused the few hours left of work on catching up with some emails. He declined several invites to charity events, galas, and that kind of thing. For his charity work, he signed checks to help causes.

By the end of the day, he noticed most of his employees were gone. Hannah was still hard at work. She'd turned the light on near her desk.

His window was partially open, which allowed him to hear the heavy beat of the music from the club below.

Sin was a popular club, one that offered late-night dancing, and if patrons stayed long enough, some of the girls offered lap dances for special VIPs.

Rubbing at his eyes, he knew what he needed to do. He wasn't comfortable with anything about it.

Leaving his office, he switched off the light and leaned against the doorway, watching Hannah once again.

All his life he felt like he'd been watching her. Not that it was a hardship. She was a beautiful woman.

That beauty had only grown in the last few years.

She tucked some hair behind her ear, looking up at him with a smile.

"Hey," she said. "Sorry about earlier."

"I pay you to work. Are you ready to leave?"

"Yeah, I think so. I've done so much already. You know." She clicked at her computer, turning it off.

She stood, and he moved quickly, taking her jacket. He helped her into it, running his hands down her arms and breathing her in.

"I missed you," she said.

He wrapped his arms around her, bringing a hand to her cheek to cup her face. Kissing her lips, he wondered if she was falling for him.

His love for her had grown in five years, and he couldn't imagine his life without her. Didn't want to. There was nothing he wouldn't do, no sacrifices he wouldn't make or hadn't already made for her.

"Let's get out of here." He didn't like what he was about to do.

Putting her in any kind of danger went against everything he'd fought for.

Gritting his teeth, he made his way out to the car with Hannah near him. Rome would be somewhere nearby, ready to take the picture. Helping her into the car, West strapped her in and made his way to the driver's side.

Climbing in, he turned to look at her.

"You're acting strange. What is it, West?"

"It's nothing. I just don't want anything to happen to you." He cupped her cheek, and she smiled.

Damn, he loved this woman so much it was a constant ache deep in his gut.

"Nothing's going to happen to me. I promise." She leaned in, but he was the one that pressed his lips to hers, consuming her.

As he slid his tongue into her mouth, her hands went to his jacket, pulling him in closer. Sinking his fingers inside her hair, he nibbled her lip, relishing her moans.

"I want you," he said.

"Then have me, West. Take me home and you can have me any way you want me."

****

The next day at work, Hannah was aware of the tension mounting inside West. Since they entered his club, everyone had avoided talking to him. If it wasn't something they could handle themselves, they put it aside.

She'd watched Rome and Cage each enter his office, leaving after about an hour of yelling. Their argument wasn't exactly clear, and it was muffled.

When Cage stormed out, the office was empty, as everyone had gone to lunch. West called her through to his office, and she wanted to run. To think of any excuse not to be near him.

She was dawdling.

"What's taking you so long?" West asked, coming to the doorway of his office.

"Nothing. I was just logging off." The lie slipped

from her mouth.

She walked toward him, trying to think of another excuse that would stop her from entering his office.

With nothing to say, she took her seat in front of him.

He slammed the door, and she couldn't help but flinch.

"Are you scared?" he asked.

"You've been in an awful mood all day. I guess I just don't want to annoy you."

"It'll take a lot to annoy me, Hannah. I have your lunch."

He pointed to the two wrapped sandwiches on his desk.

"Oh," she said. "I see."

"There've been a few complications, but nothing for you to concern yourself with." He winked at her.

"Is there anything I can do to help?"

"No. Smile. Work hard. The usual."

She chuckled. "I happen to love working for you, so that's really easy for me to do." She took the sandwich he offered. Unwrapping it, she saw it was a cheesesteak, one with slices of beef, onions, peppers, and lots of cheese. Her mouth watered, and she took a huge bite.

The flavors exploded on her tongue, making her want more.

"I also have this," West said.

She watched as he opened a drawer and pulled out two items, laying them flat on the desk.

The tube of lubricant she recognized.

The butt plug made her nervous, and she had to read the package to know what it was.

"What? Why?" She frowned, looking at him.

"You know why. You've got a tight little ass, and when I finally fuck you there, I want you to be ready."

"Oh."

Heat flooded her pussy at the thought of him working the plug into her ass.

"When are you…?" Her question faded at the hungry look in his eyes.

"Once you've finished eating."

Her cheeks warmed.

"But … the others in the office."

"Don't show them that you're wearing it."

"What about sitting down?"

"You'll get used to it."

"Have you ever had a plug up your ass?"

"No."

"Oh, so you don't know how it's going to be." She snipped out the words. She nibbled on her sandwich.

The plug didn't look that big.

"When you've taken this one, tomorrow morning you'll have a bigger size until you'll be able to take my cock. It'll stretch you. Prepare you."

"Can't we do it tonight?"

"No. Now. Trust me, Hannah. You're going to love it."

She didn't believe him. Not even a little.

"Have you heard from Emily?" he asked, changing the subject.

"She called me this morning. We didn't have long to talk. It's weird not having her around. She's been part of my life for so long. We're going to have to make a trip to see her family soon. It has been too long since I saw them."

"So, I was thinking about going away this Thanksgiving," he said.

"You are?"

"Yes, and I was wondering how you'd feel getting out of the country."

"On vacation?"

"Yes. I've got a villa in Italy. It's got direct access to a private beach. No phone signal. Just you and me."

She couldn't help but chuckle, and he joined her.

"I'm not joking, Hannah."

"I'm sorry. I shouldn't laugh. I know I shouldn't, but I can't help it. You've invited me on vacation and back to your place, and work has gotten in the way."

"I'm putting measures in place to make sure we can go. I'd love for you to come with me."

Love.

Company.

She stared at him.

Her heart started to pound.

Love.

Why did that word keep going around and around inside her head? It was like a broken record. One she couldn't shut off.

"Well, I'd love to come with you. If you do go."

"I feel you're wanting a little spanking," he said.

She chuckled.

Staring at him, she wondered what it would be like to really belong to him.

You do.

You're his.

Just as he is yours.

"Why are you frowning?" he asked.

"I just … a thought. It's stupid."

"Tell me."

"I know for me there's no one else. I guess I never really thought about it. Is there someone else for you?"

"Someone else?"

"A girlfriend. Do you have a woman waiting for

you in every single state?" Her cheeks were on fire now.

"No."

"No one?"

"No one has ever been a part of my life the way that you have."

"Oh, you don't have kids or anything?"

"If I did, do you think I'd keep it a secret from you?"

"I don't know. We've not known each other that long."

"You've seen all of me, Hannah. There's nothing else for you to see. I wouldn't lie to you about this."

She tilted her head to the side, watching, waiting. He wouldn't lie to her *about this*. Did it mean he'd lie to her about other things? Stuff he didn't think was that important.

Get a grip.

This is still all new.

She finished her sandwich as he talked to her about another potential building he hoped to purchase. It was over an hour away and one he saw had real potential. The local bars and clubs had all been shut down, and that part of the city needed a revival. They were building a tourist attraction near it as well as a mall.

"You should go for it. If you think it's a good business decision."

"I'll take you to it. Show it to you."

"I'd like that."

Their lunch was finished.

Neither of them said a word.

The dirty look in his eye wasn't hard to assess.

"Come here, Hannah."

"I like sitting here."

"You promised to trust me, remember. To do everything your boss said."

"I know I did. What I didn't know at the time, my boss was going to go back on his word."

Her tits were heavy, the buds pressing against the lace of her bra.

She wanted nothing more than to get out of her seat, walk over to him and give him what he wanted, only she held herself back. Making him wait.

West got to his feet.

He'd already removed his jacket and rolled up his sleeves. The ink on his arms stood out against the white material.

Licking her lips, she waited to see what he'd do next. Gripping the edge of her chair, she waited. Hungry.

He went to the buckle of his pants, opening it up before lowering the zipper. She watched as he reached inside and pulled out his rock-hard cock.

The vein along the side of his cock stood out.

He wrapped his fingers around the length and started to move up and down. He pulled back the foreskin, showing off the bulbous head.

Licking her lips, she heard him groan.

"You want to taste my dick, Hannah?"

Did she?

Staring at his cock, she realized she wanted to give him pleasure, all the kinds of pleasure in the world.

"Yes."

He stepped away from his desk, moving close. She pressed her legs together, creating a little friction against her clit as she did.

His cock was so close, so near her mouth.

All she'd have to do was stick her tongue out and he could slide right inside.

One of his hands was still around his cock while the other went to her head.

"Open your mouth."

She did so, tilting her head back as she did.

He fed his cock between her lips, the head going to her mouth.

"Don't use your teeth. Slowly, to start."

She took more of him into her mouth, going down as she kept her gaze on him. West thrust into her mouth, hitting her throat.

At first she gagged, but he pulled away, falling out of her mouth.

He took one of her hands and opened her fist. "Touch me, Hannah."

She'd never touched a cock before. With West's guidance, she took him in her hand and marveled at how soft he was.

Soft and hard. The vein seeming to throb.

His entire cock pulsed within her grip.

She squeezed his length, making him hiss. "Did I hurt you?"

"No. It feels good."

Running her hand up and down his dick, rubbing her saliva into his flesh, she was fascinated by him, by how he seemed to get just a little bigger.

Without any guidance from him, she took his dick into her mouth and sucked him until her lips met her hand.

Flicking her tongue across the tip, she tasted the tanginess of his pre-cum.

Closing her eyes, she let herself explore. Pulling off his cock, she licked down the vein, all over his cock, until she finally took him back him. This time when he hit her throat, she didn't immediately pull away. She felt him fill her mouth, the length of him keeping her open, wide, sucking on him.

"Oh, fuck, baby, that feels so good."

Opening her eyes, she glanced up at him. One of

his hands was now in her hair, holding her in place.

"Can you take some more?"

She swallowed, and he moved a little more.

Her gag reflex nearly kicked in. She focused, wanting all of him in her mouth, pushing past, but she couldn't do it.

Pulling off his cock, she thought she'd see disappointment there.

There was none.

"One day you'll be able to take it all."

She wanted to.

Sucking him again, she bobbed her head, loving the taste as more of his pre-cum leaked into her mouth.

He groaned and started to thrust inside her, fucking her face.

Both of his hands were in her hair, and she loved it.

She loved the power and scent of him as he rode her mouth.

"Fuck, I'm about to come. You better swallow every drop." He started to climax the moment he finished his order.

The first wave of his cum flooded her tongue, and she swallowed him down, moaning as more came.

She kept on swallowing, trying to capture it all until there was nothing left.

He dropped to his knees before her, his hands sliding beneath her skirt. His face was buried against her chest.

Her pussy was so wet. She wanted his hands on her.

West kissed her chest, traveling down to her stomach.

The chair was more of a hindrance, so he pulled her down to the floor. Within seconds he had her skirt around her waist and her legs wide open.

She cried out his name as he fingered her pussy.

Another pair of panties were snapped off her body, and he shoved them in his pocket for safekeeping or whatever it was he did with her panties. He spread her pussy lips, sliding two fingers inside her, drawing them up to pinch her clit. The sudden pain startled her before he soothed it out.

He kissed her lips seconds before his tongue replaced his fingers. She closed her eyes, thrusting her pelvis up to meet him, desperate for the pleasure he could give.

"Your pussy is so damn sweet. So perfect. I could eat you all day long."

She'd be more than happy with that.

When he lifted her legs up, she opened her eyes.

"Hold your legs?" he said.

She wrapped an arm around each leg, which opened her up.

He reached for the plug off the desk, and her nerves suddenly hit her.

"West?"

"You're going to love it. I'll even let you put your panties back on."

"You tore them."

"I've got an extra pair."

He opened up the butt plug, and she wanted to tell him no.

Her excitement replaced her nerves.

Anal sex … intrigued her.

What would be the harm in at least trying it?

Keeping hold of her legs, she watched as he opened up the lubrication and coated the plug generously.

When it was slick and ready, he put one hand on

her legs, pushing her back, which lifted her ass up in the air.

There was no escaping or hiding. The light spilling in from the window gave a clear view of her pussy and anus.

Any sane woman would be running scared.

You want this.

You crave this.

She gasped as the cold plug pressed against her anus. He rubbed the tip over her puckered hole, getting her nice and ready, and slick.

When he started to apply pressure, she knew he was going all the way.

This plug was much bigger than his fingers. She didn't know if she'd be able to handle that kind of thickness.

You can do this.

Taking a deep breath, she let out a little squeak as it stretched her open. Slowly, he pushed the plug into her ass, and even though it burned, it wasn't completely uncomfortable. Far from it.

She ached for him to touch her pussy. To slide his fingers inside her, to stroke her clit.

The moment the plug was inside, West took her ankles and spread her legs.

"How does that feel?"

"Touch me, West. Please, touch me."

"You want my hands on your pussy?"

"Yes."

"You want to come."

She was going to hurt him in a minute if he didn't start touching her.

Before she could scream at him, yell, or beg, his fingers were between her thighs, stroking over her clit.

She couldn't contain her moans. Crying his name,

she felt the first stirrings of her arousal build with just a few strokes of his fingers.

She was so close that when he leaned down and took her clit into his mouth, she came, screaming his name.

Grabbing his hair, she held him in place as she rode her orgasm.

Her release seemed to go on and on until she finally collapsed on the floor, panting for breath. Her tits felt heavy, and she'd come alive beneath his touch.

West kissed up her body.

She tasted her release on his tongue, but she didn't care. Holding his face, she kissed him hard.

He licked across her lips, and she wondered if he could taste the orgasm she'd swallowed.

"I don't know how I'm going to be able to handle the rest of the day."

"You're going to do it thinking about my cock fucking your ass. Making you scream." He kissed her lips. "Tomorrow, you move up a butt plug."

Chapter Eleven

The picture had been sent.

Tomorrow was the day West intended to meet with Enrique about the cartels. Lawrence had yet to come out of hiding, but that was more than fine. West was aware of the meeting, of the picture, and the moment Enrique entered his city, he already had eyes waiting. The deal that would be struck between Lawrence and Enrique that would guarantee his safety would be intercepted by West's team. Grabbing Lawrence, they'd bring him back to the warehouse where he'd finish him off and make him wish for death.

To deal with Enrique was a different problem.

That fucker had gone behind his back to make this arrangement. While he was talking with him, Rome and Cage had their orders where it concerned Hannah's safety.

He already had a secret apartment that he intended to take her to, one he'd signed up under an alias. There she'd be safe until he finished with negotiations.

With Enrique believing he had the upper hand in these talks and that West was none the wiser, West had already countered the plan.

Enrique was in the dark about his knowledge, and he already had a team ready to take his wife, Isabella.

The little cartel leader thought he could hide his young wife from him.

West had been underestimated all of his life, but right now it was like taking candy from a baby.

All he needed now was for everything to go smoothly, and war wouldn't break out on the streets.

Glancing over at his passenger, he saw Hannah flicking through her cell phone.

She still wasn't convinced about his

determination to take her to his villa. He wasn't surprised by it either. So far, every venture he intended to take her on had been thwarted. Again, it all came back to his own fucking mistakes.

"What are you looking for?"

"I sent Emily a text. I just wondered where she was. I've not heard from her since yesterday morning."

"I'm sure everything is fine. I got a report last night that said she was going through a couple of properties, but she'd found something that she wasn't happy with." The lies were easy to tell. It did so happen that he was looking for property in that area, only, he'd never send someone like Emily.

Hannah didn't need to know that though.

She could stay completely oblivious in her own little world.

"I guess you're right. I'm worrying all the time again." She closed her cell phone. "So where are we going again?"

"It's a surprise."

"I happen to love surprises." She rubbed her hands down her thighs.

She was on the final butt plug. This one he intended to get her used to for the next couple of days.

What he loved most about making her take each plug was her reaction.

Even now, her nipples pressed against the front of her shirt and her thighs were clenched together.

She was trying to fight her arousal, and he found it a turn-on to watch her. He'd fucked her with them in, and it made her pussy even tighter, if that was possible.

They'd been driving for twenty minutes. Traffic wasn't that bad, and as Hannah kept firing off questions about his life, he tried to answer them.

"Is there anything you wish you could have that

you don't?" she asked.

"Be more specific?"

"I don't know how to be. You're a guy who has everything. What do you get a guy who appears to have everything?"

He tried to think about it. "I don't want material things."

"So, a new tie is out of the question?"

He chuckled. "You can buy me a tie whenever you want."

"When's your birthday?" she asked.

"May."

"Ah."

"You're not going to ask me when mine is?"

"I already know."

"You do?"

"Your employment form you filled in."

"Right, right. I do have brains even though they're not working at the moment." She tapped her fingers against the door. "If it's not material things you want, what else is there? You've got the job. The business. The success."

"I don't have a family, Hannah."

"No family?"

"None. No wife. No kids."

"Do you want that?"

He'd been taking her every chance he got without using a condom. He wanted a damn family with this woman.

"Who doesn't want a family?" he asked. Glancing over at her, he saw she looked deep in thought. "Do you *not* want a family?"

"I don't know. I mean, don't get me wrong, being an only child at times sucked because I always wanted a brother and sister. I never told my parents that though. I think they regretted not having me sooner, you know. I think they felt a little guilty because I was alone a lot of the time. Especially growing up. I didn't mind. Family. My parents were in love. No one could come between them. Not that anyone wanted to. My dad always said he fell in love with her at that bistro and he never looked back."

"You want to be loved?"

"Yes. My dad was completely and utterly devoted to my mom. That's what I want."

"And if that came with a family?"

"I guess I'd love to have a family. I can't have one yet though. I'm too young. I'd like to focus on my career right now. Spread my wings. Maybe even travel for a couple of years."

"You want to travel?"

"Yeah. I've not been far in life. I'd love to go to Europe, you know, see the sights. Spend a few days checking out all the local attractions. I'd love to see the Big Ben in England. The Eiffel Tower in France. Things like that."

"I could take you."

"You could?"

"It's something we could do together." *As our honeymoon.* He didn't add that part.

"I'd like that. Emily has never been interested in traveling. Whenever I talk about it, she shoots it down."

Emily was going to get a raise.

"Where are we going?" she asked.

"The building I was telling you about. The area that they're building back up, offering some investment. I wanted to show it to you."

"Cool."

Seconds passed.

"You want kids?" she asked.

"Yes, Hannah, I want kids. I'm not getting any younger."

"I think you're looking just fine to me."

He laughed. "That's good to know."

"I never thought I'd fall for an older man, but then I also didn't plan a lot of things in life."

He saw the sadness on her face and took her hand.

"Life throws us curveballs, and we've always got to learn to dodge them."

"I'm getting tired, like, really tired, of dodging them, West."

"Then share them with me and I will do everything I can to make sure you never have to deal with them again."

She dropped her head onto his shoulder. "You're so good to me. I don't know what I'd ever do without you."

That was good.

It wasn't the words of love that he'd been hoping for, but during his time watching Hannah, he realized she never verbally expressed her feelings, not even to Emily.

He got to the building without any problem. On the outside it didn't look like much. Across the street, he saw several builders working on some new structure.

Parking the car, he climbed out and helped Hannah out of the vehicle.

"Wow, it's huge," she said.

The space was large.

"Come on." Taking out the keys he'd been given, he opened up the door, and helped her inside. There was a lot of light coming in through the windows. He found the switch that lit up the main entrance.

"It looks like a rundown hotel."

"I think it was raided a few years ago. It was a

brothel."

"You're kidding me?"

"Nope."

"You have no proof of that."

"I'll show you proof."

"It's not, like, haunted, is it?"

"No. Not haunted."

"It smells," she said, wrinkling her nose.

"It needs gutting. The main structure is safe, and there are no signs of subsidence. No damp. No damage to walls. It just needs a good cleaning." The walls had red paper peeling off them. Dust clung to the surfaces and floors. He saw the quality of the place.

Something to get him excited.

Taking her hand, he led her through several rooms. There were old chairs. The furniture was well-used and faded from the light.

There was a large fireplace, which was no longer in use as the building had central heating, but it gave an old world feel to the property.

"Did they role play here or something?" Hannah asked.

"I bet a lot of fucking was done here."

"With politicians?" she asked. "You know, the stuff they always say about getting a good Domme to tell them they've been bad little boys? I'm sorry. I really need to stop."

"You'd be surprised."

"I don't think I would."

The main floor was rather tame, but the basement was an interesting exploration. There were dungeons, chains, whips, paddles, and other equipment lining the walls.

"You want to touch them?" he asked.

She shook her head. "You don't know if they've

been washed."

He laughed. "So proper."

"I don't want to get catch anything."

"The only thing you'll catch is a spanking."

"You keep threatening that."

"One day I'll give it to you."

"Promises." She hugged his arm, kissing his cheek.

Leaving the basement, they made their way up to the main floor before going through each room until they got to the attic.

"Wow," Hannah said. "Do you think you'll clean up all the sex toys and sell them?"

"Probably not. It all needs to go."

Hannah released his hand and lifted both of hers up to the chains coming out of one of the beams in the attic. "Do I even want to know?"

He chuckled.

There were keys in the locks.

"Want to try?"

"You're not going to leave me here to starve, are you?"

"Not a chance."

He took her wrist and placed it in the cuff. Her eyes were on him the whole time that he locked her in place.

The skirt she wore was no protection and neither was the shirt.

Placing a hand on her stomach, he circled around her. Her hands were in the air, and she couldn't get them close. There was a bar between them that stopped her from opening them.

"Okay, I have a feeling I know what this is for," she said.

He smiled, standing in front of her. "I rather like

this. You're at my mercy."

"I've always been at your mercy."

She didn't even realize how true that statement was.

Pulling her shirt out of her skirt, he began to work the buttons, opening it. Hannah didn't tell him to stop. Her breathing deepened. Running the back of his fingers across her breasts, he heard her gasp.

With the shirt open, he pulled out his knife and cut the bra away from her flesh. Her tits sprang free, and he dropped the offending garment on the floor. Nothing should be trapping those beauties.

He put his knife away, cupping her tits together. Licking her nipples, he flicked each bud in turn, hearing her moan. Releasing her tits, he slid his hands down, cupping her hips. Dropping his hands down to her knees, he started to lift up her skirt until it was around her waist.

"You're always doing this to me." She moaned, and he laughed.

"That's because I'm always wanting inside your pussy." He cupped her through her panties, feeling how damp they were. Sliding a finger beneath the fabric, he touched her clit. "You love having that plug in your ass, don't you? Do you think about what I'm going to do with you when I take it out? How I'm going to fuck your ass?"

"Please, West. I can't take anymore."

He thrust a finger inside her. Her pussy tightened around him.

His cock pressed against the front of his pants. He was so hard and aroused it was near the point of pain. He didn't pull himself out yet.

Moving his finger from inside her, he stroked over her clit, using two fingers to heighten her arousal.

Her tits swayed, and the chains kept her in place.

He was going to have to invest in some of those chains.

"Do you want my cock inside your pussy?"

"Yes. Please, West. Please."

Holding the fingers that had been inside her pussy up to her mouth, he stroked his slick fingers across her lips. "Suck them. Taste yourself. Taste how wet you are. How desperate and horny you are."

She opened up, and he plunged them inside.

Once she had them clean, he worked on his pants, getting the zipper down and taking out his cock. Running his fingers over the length, he wrapped an arm around Hannah. "Put your legs around me."

He lifted her up. With one hand on his cock and the other holding her, he found her entrance and seated her on his dick. Whoever put the chains in place wasn't thinking of ease of fucking.

With his cock inside her, he used two hands to hold her. Her arms were wrapped around his neck. She could get to the cuffs this way.

"Take them off," he said.

He heard the click of the cuffs, and then, slamming her against the wall, he started to fuck her. The leverage of the wall gave him all he needed to start fucking her, to pound inside her.

Her pussy quivered, tightening around him.

He couldn't hold back.

Slamming to the hilt, he came, once again flooding her pussy with his release. When his orgasm started to subside, he wondered if this would be the one to take, if he'd finally gotten her pregnant.

****

"I can't live with you forever," Hannah said. "I've got to go back to my apartment." It was lunchtime on Friday, the last day of the week. It had been a long, hard one. She couldn't wait to get home to relax and put her feet up.

"It doesn't have to be tonight. Please, go back to my place."

West was being difficult. She didn't know why it mattered so much to him where she stayed the night. She just wanted to go home and relax. Chinese food was calling her name, and she hoped to phone Emily as well.

She'd started to feel like a really shitty friend. West had come into her life and completely dominated every single part. She loved it though. Waking up with his arms wrapped around her or going to sleep with his warmth made her feel complete. The only problem was she hadn't been home in a couple of days.

The clothes she wore were the ones he'd purchased for her.

If she sat back and thought about how easy it was to lose herself, she started to feel afraid. She'd never been the kind of woman to fall for a man so hard and so quickly.

It no longer felt like weeks but actual years that she'd known him.

"I don't know when Emily's going to be back. All I want to do is go grocery shopping. Clean my place. Please. You're not going to be there." She placed a hand against his chest, feeling his heart beat.

Whenever she was around him, hers always seemed to speed up.

"I don't want you to be alone," he said.

She laughed. "West, you've got an important meeting. I'm not going to be the kind of woman that can't function without you." She pressed a kiss to his lips. "This will mean that you miss me and maybe we'll be able to get on that vacation after all?"

West wasn't happy. It didn't take a rocket

scientist to figure that out. Stroking her fingers across his chest, she didn't back down.

She didn't get why he seemed determined to make her stay at his apartment.

"Okay, fine. Rome's going to be with you though. He'll take you to the supermarket and to your place. I don't like this."

Rolling her eyes, she shook her head.

"It's a shame, really," he said.

"What's a shame?" she asked.

He shrugged. "I just had plans is all." He pulled out of her arms, and she watched him.

"What are you hiding?"

"A surprise."

"You have another surprise?"

"Just a little something."

He opened his desk drawer, and she tensed up. Her ass had been given a reprieve today. She'd already taken the large plug and begged him to stop. That she needed one day to just be able to walk around without a huge plug up her ass. He'd relented.

He held out a black velvet box. It was too big to be a ring, so she wasn't overly concerned.

If he *was* to propose to her, would she accept?

What are you doing?

Why are you even thinking in terms of a proposal?

They were not at that stage yet. Not even close.

"What is it?" she asked.

"Why don't you open it and find out?"

Letting out a breath, she stepped up to his desk and picked it up. Flicking open the lid, she saw a key.

"This isn't a car, is it?"

"No."

"You got a new apartment?"

"I got *us* a new apartment."

She stared down at the key, tilting her head to one side.

"How did you get us an apartment when I didn't even agree to living with you?"

"Because you're going to agree?"

She laughed. "I am?"

"Yes." He wrapped his arms around her waist, pulling her close. "You see, I know what is going on here. You know what is going on here, and one day you're going to admit it. I'd like you to let Rome take you here."

"But my place?"

"Go to the grocery store and stop by your apartment. Do what you need to do, but please, promise me you'll go here."

She heard the desperation in his voice, which shocked her. "It really means that much to you?"

"I'll go to my meeting feeling a lot happier, yes."

"Wow." She stared at the key. "This is all too much." *Just say thank you. He wants you to live with him. He wants an actual commitment. What the hell are you doing?*

"I'm laying my cards out on the table for you to see. I'm not holding anything back. I want this, Hannah. With you. Me and you."

She couldn't say anything. It was on the tip of her tongue to tell him the same thing, but she held back.

Why did she keep holding back?

"This is amazing, West. Thank you."

"You've not seen the apartment. I have a feeling you're going to love it."

"Then why don't we wait until we've seen it together? Why do I have to go now without you?"

"Because I want you to see it. Please, Hannah.

For me."

He kept repeating the same words, and she didn't have the heart to keep on fighting. She didn't even know why she was.

"Fine. Fine. I'm not going until I've gone to my place though. If Emily returns before I get the chance, I don't want her to have to go get food and stuff."

"Thank you." He pressed a kiss to her lips, and she sighed.

Pleasure flooded her body, reminding her of all the sinful things he'd done and would keep on doing.

Just the thought of him coming to their apartment to wake her up to have his wicked way with her filled her with need.

Pulling away from him was hard.

"I'll be fine." Patting his chest, she went back to her desk and continued working on the figures HR had sent to her.

This wasn't the job she wanted long-term. She didn't offer anyone financial advice, but it was a good place to be. The salary was amazing, and she didn't have to worry about being fired.

Of course, it helped that she was dating the boss.

Dating West Gallo.

Everything was crazy right now.

Near the end of the day, Emily called her.

"Hey, I thought I'd check in. I got your text messages. What's up?" Emily asked.

"There's nothing wrong. I was thinking when you come back maybe you and I should have a girls' night. You know, just you and me."

"That sounds cool. We've not had one of those days in, like, forever, and I've been a bitch to you."

"You have not been a bitch."

"I totally have. I was going through a tough time,

189

and I shouldn't have blamed you and I guess in a way I did. It is entirely my fault. I'm a bad person."

Hannah couldn't help but laugh.

"It's the change in scenery. You had to keep looking at my ugly face all the time."

"Hannah, you're not ugly. So, how are things going with your hot stuff of a boyfriend?"

"They're going great." She looked down at the key he'd given her. "Do you think things can move too fast?"

"Things?"

"You know. Moving in together. Dating. Sex?" She wished she'd not said anything.

"Does there have to be a time limit or is there a recommended time for anyone who wants to date? I don't know what you're trying to ask."

"West. Things are moving really fast. Incredibly so. He's amazing. I mean, so good." She wasn't even thinking solely about sex then either.

"Do you have feelings for him?"

Hannah stopped.

Feelings.

Love.

Like.

What *did* she feel for him?"

"I do," she said.

"Do you love him?"

"I don't know. I've never been in love before."

"I don't know either," Emily said, laughing. "I've never been in love. I guess we'll be doing a romance marathon when I get back."

"I'm going to head to our place."

"Oh, you don't have to do that. I'm going to be here a couple more days at least. Have some fun with West."

Hannah paused. "You're not?"

"No. There's no need to go shopping or do anything you want to do."

She looked toward West's office. He was behind his desk, typing away at his computer.

Why did she have a feeling that he'd done this?

"Okay," she said.

"Cool. What are you guys' plans for tonight?"

Hannah didn't want to talk anymore. Something didn't sit right with her. Once again, she had that twisted feeling in her gut like she was missing something, but again, not exactly sure what the hell it was.

"I've got to go, Emily. Something's come up. I'll talk to you real soon." Hanging up the cell phone, she stared down at her desk.

It couldn't be a coincidence, could it?

Before she had time to really think about it, Rome entered the floor.

He was wearing a leather cut jacket, a pair of jeans, and a white shirt. He looked ready to blend into a crowd. She was used to seeing him in a suit.

West came out of his office.

"You're ready to take her?" West asked.

"Yep. Where are we heading first?" Rome asked.

"To the supermarket and my apartment. Actually, make that my apartment and then the supermarket."

"You still want to go to the supermarket?" West asked.

Again, her senses were tingling all over.

"Of course. Why wouldn't I want to?"

"I don't know. Just a feeling. You know, I quickly checked Emily's schedule, and she's not going to be back for a few days."

"I still want to go if that's okay." She stared at him, but she couldn't detect anything. She wished she knew what he was thinking, but alas, mind reading was not on her list of skills. "I'm ready to go." She stepped up to West. "Have a good meeting."

West caught her around the waist, pulling her close. "Be careful."

"Always."

Why was he always insistent that she be careful? She wasn't a klutz.

She'd never given him any indication to worry about her.

Pushing some hair off her face, she followed Rome into the elevator. He didn't say anything, and she wondered if he knew she wasn't in the mood to make small talk.

Once at the car, he opened the door to the back seat. Buckling her own seat belt, she sat back and waited.

"Are you okay?" Rome asked when they joined traffic.

"Of course. Why wouldn't I be?"

"I don't know. You're usually really chatty."

"It has been a really, really long day."

She also didn't like the thought that Emily and West were somehow working together to … what? To manipulate her?

He said there was no one else.

She believed him, but why would Emily call her not long after her conversation with West?

Not only that, the time back at Dirty.

She'd been worried about Emily, and when West disappeared, Emily called her.

You're starting to get all paranoid. This is not good for you.

Your life is not one big conspiracy theory.

"Do you know anything about this meeting West has?"

"Not much. I know it's really important to him."

"If it's so important, how come you're not with him?"

"I'm needed elsewhere. You shouldn't worry about a thing though. West knows what he's doing."

She had no doubt that he knew what he was doing.

She was more curious as to what he was doing in her life. "You've been working with him for some time, right?"

"You know I have."

She'd already asked him about it before.

Biting her lip, she stared out the window. "Do you know if he's purchased an apartment for another woman before?"

"No, he hasn't."

"Do you know Emily?" she asked.

"I've met her, yes."

"Do you even know who I'm talking about?"

"West has made it our business to know your friends. What's wrong, Hannah?"

"Nothing."

"You seem a little ... distracted."

"I'm fine."

She didn't have a clue what was going on. "Have I ever met you before?"

Did she see him tense? Was that a trick of the light?

"No, we've never met."

"I feel like I know you."

"We'd never met before you started seeing West. We had no reason to."

He pulled up outside her apartment building.

"Okay." She climbed out of the car, not wanting to talk to him right now. She was going crazy.

Sickness filled her, and she rushed up to her apartment. Why was she feeling weird and like someone was lying to her?

Entering her apartment, she saw everything was exactly how she left it.

Rome had followed her up and closed the door behind her.

She went to the kitchen.

Opening the fridge, she saw a couple of items were spoiled. Grabbing a trash can, she filled it with the out-of-date stuff.

With the bag full and the fridge cleaned out, she excused herself.

Entering her bedroom, she closed the door and went straight to the bathroom. Emily's main door was closed. She opened the door that connected both of their rooms to the bathroom.

What are you doing?

Staring into Emily's room, she stepped inside.

Beside her friend's bed, there was a picture of the two of them. She was smiling, as was Emily.

Glancing around the bedroom, she saw nothing that seemed out of place.

Going to the first drawer, she opened it up and found nothing but lingerie. She tried to snoop as quietly as possible.

She didn't find anything in the drawers or in the desk. Next, the small closet. Opening the doors, she switched on the light. There were several boxes. She went to her knees, opening up one box and checking through it before moving onto the next. She dropped something on the floor, and she picked it up. Glancing under the bed, she saw another box. This was wooden, and it looked like it had been pulled out recently.

Closing up the closet, she went to the bed, and

pulled out the large crate-like box. Running her hand across the wood, she lifted it up. There were a couple of folders. Taking them out, she opened them up, seeing old bank statements.

She saw the date went back five years. That was the start of the files.

Pulling one out, she stared down at the figures and frowned. The day she met Emily, which she remembered as it was the start of a new semester and they shared a dorm, Emily was transferred a large sum of money. Every month, Emily was sent money, but it was the account that made her pause.

The company that offered her the scholarship that paid for her tuition, her books, and her rent money, was the same account.

She would recognize the numbers anywhere.

Sitting back, she didn't know what to make of it.

"Hannah, you okay?"

Shit.

Putting the files down, she padded back to her room.

"Yeah, I'll be out in a minute."

She placed her hands on the door.

Something wasn't adding up, and now she felt even more sick.

Maybe Emily had the same scholarship?

No, Emily didn't.

Her friend had told her that her family funded the entire college tuition.

Hannah ran fingers through her hair.

Whatever was going on between Emily and West, she was going to get to the bottom of it.

She didn't have time right now though. Not with Rome there.

She rushed back to Emily's room, put away all

the documents, and slid the box under the bed, careful not to make a single sound.

With the box back in place, she got to her feet and entered the bathroom.

A little over five years ago, her life had changed completely. The scholarship she had originally applied for got taken away as the company that supplied it crashed. She'd struggled to find a replacement until she was contacted and given another.

Quickly shoving clothes into a bag, she changed into a pair of jeans and a shirt.

Rome was waiting for her.

She'd get to the bottom of what the hell was going on.

Until then, she'd be careful.

Chapter Twelve

West glanced down at his cell phone. Lawrence should have been taken by now. He didn't like not knowing what was going on. He'd arrived at the location where he was set to meet Enrique. He'd already checked all the escape routes. Some of his men were on standby and close just in case he needed them.

This was not his and Enrique's first rodeo. They'd encountered each other many times, and it had never ended in bloodshed. Their negotiations were always brutal, but neither of them wanted to bring about a war. For the most part, he admired Enrique's dedication and loyalty to his men, but he'd crossed the line when he listened to Lawrence.

After double-checking the escape routes, he did a quick check of his weapons. His deal with Enrique was that he came alone. Again, he doubted that would be the case.

This was fucking dangerous. If he'd not done business with Enrique in the past, he wouldn't have even considered a meeting. Without many escape routes, and with what was at stake, he'd be lucky to get out with his life intact but certainly with plenty of wounds.

The only good news he'd received tonight was his men had gotten Isabella and she was in containment. No harm had come to her. In a few minutes he'd call her. His men had only confirmed extraction, not being in the safe location away from Enrique's spies.

Rome hadn't called him about Hannah's safety.

He didn't understand why she'd felt the need to go back to her apartment. He'd called Emily to dissuade her, and it hadn't worked.

Rubbing his temples, he wasn't in the mood to deal with any fuckups tonight. There had been too many in the past few weeks. Lawrence should have been easy, but his biggest fuckup was biting him in the ass over and over again.

Who had known the piece of shit would know what to do to protect his ass? The moment he got this dealt with Enrique, he was taking Hannah away. He'd get her to finally admit that she loved him and they'd get married.

The plan was so simple in his mind.

Tapping his phone against his leg, he counted down the seconds, waiting for someone to come.

Checking the time on his watch, he saw it was now a little after seven.

If Enrique didn't turn up in the next five minutes, he was gone. Simple as that.

While he waited, he put a quick call to Rome, who answered on the second ring.

"Yeah, boss?"

"Update."

"I'm waiting for her and then we're heading to the supermarket. I've asked her to change her mind, but she's not budging. Have you two … talked?"

"What do you mean?"

"I just wondered if you'd talked about something."

"Why?"

"She's acting weird," Rome said.

He didn't need the fucking cryptic questions right now but actual answers.

"What the hell is that supposed to mean?" He didn't have time for this. There was a shitload of stuff going down. What he actually needed was for Enrique to turn up, confirmation that Isabella was safe at one of his locations, and to finish off with Lawrence caught. That's what he needed on all fronts. Nothing else.

"She's asking about you. About us. About Emily. I believe she's starting to see some of the lies," Rome said.

"No, you've got it all wrong. Just do your job. Get her to the supermarket, keep her safe, and then get her to the apartment. It's not that hard. Now do it." He hung up his cell phone and before he'd even taken another breath, another person was on it, and it pissed him the fuck off.

"What?" he asked, yelling into the phone.

"We've got Isabella, sir. Is everything okay?"

"Yes. Put her on the phone."

He heard some shuffling before someone spoke. He was already annoyed and pissed off. If he'd been with Hannah, none of this would be happening right now.

"Hello," Isabella said, sniffling.

"Hello, Isabella, how are you?"

"What do you want?"

"I want you to play along. If you do as I ask, you'll live. If not, one of my men will put a bullet hole right in your skull right now. Got it?"

"Why are you doing this? Enrique will kill you if anything happens to me. Why?"

He chuckled. If this had been Hannah's tears, his heart would be breaking and he'd try to think of a way to fix it. This woman was not Hannah, and he found her tears pitiful. "Because your precious little beau thought he could take something from me without my figuring it out. He'll soon learn you don't mess with the king of the street without getting burned yourself."

"This is complete madness," Isabella said.

"Let's hope he loves you as much as you think he loves you." He hung up the cell phone, and was once again waiting.

His patience was fast running out.

He was about to leave when his cell phone rang once again. It was Cage. "Tell me what I need to know."

"He's gone, Boss. No sign of him."

"Fuck!"

"You need to get out of there. Enrique is coming, and I don't like this."

He cut Cage off. There was no way in hell that he'd ever back down from a fight. He thought about Hannah. His men would take care of her.

In that moment, he wondered if she was pregnant.

He'd done everything in his power to knock her up and now he just had to wait. Being inside her was like going to heaven. Her tight cunt pulled him in every single time, making the past five years worth it.

After that first time meeting her in the burger joint, he never expected to see her again. When he did, he knew he had to protect her, have her, take her, but she wasn't ready, not for him.

Pushing those thoughts aside, he heard the car pull out, doors opening and the sound of footsteps.

"Stay," Enrique said.

This made his brow rise.

In the next second, Enrique entered the abandoned basement, surprisingly alone.

West had a grip on the gun at his back.

"You're alone."

"That's what you requested."

"I never expected you to follow through with my request."

"We come from different worlds, West. There have been many times that you could kill me, and I know if I came in with men, you'd have no problem firing at every single one of them before they'd even drawn a gun. You don't get where you are without being the best at what you do. We've done this dance before. I have something you want, and you know what I want. So why don't we talk business?"

"What do you have of mine?"

Enrique sighed, opening up his jacket for him to see. He reached inside and pulled out a piece of paper. He opened it up and West saw the picture that he'd posed for with Hannah. He'd not hidden his feelings for her. His men had been waiting to take the snap for this very moment.

"You know, it's funny you should talk about having something of mine. I'm rather shocked at how easy it was to get something of yours." He dialed the number as he looked at Enrique. "Just a moment and you'll see what I mean." He waited for his man to answer. "Put her on the phone."

He waited a few seconds.

"Hello."

"Hey, sweetheart, let's hear you for a second."

He put his cell phone to speaker and her voice came over the line.

Enrique was good at hiding his feelings, but West saw the panic, the fear as it flashed across his eyes before he hid it.

"Bella," he said.

"Enrique, please don't do anything stupid. I don't want to die." She started to cry. The sound grated on West's nerves.

He closed his cell phone. "My men will kill her if I don't leave this place alive and well."

"You son of a bitch."

"My mother was no bitch. My father was a fucking whore and a bastard, but not my mother. Now, let's put something into perspective, shall we? You thought you could come into my fucking city, tell me how I'm going to pay you, and that I'd follow behind all the bullshit you wanted me to?"

Enrique's jaw clenched.

"Lawrence has been in hiding for a few weeks now. His death sentence is coming the moment I get my hands on him. He tried to rape my woman. Now, I can tell you, Isabella is safe from that happening to her, so now tell me why I should let you fucking live when you were going to help a rapist that is on my shit list and due to die?"

****

"That's never going to happen," Rome said.

"Why not?" Hannah placed the large joints of beef into the cart, along with lots of chicken, which were on a half-price sale and no one could ever turn down a bargain. She'd bag them up and place them in the freezer for when she needed them. Her mother had taught her how to do this, and even to this day, she followed her mother's advice for shopping.

"I know the boss, and he won't go for that."

"I've never met any of his friends. He must have them."

"You're confusing West for someone else."

"And if I want to give this dinner party, you're telling me you wouldn't come?"

"I'm saying to you that West will figure some way out of not going or you not giving one. It's as simple as that."

Hannah followed behind him, staring at the shelves, but she wasn't paying attention to any of the labels.

Rome's words rang inside her head like a broken record. Emily's bank statements, the coincidences, everything seemed to be confusing her and making sense at the same time.

"You're saying West manipulates people to get

what he wants?"

"He's not been on top playing fairly."

She picked up a couple of cans. She didn't know what they were. Putting them in the cart, she tried her hardest to force a smile.

"So, has he ever tried to manipulate me?" She tilted her head to the side, hoping her look came off as teasing and not snooping.

He opened his mouth and closed it. "Are you done? We need to head back so I can take you to the safe apartment."

"Nearly. Don't think I didn't notice you didn't answer." Her hands shook a little as they finished their shopping. She tried to draw Rome out a bit more but he'd closed himself off, and that only annoyed her.

Once they were finished and as she went to pay, Rome took over, handing a card to the woman.

The woman behind the counter kept blushing as she looked at Rome, who didn't seem to notice anything.

With the groceries paid for, Hannah followed him outside. It was already dark, and this was the time she loved to shop. The supermarket was rarely busy at night so she got her pick of the store.

"You know, that woman liked you," she said.

"What?"

"That woman. Back at the register. She, like, really liked you. She was trying to get your attention."

He glanced back at the store.

"I don't have time for silliness."

"Please, flirting is fun, you know." She shrugged. "How come you're in a sour mood?"

"We've got to get you to safety."

She rolled her eyes and saw the car. Reaching into his pocket, she pulled out the keys and rushed toward the car.

"Hannah, wait."

She beeped the car and rushed toward the trunk. Just as she was lifting it up, movement caught her attention, and when she looked, Lawrence stood there. He held a gun pointed at her head.

At first, it didn't seem real to her. A gun pointed at her head.

Fear rushed down her spine as she stared at him.

"Do you have any fucking idea what you and your pussy caused me?"

She remembered the feel of his hands touching her, of the sick to her stomach feeling.

"The cops are looking for you."

"They're the least of my problems. Your little boyfriend is my biggest, and if he thinks for a second I'm going to him to beg for my life, he's mistaken. The only thing he cares about at all is standing right here."

"You better back away," Rome said.

Hannah turned and saw the gun in his hand.

Why did everyone have guns?

"I have no idea what is going on here. Rome?"

"Hannah, get in the car."

"No," Lawrence said. "She stays." He stepped toward her, and before she could do anything he had a hand tightly wrapped around her throat, cutting off some of her air supply. She gripped his hand, taken aback by his strength. "Does she even know what he's done? What he's been doing for some time?"

"Enough," Rome said.

"What is going on?" she asked.

"I wonder how you'll feel when you realize none of your life has been real."

She frowned, looking at Rome.

"She doesn't know because no one is allowed to tell you. West Gallo isn't some businessman. He rules these streets."

"He told me about the fighting. How he won every single fight," she said.

Lawrence laughed, his grip bruising as she choked.

"You have no idea of the monster you're in bed with. You really are a stupid fucking bitch, aren't you? I can see why he likes you. You can't even see how much he's controlled your life. You really think you were intelligent enough to get a scholarship? There are a lot brighter women out there that are worth the time and money, believe me. You're not one of them. You'll never be one of them."

"Enough, Lawrence."

"I see his little cronies keep you in the dark. You see, West wasn't just a random guy, Hannah. He's been watching you for a long time now. Longer than you even realize. He's the one that made sure you didn't fail out of college. He even gave you a roommate. He thinks when he talks people listen. I listened. I fucking investigated him. That's my job, to find out where money is being leaked, and I know that he's been pushing money your way for fucking years. It didn't take long to put two and two together when you came to my office. I already had your name on file for one of his businesses. With him looking the other way, I was able to piece everything together. Yeah, Emily too; it's all part of his clever plan to have you in his life. Nothing you know is the truth. It's all fabricated lies for him to own every single part of you. There's no one you can trust. You think you know him, but he's got more kills under his belt than a fucking army sniper."

Her heart pounded.

She listened to every single word that Lawrence said.

Staring at Rome, she tried to see if what Lawrence said was the truth.

Rome gave her a look of pity.

Was it pity?

There's no way she could trust what Lawrence was saying, could she?

All lies.

"Now I'm on his shit list for wanting to take a taste of the pussy he's been wanting, and my life is in danger."

"Let her go."

"Nah, I'm not fucking stupid."

"Following us here was fucking stupid."

"Yeah, well, I'm taking my chances."

"Hannah," Rome said. "I know right now you're feeling hurt and you're trying to figure out what the hell is going on. I get that, but you can't leave with this man. He will kill you just to make it out. Do you know what I'm saying?"

He wanted her to move. To do something that would give him the chance to take Lawrence out.

Did she want this man dead?

The memory of his attack in his office made her close her eyes and slump to the ground. She covered her face as she heard the silencer on the gun. There wasn't a loud bang, but she heard the single shot—next, the sound of a body falling to the ground.

Before she could turn her head or do something, Rome had her hands locked in his.

"Get in the car."

"I want to go home."

"No. Get in the damn car and don't make me force you, Hannah. Right now, I'm not in the fucking mood." He didn't give her a chance to argue as he shoved her into the back of the car.

He'd put the damn child lock on. She slammed her hands against the window. She watched as he lifted Lawrence's body and dumped it into the trunk of the car. There weren't too many people around, a few cars here or there. It wasn't a very popular supermarket but it was one she always liked. She was never going to see this the same way again.

"Let me out of here."

Rome didn't answer. The moment he dumped the body in the back of the car, he rounded to the driver's side and climbed in.

"Let me out, Rome. I don't want to go anywhere with you."

"You don't have a choice."

"Rome, please, was it true?"

"This is not a conversation to have with me. Sit back and relax."

"Relax? You killed a man."

"Who was going to kill you the first chance he got. I did you a favor, and this is how you repay me? For fuck's sake. Your life was in danger."

"How long has my life been my own? What he said? All of it. I saw something in Emily's bank statements. It's true, isn't it? West has paid her to be my what? My friend?"

"Hannah, you need to talk to him."

"Why? Is he really that dangerous? Should I run? What should I do?"

"Not panic and trust me to take care of you. Can you do that? I've only ever wanted to take care of you and make sure you stay safe."

She stared at his reflection in the rearview mirror. He did look genuinely sorry. "Do we know each other?"

"No, we don't know each other. I've been trusted to care for you, and that is exactly what I'm doing. It has been nice to finally meet you though, Hannah."

"Finally?"

"I can't tell you any more."

Sitting back in her seat, she wondered what she was going to do. Who she could trust? Emily? Emily's family? West?

Since her parents died, she hadn't gotten close to anyone.

"Does West hold the scholarship?" she asked.

"Hannah, please, just, calm down. Relax."

She had sex with a man she didn't even know. What the hell was wrong with her? Running hands down her face, she tried to think clearly. To understand all that was going on. There was always something vaguely familiar about West. There were movements that always gave her a feeling of déjà vu.

Staring out of the window, she tried her hardest to ignore the dead body in the back of the car and that feeling like she couldn't breathe. Rubbing her chest, she kept taking deep breaths.

Calm down.

Don't panic.

It'll be okay.

What if it wasn't okay? What if it was all true? What if she had no one?

Biting her lip, she ran her fingers through her hair, wanting nothing more than to pull the strands out.

This wasn't what she wanted. This wasn't how she imagined her life.

She should be happy, not feeling so alone.

Chapter Thirteen

After careful negotiation with Enrique, West was able to stop any potential threat of war. Of course, it helped that Isabella was in his care, and before Enrique left, he made sure she was at a secure location before they concluded their business. With Isabella held by his men, he'd made sure that Enrique couldn't sell any of his dope in his city. However, they did talk profit for transporting it through the city and out to where he needed it to go. For twenty-five percent of the profit of all the dope sold, Enrique got one of the MCs he had dealings with for a lump sum payment.

"I wouldn't have listened to that piece of shit if I knew what he'd done."

"We live and learn." He shook hands with Enrique, and considering he expected to leave injured, coming out with a business arrangement was pretty good going. Neither of them wanted to die. West's death would not only guarantee Isabella's death, there would also be a hit placed on Enrique as well.

He always made sure he had several backup plans. First, his men would put a bullet in Isabella's head, tear her limb from limb, and display her outside Enrique's mansion. After that, the hunters would come for the price on his head.

Leaving the building, he watched Enrique depart. Without their men there, they didn't have to throw fights or insults. They could talk shop without needing to look like the bigger man.

His cell phone had done nothing but buzz throughout it, pissing him off.

Now that he was alone, he opened up his cell phone and saw Rome had been calling. With over fifteen missed calls, he couldn't put him off much longer.

"What's up?" he asked, finally answering a call.

"Lawrence is dead, but you got to get over here to the safe house." The house actually being an apartment.

"Wait? What?"

"He was at the supermarket. He'd clearly tracked us down. She knows, West. She's freaking out, but you need to come here. I've not told her anything."

"What does she know?"

"About the scholarship, Emily, most of it. You're needed here."

"Fuck!" He rushed toward his car. This was not part of his plan. He never wanted Hannah to find out the truth of what he was capable of and what he'd done to put himself in her path.

This was going against everything he'd been planning.

"Piece of fucking shit. Keep her there. Don't let her move."

"I won't."

Hanging up his cell phone, he put his foot to the gas and started driving fast. He ignored the speed limit, making his way along the busy roads, careful not to kill himself.

Pressing down on the horn, he urged people out of the way. This was not how he expected his plans to go, not even fucking close.

He was so angry.

All they had to do was one job.

To keep her safe.

None of them could even do that right, and now he was going to have to deal with this current fuckup.

Breaking the speed limit and nearly every other traffic law, he arrived at the apartment building within twenty minutes. Pulling up, he didn't bother to park correctly. Rushing to the door, he typed in the code to enter the building. Once inside, he ran up the flight of stairs to the apartment.

He didn't knock. Using his own key, he opened the door, and there Rome stood.

As West closed the door, Hannah was suddenly there, her hands folded as she glared at him. Her long, brown hair was a mess from her running her fingers through it repeatedly.

"You're finally here?" she asked.

He heard the attitude in her voice.

"Rome, you can go and deal with that dead body in the car."

She shook her head. "Oh, my God, I can't believe that just happened. What … what do we do? I don't know what to do. This is too much. Oh, my God. I'm panicking. Think, Hannah, think."

"You don't have to worry about a thing," West said. He saw her panicking. Her hand went to her chest, rubbing at her heart. Fear and shock stared right back at him. "It's okay, Hannah."

"He shot someone."

"Rome was doing his job."

She nodded. "Like Emily? Like the scholarship company? Like Lawrence? What about you, West? What job did you have?"

He saw the hurt in her eyes.

"You're overreacting. You don't know—"

"Don't even try to pretend this isn't real. It is. Isn't it? You have been pulling the strings like some puppet master for a long time now." She stared at him. The sound of the door closing let him know they were in private once again.

He stepped closer to her.

She shook her head, held a hand out, and took a step back.

"I'm not going to hurt you, Hannah. You should know this by now."

"What do I know? Really? What exactly can you tell me? I don't know anything. I don't know who you are. My best friend. It all makes some weird kind of sense. The scholarship company. No one else would take me. My grades were not the greatest. My parents had died. Out of the blue that scholarship was a lifeline I needed. It's run by you. One of your shell companies? That same scholarship also paid Emily. She told me that she didn't need it. Her parents paid it."

"It was a good investment."

"You really did," she said. "You paid people to be part of my life? Emily's not really my friend. I'm a job to her? My job. Everything. Are my grades even real?"

"Yes. All your grades were you. I never manipulated that. That was all your hard work. I just made sure your professors knew how to guide you."

"How much of my life did you invade?" she asked. "I don't want lies. I thought … I thought we met in a random bar."

"We met a little over five years ago. It was your eighteenth birthday. That's when we first met."

"You're crazy," she said. "I would have remembered."

"I thought you might, but it wasn't that significant an encounter. I was sitting, nursing a wound. No one had come to your birthday party. Your parents still thought it was cool to, erm, for a burger place to have a teenagers' party."

He saw her face pale.

She stared at him and shook her head. "Your hair was longer, and you had a beard."

"That I did." It had been a rough couple of weeks

for him.

"No. I can't. You decided then?"

"No. That was a few months after. I wanted you. I had fallen in love—"

"No, it can't be love."

"Why not?"

"When you love someone you don't lie like that. You don't manipulate."

"I've done everything in my power to make your life better."

"Better? How is it better?"

"You got your college education. You don't have to pay a cent of that money back. You're in a job you love. Emily is always there for you."

"Emily's a fraud. She can't stand to be around me."

"That's not true."

"It is true." She placed a hand to her stomach. "These feelings I have for you, are they real? I don't … I can't even trust them."

"You can trust them."

"How? How can I trust that these are real? How can I trust anything? I have no one. I have nothing. The apartment." She stopped and looked at him. "You organized the apartment. The killer rent?"

"Yes. I am your landlord."

She took a step back, and he watched as she collapsed into a chair. He didn't like to see her like this.

"Was Lawrence part of your plan too? Did you intend for him to attack me?"

"He shouldn't have fucking touched you. None of that was planned, not even a little bit."

"I don't know if I believe you."

He moved toward her, kneeling down. She flinched as he put his hands on her thighs, and he ignored

213

the action. He got that she was angry, that she was upset, but he wasn't going to let her go, nor was he going to allow her to try to hide.

Their feelings for each other, that was real. Everything else, that didn't matter. He loved her more than anything. Had done absolutely everything in his power to make sure she had a good life, a safe life. He'd never let anything happen to her.

"I love you, Hannah."

"No."

"Please, don't say no."

"How would you feel if I did these things to you? If I lied to you about who I was. About what I'd done. I don't even know the real you. The one people are afraid of. Lawrence was afraid of you, wasn't he?"

"Hannah."

She pressed her hands to her ears. "I need you to stop lying to me. I need the truth. To know who you are. To know everything. Why don't I remember you? You said we had another meeting after. I don't remember anything."

"You won't."

"Why?"

"Because I made sure you wouldn't." He gripped her thighs.

Even with her whole world turning upside down, he saw the reaction of her body. Her nipples pressing against her shirt. The dilation of her eyes. Running his hands up and down her thighs, he felt her tense up.

"Stop it," she said.

He stopped moving his hands, but he didn't let her go.

He refused to let her go.

"You know you want me."

"I don't even know the real you." She bit her lip.

Her hands covered his, turning them over so that she placed her palms against his.

Seconds passed, and she finally growled, thrusting his hands away and standing up. "No. I'm not going to do this. I want to go home."

She got to her feet, and he watched her storm away.

He let her get to the door before he was behind her, his hands on her hips, trapping her.

"You can't leave."

"West, you don't control me. Is that even your real name?"

"Yes."

Her hand lay flat against the door.

Stroking his hands up the sides of her body, he grazed against her tits. He heard her muffled moan.

"I know right now you're hating me, and that's fine. I don't mind. You can hate me. I accept it, but I'm not going to let you leave."

"You call this love? West, stalking someone, changing their lives, putting people there, that's not love. It's far from love."

He closed his eyes, hating the words spilling out of her mouth. This *was* love. She had no idea how he felt about her.

"I never wanted this to happen."

"You never wanted me to find out."

He gritted his teeth. "Hannah, I'm not like normal men. I never have been. Everything I've ever wanted in life, I've had to take."

"You shouldn't have to take love, West. It's given to you or earned. It's not something you're supposed to manipulate into getting."

He heard her sniffle. "Please don't cry."

"I'm so confused."

Slowly, sliding his hand around her body, he cupped her breast. "Your body isn't confused." The puckered bud of her nipple pressed against his palm, and she released a little moan. "No, you're not confused. Your body wants me."

"My body isn't the one in charge."

"It wants to be, Hannah. Your body knows what it wants." With one hand on her tit, he slid the other between her thighs. The jeans she wore kept him from touching her naked pussy, but rubbing her through the fabric, he felt the heat. Reaching up, he unsnapped the button.

She didn't fight him.

Her hands clenched on the door, and he kissed her neck.

"You can stop me anytime."

She whimpered, and he slid a hand inside, going into her panties and finding the warmth of her pussy. She was so wet, so hot, so fucking tempting.

"Right now, you may hate me. You may hate what I've done. I'm not going to lie to you, I've done some unspeakable things. I've killed people. I've done what I needed to do to survive. I'm a fucking king in this city. I can have what I want, when I want. The only woman I need, the one I crave, is you. You think I've not thought about letting you go. That I've not been tempted to let you run. You should run far from me, but here's the thing—it'll last a day at best before I need to see your smiling face. I can never let you go." He sucked on her neck as he teased her clit. Sliding down, he filled her wet pussy. "Tell me to stop, Hannah. If you don't want my touch, if you don't crave it, tell me to stop. I will."

She whimpered, and as he plunged a finger deep inside her cunt, he felt her tighten around him.

She couldn't ask him to stop because it was

simple. She didn't *want* him to fucking stop, and neither did he. He wanted to take her, to fuck her, to consume her, to give her everything her heart desired. All he wanted in return was her love.

Tugging down her jeans, he kicked her legs open.

Placing her hands on the wall in front of her, he ran his hands down her hips, over the curve of her ass. Spreading the cheeks wide, he stared down at her asshole. He'd been preparing that for his dick. He wasn't having her there now, though. He needed to be inside her, had to feel her dripping pussy clutch him, especially after what she'd discovered.

He just had to have her any way that he could get her.

To drown in every single part of her.

Letting go of her hips, he released his belt, sliding down his zipper and pulling out his already rock-hard dick. He needed to be inside her.

To take her.

Running his fingers up and down his length, he gripped her ass, spreading her cheeks, and placed his dick against her slick entrance.

Sliding inside, he heard her moan.

Her pussy squeezed him, trying to milk him dry. When he was more than halfway in, he grabbed her hips once again and slammed to the hilt deep within her, feeling every single pulse as she wrapped around his dick. Closing his eyes, he saw stars as the pleasure rushed through his body.

Pulling out, he saw his length covered in her cream and pounded back inside her. Holding her tightly, he didn't let up or stop as he took what he wanted.

"Please," she said.

"What do you want, baby?"

"I need you to touch me."

"You want my hands on your pussy. Stroking your clit."

"Yes!" She let out a scream as he wrapped one hand around her hair, pulling her back so that she could see her face.

"Do you love me?" he asked.

She shook her head.

"You're a fucking liar."

Sliding one hand between her thighs, he found her clit. His cock was still deep within her. He used his grip on her hair to use as leverage to keep on pounding away inside her pussy. If he thought for a second that he was hurting her and that she wasn't totally loving every tug and thrust, he'd have stopped.

Her pussy kept getting wetter the more he used her.

He touched her clit and she screamed, the sounds echoing around the room and urging him to continue.

"You can lie to me all you want. You and I know the truth. I know that you want me, that you love me. It's why you're so angry. If you didn't care, you wouldn't be hurt." He sucked on her neck as he pinched her clit before soothing the bite with his fingers. "I made sure I saved you for myself. All of your dates, I stopped."

"What?"

"They were pricks because I let them know they were not getting inside your pussy. You belong to me. Always have. No one was having you but me. I stopped you getting your heart broken. None of them deserved you. Only me. You're mine."

He felt her orgasm, and it went straight to his balls, setting off his own orgasm. He thrust to the hilt within her, shooting load after load of his cum deep within her.

West hoped it took.

He hoped she was so fucking full of his cum that there was no way she couldn't be pregnant.

After the orgasm started to ebb away, he pulled out of her and lifted her up in his arms. She didn't fight him as he carried her through to his bathroom.

Hannah didn't say a word.

Turning on the shower, he stripped out of his clothes and then helped her out of hers. With them both naked, he tugged her into the stall, moving her so that she was near the hot water.

Tilting her head back so the water cascaded off her shoulders, he stared into her eyes.

"I don't know what to do anymore," she said.

"What do you want to do?"

"I want you to leave me alone and hug me all at the same time. You never gave me a chance to fall in love with you. You just manipulated everything so that I would, and now I don't know what to do."

"Those books that you love so much. Why is this any different?"

"They're fiction. This is not. You … took away my choice."

"How did I do that? I've not once taken your feelings away. Everything you feel for me is real. I've not lied to you about who I am."

"You own the streets. You've killed people. You admitted it."

"I'm also a businessman. You just never saw that other side of me. You've never had to."

"Emily knows that side of you."

"Emily was a whore and an addict who I helped to save. You can try and hate me all you want, but I could have left her in the street to rot."

"None of it's real. You don't seem to grasp that it's all lies. How can I know for sure if Emily wants to be my friend if I'm always wondering if you've given her instruction?"

"It wouldn't be like that."

"Then what would it be like?" she asked. "Did you not ask Emily to call me up to stop me going grocery shopping? How about all the times I've wanted to go out on a date and she's convinced me not to go out? Or how about how she always said nothing but nice things about you?"

"I'm a nice guy."

"You've just said that you're not a good guy. That you've killed people."

"I've done what I've needed to do to survive."

"People don't need to kill others to do that. That's not survival, West."

"You've never walked in my shoes. Don't even pretend to know what I've been through. I've done everything I can to be out on top. Where I come from, if you're not on top, you're under someone's boot. They're the ones with the power and get to choose who lives and who dies. You think I don't know what it's like looking in, seeing the world I'm part of? You think there are not moments I fucking hate what I have to be? I loathe it, but I do it because if I don't, someone else will, and I can't live that way. I can't live knowing there's someone like you out there and there could be a depraved fucking asshole who'll do everything to destroy who you are."

He stopped, and silence rang out between them.

"I know you can't stand what I am right now, but know this, for all the bad I've done, you're the part of me that makes everything good. You make me good."

He didn't have anything more to say. After the night he'd been through, there was nothing more for him to give.

****

The following day, Hannah stared at her empty apartment. The night before was still raw inside her head. West hadn't allowed her to sleep in the spare bedroom, and the truth was she didn't want to sleep away from him.

Waking up without him there had stung.

Their first argument.

Wrapping her arms around her waist, she assessed the place that she'd called home.

Was it a real home?

Did this make her life complete?

Knowing that the past few years had been a lie, she didn't know what to do.

Her parents were gone.

Besides Emily, there was no one.

She'd been surprised West allowed her to come here.

Of course, Rome was stationed outside, and West had told her that Rome would stay for as long as she remained out of his company. Running fingers through her hair, she felt empty.

Alone.

Lost.

Pictures were on the wall, and when she thought she saw two best friends, laughing, joking, having fun. She wondered if there was any truth in it.

How much of her life was real?

Not only did she have to deal with the truth of how her life had been mapped out without her consent but now the real West.

He wasn't just some businessman.

"I know you think you hate me. I never wanted you to find out like this. If you have any questions, please don't hesitate."

Those had been his parting words.

Well, not his only parting words.

"Hannah, I get that you're in shock. I'm giving you some concessions with regards to that, but be under no illusion, you belong to me. You're mine, and I won't wait forever."

She hated that she liked his possession.

The sound of the apartment door opening had her turning. Emily was finally home, and every single part of her wanted to do nothing more than hug her friend.

She's not your friend.

Emily let out a sigh. "West told me everything."

"Do you love him?" Hannah asked.

A sharp spike of jealousy rushed through her, shocking her with the ferocity as it hit her. She didn't like the thought of Emily and West being anything.

"No. I don't love him. Did I want to fuck him? That's a question you can ask me."

"I don't know you."

"Yes, I wanted to fuck him, if you'd like to know."

"I didn't ask," she said.

She stared at Emily and shook her head. "You don't have to be here."

"I do, actually. This is my apartment, and for what it's worth, you are my friend."

"We're not friends."

"You're hurt."

Hannah burst out laughing. "Nah, you can't tell?"

"You're not a little impressed, turned on, and swooning about how much this guy has done for you?" Emily asked.

"Has done for me? Are you kidding right now? I have nothing that I can call my own. You're not my friend. You're a damn plant that he put in place."

"So you didn't have a horrible time. News flash,

Hannah, you're not the easiest person to get to know. He wanted you to have a normal life. To enjoy being young. To have a college education."

"What did you get out of it?" Hannah asked.

"I got a decent wage, a college education, a clean slate on everything, and I no longer had to suck gross, infected dick to make a living."

Hannah wrinkled her nose.

"Believe it or not, Hannah, you were hard work, and at first, I *didn't* want to be your friend. I didn't get you. You were weird and had no personality. All you wanted to do was study and be boring. Then I waited it out for the money, and little by little, I grew to like you. When we left college and moved here, I was a little scared," she said.

"Why?"

"Because I knew his plan. I knew there was going to be a time when you were going to fall in love."

"You don't know that. You don't know anything."

"I know that West Gallo would move the damn earth if it would please you. He'll do whatever it takes to make sure you're happy, and yet it doesn't help you, does it? You don't see how devoted he is to you."

"He kills people."

"Oh, grow up, Hannah. This world is not all black and white. It's grey. People have to do shit they don't like. It's the way of the world. West, he's not a good guy. You're right. He's killed people. He's done unspeakable things to a lot of bad people. Never innocent people. Only to those that would betray him. Who would cross him. Can you even blame him for that?"

Hannah glared at her friend. "That doesn't make it right."

"He helped me, Hannah. He helped me when

most men would smash my face into the ground, grab my ass, and fuck me in both holes. You think what West has done to you is bad. Try being a fifteen-year-old girl, screaming for help, knowing her dad won't come because he's the one that sold you to the men that wanted to get their kicks off fucking a minor."

She stared at Emily, shocked.

Taken aback.

Horrified.

What the hell had just happened?

Emily nodded. "That was my life. My dad needed money, and to him, women were nothing. In fact, we have handy little holes that every man wants a piece of. That's what I was taught. When you were being loved and kept warm and safe by your parents, my dad was passing me around. Teaching me how to suck cock, to deep-throat a man until he came and I had no choice but to swallow. The word 'no' wasn't allowed in my dictionary, sweetheart. The stuff I had to do before I turned eighteen, I don't even want to think about. It got harder when the men wanted to gang up. To do a train on me. It's why I got addicted. There was nothing better than the high in my blood to numb the pain of the dick riding between my legs."

Tears filled Hannah's eyes.

This was real.

This was who Emily was.

She wasn't horrified at her friend.

She wanted her father to hurt, to have pain unlike anything this woman had ever felt.

"So, you see, that's why I can't hate West. Yeah, I love him a little bit. I'm actually so glad that I was the one near the dump that day. That I wasn't dead. He took me in when most men would just use me." Tears were in Emily's eyes. "I had to be your friend. To stay clean.

And he'd make my other life disappear. I got a family. It's not real, but when I go home with you, it felt real. I wasn't your friend to start off with. I didn't know if I even liked you. In time I realized you were an amazing friend. When we moved here, I wondered what he saw in you. Why he wouldn't give me a chance, but now I know. Five years ago, he fell for you, Hannah. These are my words. From now on, all you will get is my words. No one else's. He doesn't control me." Emily held her hands out, giving a turn. "This is me. I'm an ex-whore and addict. For the past week and a half, I've been in a rehab facility. Lawrence, the guy they dealt with, he cornered me in one of my favorite spots and asked me questions about you. When I didn't give him what he wanted, he gave me a shot. Nice guy, huh?"

"I'm so sorry," Hannah said.

"I thought you'd lost your voice there." Emily sighed. "I'm clean. There's no drugs here. It was nice to have a break though. You know, to get away but to also realize the drugs don't control me. I didn't want them in the first place. The moment it happened I went to West, and he helped me."

"I'm so sorry."

"You keep saying that."

"If it wasn't for me, Lawrence wouldn't have gotten to you."

"Technically, if it wasn't for West he wouldn't have known you existed. He thought Lawrence would help you and guide you in the field of finance so you'd get to live your dream. He had no idea that you'd end up in that kind of situation."

"Hearing what you went through, I can't complain."

"Don't do that. Don't think of your situation as being the same as mine or less than mine. When a guy doesn't take no for an answer, then he's the one that should suffer. Not us. It's not our fault."

Hannah smiled as she wiped the tears off her cheek. "You ever thought about preaching about women's rights?"

Emily burst out laughing. "Yeah, I thought about it but decided it's too much hard work."

There was still a pretty big gap between them. Hannah stared at her friend.

"Would you like me to leave?"

Hannah shook her head. "No, I don't want you to leave."

"Good. I'm going to come over and hug you, okay."

Hannah didn't stand still waiting for her friend. She walked across the living room, and threw her arms around Emily, holding her close.

"I can't believe all of that happened to you. I'm so sorry I didn't know."

"It's not your fault. Stop saying you're sorry. You've got nothing to be sorry about it. It wasn't you."

"Your dad? Where is he?"

"You don't want to know."

"If you say he's enjoying retirement I'm going to get angry. He should be in prison and rotting in some hell somewhere."

Emily laughed. "I don't think you should be worrying about your and West's compatibility. I'd say you're both pretty much suited."

Hannah pulled away a little, her arms still around her friend.

"What do you mean?"

"When he found out the truth of what my life had been like, he went about resolving it. He located my dad and made him pay, Hannah."

"He killed him?"

"Yes."

She couldn't believe she was about to say this. "Good."

"Good?"

"Yeah. He had no right to, erm, to hurt you. To put you through that."

"You're happy that he's dead. That he was killed?"

"Not if you're not."

"I got to see it happen," Emily said.

"You did."

"Yep. I was in the room." She smiled. "West was there, along with Rome and Cage. They all know the truth of who I am and what I've done."

"I wish you'd told me the truth. I can't believe you went through all of that and I never knew." She stroked a hand down Emily's long hair. "I'm so sorry."

"If you do want me to leave, I can."

"No. I told you no. Listen to me. I don't want you to leave. I don't want you to ever leave. You're my best friend. You're my only friend. So it was organized by a complete control freak, but whatever. I want you in my life."

"How about I order Chinese food and we have a girly night? Would you like that?"

"I'd love that."

While Emily ordered the food, Hannah took a quick shower and made her way into the main apartment.

Rome was there, carrying a huge box of food.

"This arrived."

"You're still here?"

"West wants to make sure you're both safe."

"Oh."

"He's a good guy, Hannah. You'd understand that

if you got to know him a little." She was in her skimpy pajamas, but with Rome she didn't feel exposed. He didn't look at her like he wanted her.

"I don't know what he wants from me."

"You know what he needs. He loves you."

"In the car yesterday, you said it was nice to finally meet me."

"Yes."

"You'd been following me for some time?"

"'Following' sounds like the wrong word to describe it. I was making sure you were safe and protecting you. That will never stop."

"It was nice to finally meet you as well. I have these moments, these flashes where you or Cage or West will do something that I think I've seen before. Is that crazy?"

"No, but if you want to know why you recognize it, ask West about the second time he met you. He'll tell you if he's sure you're ready."

"The time I don't remember?"

"Yes."

"I'll do that."

Emily came out of the bedroom. She had a towel in her hands, drying her hair. "Hey, Rome. It's really cool now that she knows the truth. I don't have to keep pretending everything."

"It certainly is."

"You want to stay for dinner?" Emily asked. "We're going to pig out. Watch a couple of chick flicks and a few of those action movies she loves so much. You don't mind, do you?"

"Not at all," Rome said. "I have to protect the two of you."

"What better way of protecting than being in the same room as us? Your big gun will work here just as it would in the hallway."

"You're bad for a man's concentration," Rome said, lowering himself into the only available chair.

She and Emily took the sofa.

"You won't get into trouble, will you?" Hannah asked, nibbling her lip.

"Only if something bad was to happen to you."

"Is he still going to punish you over Lawrence lurking and you not knowing?" Emily asked.

Hannah looked from her friend to Rome.

"I don't know."

She saw his jaw flex.

"No. He can't do that. It's impossible for you to have known."

"I let my guard down shopping with you."

"Please, Lawrence was a wormy piece of shit. He thought he had the cartels in his pocket. Of course West knows how to deal with pieces of shit like Lawrence. He already had a plan in place, am I right?" Emily asked.

"Yes. It just so happens West did. When it comes to your safety, West doesn't like to take any chances."

"This is all crazy. I mean, you're talking about a guy—"

"That will do anything to protect you. That loves you more than anything else in the world." This came from Emily.

"Who will turn his life upside down and left to right if it so pleases you." This from Rome.

Hannah looked at both of them, not knowing what to say or do.

"You have to admit he's dreamy," Emily said. "I mean, he's that much in love with you, he will do whatever it takes just to see a smile on your lips. That's the stuff of romance movies and books."

"You don't think it's verging on stalkery?"

"Nope." Both Rome and Emily spoke in unison.

Hannah couldn't help but laugh. "And you're sure West isn't telling you what to say or do?"

"He's not." Again, they both spoke together.

She found it oddly sweet and comforting.

"You should give him a chance," Rome said. "I've never seen him be like this with anyone else. He loves you. There's no doubt about that. It's not a sweet, kind love that kids are used to. But it's there. He loves you, and he'll do whatever he has to for you. That's got to mean something."

Hannah didn't say anything.

The truth was … she was finding it a lot easier to like. There had been a man in her life that had kept his distance until he had to. He'd been there as some guardian to her without her even knowing it.

"Let's just watch the movie."

"She's totally falling for him," Emily said.

"Totally."

"I think he'd walk over broken glass for her."

"A lava pit if you ask me," Rome said.

She laughed at some of their suggestions, finding their banter comforting. They were her friends, and even if West had brought them into her world, she was pleased that he had.

Chapter Fourteen

Work had no appeal to West the following week. Hannah had stayed at her apartment over the weekend with Rome and Emily for company. He'd known about their little sleepover because he got to watch it.

The only reason he didn't storm over there, kick Rome's ass, and force Emily to her room was because he heard their conversation. He heard the truth from Emily. The reality of Hannah's feelings. He even saw the happiness in her eyes that he'd taken care of Emily's deadbeat dad.

He witnessed it all and was so fucking happy that he'd stayed away just to watch her. Rome stayed alert, and Emily snuggled up against her friend. They looked good together again.

He was glad. He may have brought them together, but their friendship was on the two of them. It wasn't about him at all. It was about each other and the love they had for the other.

Staring outside of his window overlooking the city, he ran fingers through his hair. Staying away all weekend had been sheer torture. The only way he'd gotten through was to watch her. To observe.

To know that she was happy.

What he'd done wasn't conventional. He was aware of this. He knew that he'd crossed a damn fine line, but that didn't matter. Not to him.

Hannah needed someone.

She needed him.

He heard her clear her throat, and he turned to see Hannah standing in his doorway. She wore her usual skirt and crisp white shirt. Her jacket was probably over the back of her chair where it would stay.

"Morning," she said.

"Morning."

She held an envelope in her hands, and he wasn't interested in looking at whatever it was she wanted to give him. That shit wasn't going to happen to him.

"I wanted to thank you," she said.

"Thank me?"

"Yeah. For helping Emily. For giving her a life. For being her hero."

"I'm not a hero."

"You are."

He snorted. "You know her father isn't breathing."

"I know." She glanced down at the envelope in her hands.

"You better not give that to me."

"I can't take this job."

"Hannah, I'm giving you time to get used to the idea of being mine. Don't for a second push me too far."

She rolled her eyes, and the letter still in her grip, dropped to her side. "Why are you making this so difficult?"

"Why don't you just accept that you love me?"

"You don't even know love."

She turned on her heel, about to storm to her desk.

Oh, no.

He wasn't having that.

Before she even got to her desk, he grabbed her around the waist and hauled her back to his office.

"Stop it. Help."

The rest of his employees stayed in their seats.

"Aren't you going to do something? He's taking me against my will."

Still, they did nothing.

"You may as well stop trying to get them to help

you. They already know who you belong to, and getting them on your side is not going to work."

"I fucking hate you. You asshole. I can't believe you're doing this to me. It's so unfair. Let me go!"

He slammed the door closed. They knew not to disturb him. Pressing her up against the wall, he captured her hands as she tried to push him away.

Keeping them above her head, he stared into her dark brown gaze. He'd never thought much of brown eyes until he met her. Now he'd gladly spend all of his days looking into hers.

"You can fight me all you want to, but you and I both know who you belong to. Who makes you wet. Who you think about in the darkest night when your books won't get you off."

"You need to stop watching me."

"I will never stop watching you. If you think for a second this is me backing off, giving you time, you're fucking mistaken. I'm not going to be your fucking whipping boy, Hannah. I'm not going to be the one you blame. So I took things a little extreme. I gave you a college education free of stress and needing to find a job. A friend that adores you. Emily is different. What do you expect after all you've been through? You don't like her, then I'll kill her."

"You can't do that."

"But I can. I can do whatever the hell I want. That's the kind of man I am. I'll take out anyone who hurts you. I will tear this world apart to be with you. There's no getting away from me. So, go to your desk and if you even try to leave, I will make it impossible."

"There's nothing you can do."

"I've got eyes on you."

"I know Rome and Cage."

"You don't know everyone I've got keeping an

eye. They all know what their job is. What I require of them. Everywhere you go, I will make the people know that you're unfit to work for them. Your reputation in this town will be ruined, and I'll make sure of it."

"How can you do that?"

"Simple, I will do that to keep you here where you fucking belong. Test me, Hannah, try me. I'm willing to wait so long but not forever. Now get out there and do some work." Before he let her go, he slammed his lips down on hers, taking the kiss he'd been wanting to from the moment she walked in. "And you're welcome."

He opened the door and watched as she walked to her seat with her cheeks the red of ripe strawberries. He shot a glare at the rest of his employees. They better keep their damn mouths shut if they knew what was good for them.

With that, he took a seat behind his desk.

He wouldn't ruin her.

Not even a little.

Her reputation would always remain intact, but he wouldn't allow her to think she could walk away from him without any consequences.

He had no doubt she was confused about her feelings for him, but that didn't mean he wasn't going to make it perfectly clear to her.

She belonged to him.

If he had to repeat it to her over a thousand times, he would.

She'd been his five years ago, and now that he had a taste of her, he wasn't letting her go, not ever.

****

One week later

Hannah's feet hurt. Rome had dropped her off, and she knew he hadn't left the building. Like every other day the past week, he'd wait until she was safely indoors and then take a seat outside. West's orders.

Someone had to be with her at all times, and it was driving her crazy.

She didn't have any time to think.

If it wasn't West, then it was someone else, Rome, Cage, Emily. They were always there, asking her how she felt and what she wanted to do.

None of them seemed to understand that she just wanted to have a few moments of complete privacy to do her own thing. To be allowed to think about all the changes going on in her life.

Entering her apartment, she closed the door and flicked the lock into place.

She walked down the short corridor, rounded the kitchen and there was Emily. She reached into the cupboard on the highest shelf.

It wasn't her friend that got her attention though. Nope.

It was the large display of flowers in a vase on the table.

"Are those for you?"

"Oh, hey, Anna, I didn't hear you come in."

"The flowers? You got a secret admirer?"

"I wish. They're all for you, girlfriend."

Hannah sighed, walking up to the large bouquet and looking at the card.

You can't hate me forever. With all my love, West.

"You accepted them?"

"Of course. They're beautiful and expensive, and they'll look great at the table that we never eat at anyway."

"I wish he'd stop this."

"He's never going to stop, Anna."

She turned on her feet and walked back into the

sitting room, slumping down into her position on the sofa.

Seconds later Emily joined her, handing her a steaming cup of coffee.

"What's the problem?"

"We've been through this already. It's not like he's not going to hear," she said. She pointed around the room to all the hidden cameras.

"There's not one in my room or the bathroom."

"There's not?"

"Nope. We can talk in private if we really want to."

Getting to her feet, she walked into the bathroom as she believed that was the safest option.

"You don't want my bed?" Emily asked.

"I wouldn't put it past him to install something after this."

Emily chuckled, but they sat on either side of the small bathroom. Emily's back leaned against the bathtub while she leaned against the cupboard near the sink.

"So, let's have it all out. Why do you have a problem with the flowers?"

"Don't you think it's creepy that he keeps sending me things?"

"He loves you. I don't think that's creepy at all."

"What about the way we first started? You don't find that at least a little strange?"

"So the guy has some controlling issues. I'm not going to judge him, Anna, you know this. You and him, it's going to be."

"I don't get a choice?"

"You get one hell of a choice. We've been through this. I get that you're upset about how it all ended up, but you love him regardless."

"How can I love someone who lies to me?"

"To protect you. We live with our parents all the time and they lie to us."

"No, they don't."

"Okay, normal people's parents lie to them. Let me think." Emily stared up at the ceiling. "They lie about Santa Claus. About if you're a good singer and you're not. The talent you may not have but really want. How awesome your picture is when we all know it really wasn't."

"That doesn't count."

"It does too. So, come on then, tell me what really bugs you about this whole 'West lied to me' thing?"

"The scholarship."

"Why exactly?"

"I thought I earned it."

"So it's an ethical issue."

"I worked my ass off for those grades."

"No one is disputing that. Does it matter if it came from him or some loser guy down the street? You got the scholarship and the grades. That was all you. Move on."

She saw that no matter what she said, Emily was going to have a reason for why he did those things but also the positive outcome for herself. She didn't need her friend to point out the obvious to her, as she was doing it herself repeatedly and it was driving her crazy. She couldn't exactly pinpoint where it was in her life that she'd started to be ungrateful.

West had done all these things for her when no one had, and it upset her.

He'd been the only one she could rely on.

"He's killed people. He's not who he said he was, and that scares me. It scares me that I feel for someone that one day could lose their temper and I end up dead," she said.

"Oh, sweetie," Emily said.

"It scares me. Seeing him every single day so far, I want to run into his arms where I know I'll be safe, but at the same time I'm afraid. What if it's not safe? What if he gets fed up with me and I end up at the bottom of some pit? I don't want to die. I have fallen in love with him, and I don't know what to do. Everyone is telling me all the time what to do. That I should love him and trust him."

"He won't kill you."

"You don't know that. Twenty years from now, ten, maybe, I don't know." She shrugged and sipped at her hot coffee.

"At least you've now admitted that you love him."

"What do you think I should do now?" Hannah asked.

"Whatever you need to do. There's no getting away from this. The question really is, Hannah, do you really want to?"

Pressing her lips together, she refused to think of the answer that sprang to mind.

"You know what we should do?"

"Not talk about this?"

"Besides that, I think we should totally go out and party."

"It's a Monday night."

"I don't care." Hannah laughed. "You're always telling me I should live a little. Why wait until Friday or Saturday? Let's party right now."

"I only have one question for you?"

"What?"

"Sin or Dirty?"

"Dirty it is."

The club where she'd met West. She didn't know

why she was doing this, just that she had to get out.

To go and have fun.

To not think about the monster lurking behind the camera.

Emily got to her feet, pulling her up.

"Then get into your sexiest outfit ever."

"Wait, wait, wait," Hannah said. "What are we going to do about Rome?" There was no way he'd let them leave.

"He's been told to protect you, Hannah. Not keep you locked up where you can't have fun. You can do whatever the hell you want, so long as you know what it is you do want, and also tell him this was totally your suggestion and we'll be fine."

Thirty minutes later, heading downstairs with Rome in front made her even more nervous.

She wore a small cocktail dress that showed off more of her cleavage and legs than she'd ever worn before. The dress molded to every single curve like a second skin, and she felt sexy in it even. Her long brown hair was curled, and she'd let it down completely.

Rome had tried to think of a million different arguments and arrangements that meant she stayed indoors.

There was no way she was playing the nice girl. Not even close. Not anymore.

Hannah sat in the back of his car, and Emily rode up front.

Staring out of the window, she felt her heart beating so fast as they neared Dirty.

Would he be there?

Would he even care that she'd decided to party on a Monday night?

Biting her lip, she couldn't help but smile at the thought of him being crazy, wanting to take her into his office and punish her for being naughty.

Not that she was being naughty.

She was a grown woman who could do whatever the hell she wanted to do.

She didn't need a man ruling her life or telling her what she could or couldn't do.

"How are you holding up?" Emily asked, turning in her seat.

"I'm doing good."

"Do you know if West is at Dirty?"

"No," Rome said.

"Aw, what's wrong, handsome?"

"Don't even start with me, Emily. You know he won't like it."

"Won't like what? Her having a good time, or should I say attempting to have a good time? You're totally ruining our buzz, you know. Totally."

Hannah laughed. "Yeah, Rome, we just want to have a good time."

"I hope you ladies know what you're doing."

"We totally do."

Hannah wished for just a moment she could have Emily's confidence. She didn't have a clue what she was doing, only that she wanted to do something reckless.

Maybe to even see how he'd react if she wasn't doing what she was told.

She sat back, listening to Emily and Rome banter.

By the time he pulled up to the nightclub, her nerves were on edge and she felt a little sick.

Emily was out and pulling her along. They didn't even have to wait in line. The guy on the front let them go, much to the annoyance of the people already waiting.

"See, some perks to being the girl West Gallo wants. Come on." Emily marched on ahead and she just followed behind her.

They grabbed a drink, and she downed her cocktail in one gulp in the hope of it doing the trick and not making her nervous.

Within seconds she felt lighter, happier, looser.

When Emily next dragged her onto the dance floor, she went willingly.

All thought of West's bad temper disappeared from her mind as she focused on having fun. Of not thinking about what could be or if he had a temper.

Dancing with Emily helped a lot. She threw her head back, hands in the air, and just let the song take her to the next level. Sweat clung to her skin, and by the third song, she needed another drink.

Making her way to the bar, she saw Rome sitting all by himself.

The nightclub was crazy busy considering it was a Monday night.

"Hey there," she said.

His gaze was on the dance floor where Emily stood. Glancing back at her friend, and then at Rome, she wondered if she was detecting a little hint of jealousy.

Two men were dancing with Emily right now.

Her friend wasn't flirting, but she was having a good time.

"You okay?" she asked.

"Yeah, I'm fine."

"You should totally ask her out."

"Excuse me?"

"Emily. The way you're looking at her right now. It's like you're wanting to eat her."

"I will never date a woman like Emily."

"How come?"

"We work together."

"Ouch, that stung. That wasn't very nice." She stuck out her lip to pout. "If that's the case, seeing as you're both here to make me happy, you should totally ask her out."

Rome and Emily would be a pretty serious couple.

"Not going to happen."

"Oh, please. This doesn't have anything to do with her past, does it?"

"No, of course not. We all have a past."

"Do you?"

"I work for West Gallo. Anyone that doesn't have a past doesn't work for him. Why do you think you were so enthralling to him?"

She stared at him, not liking the way this conversation was going.

"I don't know."

"You were everything innocent in his world. A virgin. Untouched by the cruelty of the world. Your parents kept you safe, and you can even see it now when I look at you. You don't see that we're working together to make you happy. You're just seeing a lonely guy and a friend that would totally be amazing together."

"What's wrong with seeing it like that?"

"Because you don't understand that for us, it's not that simple. We don't get to just wake up and the past be forgotten. It's not easy like that for us. Besides, Emily is damaged goods."

"No, I guess it's not." She looked over toward Emily.

Did Emily even like Rome?

She didn't know, and here she was encouraging him to go and dance with her.

"Excuse me." No longer in need of a drink, she made her way back onto the dance floor.

Before she made it to Emily though, someone banded an arm around her waist, holding her close.

"Hello, baby," West said.

She should have known it was him. The sheer power of his arm around her waist and the feel of his rock-hard body against her back had her melting just a little bit. Not too much. Who was she kidding? Her body was on fire for him.

Just that one touch made her go putty in his hands.

"So, you decided to come out and party."

"We wanted to dance. Nothing wrong with dancing."

"You've got work tomorrow."

"And I'll be there."

He spun her around, his hands on her back, near her ass.

Staring into his blue eyes, she felt herself want in ways she never had before. Would it be so bad to give herself to this monster?

"You look stunning tonight."

"Thank you." She hadn't dressed to please him. That was wrong. While finding the perfect dress, she'd tried to think of what would drive him crazy. Suddenly, he turned her so that her ass was pressed against his dick.

"You feel what you do to me?"

She couldn't help but close her eyes for a second. His cock was rock-hard as it rubbed her ass.

"Please, West," she said.

"You can't beg me like that with your sweet voice and not expect me to want you. Are you wet for me right now? Do you want my cock deep inside that tight little pussy?"

She loved it when he talked dirty to her.

"Yes. I want you. I want everything."

His hands moved to her stomach, and she lifted her hands to wrap around the back of his neck.

His fingers skimmed beneath her breasts, slowly stroking the underside of the curve. She wanted his hands on her body.

Swaying her hips, she felt his cock, needing him inside her.

She'd only been in his arms a matter of seconds and already she was desperate for him.

"Do you want to come up to my office?"

"Yes."

He released her, taking hold of her hand, and she followed him, refusing to look back at Emily and Rome. She didn't want to see the smiles or the knowing looks.

The moment they were in his office, he pressed her against the door. Sinking her fingers into his hair, she gasped as he lifted her up. The dress she wore was no match for him. He lifted it up, and his hand cupped between her thighs. The panties were flimsy as well. He tore them off her with ease and dropped them to the floor. His fingers pushed inside her pussy, two going deep to the knuckle.

She cried out his name as his lips sucked on her nipple even through the fabric of the dress.

He pulled his hands back, grabbing her hips and marching her toward his desk. He turned her around so that her hands were flat on the desk. He lifted up her skirt, running his hands down over her ass. He'd already flipped the dress over so that it lay at the base of her back. She was open and exposed to him.

West spread her ass cheeks. His fingers slid inside her before going up to her clit, stroking her, teasing her, drawing every ounce of pleasure from her.

With his other hand, she heard him working his belt, sliding the zipper down.

"Tell me you want me."

"Please, West, I want you."

"No, Hannah, you fucking need me." His cock went to her entrance, and he slammed inside, not giving her a chance to get accustomed to his large length. He pulled out, only to push back inside, pounding deep and hard.

The hand on her hip grabbed her hair, wrapping it around his fist as he pulled her hair back. She had no choice but to hold onto the desk or fall as he started to fuck her hard. His other hand was still teasing her clit, and she felt completely taken over by him.

Surrounded.

Controlled.

Safe.

Shaking that last thought from her mind, she cried out his name as her orgasm started to build. There was no one else, nothing else.

Just him.

It was always about him.

She wanted nothing more than this man.

Against all odds, she knew she loved him.

He'd invaded her life, taken over everything, and yet she still loved him.

She wanted to hate herself, to stop these feelings, but with every pound of his cock, she knew without a shadow of a doubt she couldn't give this up. He made her hungry for more, desperate, aching, needy.

In his office, getting fucked from behind, knowing that he wasn't wearing a condom, that he was going to flood her pussy with his cum, she loved being used but also knowing that he loved her. That a part of him was so obsessed that he had to see her. That he had to know her. She liked it, and she didn't know if she could handle that part of herself.

Would she ever be able to handle a man so deeply obsessed with her that he'd put people around her like

Emily and Rome?

How could she not love when he touched her? Knowing no other woman would ever do for him. That he wanted her to the point of crazy.

She loved it so much that it scared her. She'd never known anything like this kind of feeling. West was breaking down her own barriers, smashing down the walls that she'd tried to build to protect herself.

"That's it, baby, come all over my cock. I've got you. Oh, fuck yeah, that feels good. So good. Yeah, push back. Take it all."

She cried out as he brought her to orgasm, his cock seeming to brand her as he rode her even harder. She didn't know where he ended and she began.

Her emotions were all over the place, and as she came down from the peak of release, she felt his cock jerk within her, flooding her with his cum.

There really was no getting out of this.

He'd never used a condom, and she wasn't stupid enough not to realize he hadn't either.

Chapter Fifteen

"Get your own coffee. The machine is right there." Hannah spun on her heel and clicked out of his office.

West sat back watching the curves of her ass as he walked away from him. Over the past four days, since he fucked her hard and fast, her patience with him every passing day had started to wear down.

On Tuesday she'd been polite, almost flirty with him. He'd thought it was cute. Wednesday, she'd snipped at him over a question about the mail. Thursday, she'd growled at him. It had been the cutest sound he'd heard from her. Today, she'd just ordered him to go and get his own coffee.

He didn't mind getting his own coffee, but he liked watching her tits as she walked into his office and when she left, her ass.

It was his own little treat, and he also got a coffee out of it. As far as he was concerned, win-win for him.

Hannah, however, wasn't happy.

He knew the problem.

Emily and Rome knew the problem.

Everyone who knew her knew the problem.

Only Hannah kept to herself. She didn't come to him to talk or even request what she needed. Each night she'd leave here and he'd get a report from either Cage or Rome about her progress.

She wasn't even talking to them either, nor did Emily have much in the way to report. Since the truth had come out, their friendship had grown. It was nice to see his woman so happy, but it had been two weeks now and he was growing tired of watching her on the damn cameras. In the past four days she'd tried to pleasure herself each night only to be disappointed and left aching.

He saw her erect nipples and could only imagine how wet her cunt was. Not to mention, he'd already done a count and she hadn't started her menstrual cycle yet either. He knew she was either pregnant or very late.

Stress could do that.

He had a pregnancy test in his desk drawer waiting just for her.

She wouldn't like it, but then he didn't buy it for her to like it.

This had to stop.

Hannah needed him, and she was being too damn stubborn to come to him.

Getting to his feet, he stood in his doorway. His other employees kept their heads down. They were paid well to do as they were told.

Arms folded, he watched Hannah. She hadn't looked up. She kept running her fingers through her hair. She looked agitated, frustrated, and just plain moody.

"Hannah," he said.

"What could it possibly be now?" she asked.

Those beautiful big browns narrowed into slits as she glared at him.

He tried to hide his smile.

"Get in my office. Now!"

She released a sigh, and she got to her feet. Her legs seemed heavy as she stomped toward him.

She wasn't impressed.

No one came to her rescue.

No one said anything.

They didn't need to.

Closing his office door, he didn't bother to lock it.

There was no need.

She stood before his desk, one foot tapping on the

floor and her arms folded.

"Well, what is it you want?"

"Go around my desk."

"Excuse me."

"Do as you're told," he said.

"Ugh!" She stormed around the desk. "I'm here, happy?"

"Bend over and lift your skirt over your ass, remove your panties, and spread your cheeks wide."

"What?"

"You heard me, Hannah. Don't make me give you another instruction. You won't like how I deal with it."

Her cheeks were on fire as he moved toward her, going around his desk on the opposite side. Opening up the drawer, he grabbed the fresh tube of lubrication that he'd purchased the other week.

Opening the cap, he checked to make sure there was nothing stopping the gel-like liquid from seeping out.

With Hannah's skirt around her waist and her hands holding her ass, he opened his belt, pulling out his already rock-hard cock.

"Spread them wider. You can do it."

She didn't argue with him this time.

Hannah opened her ass, and he took a seat, working some of the lube into his dick. Staring at her tight cunt and asshole, he knew he wanted inside both.

He'd take her pussy later.

She wasn't going home tonight.

No.

She was going home with him, and regardless of if she liked it or not, that was what was going to happen.

With his dick nice and slick, he ran his fingers between her thighs, watching her pussy open up around his fingers. She sucked him in, and he added two fingers, stretching her.

Using the tip of the lubricating bottle, he placed it near her anus, and coated the tight, puckered hole with a nice lot of gel.

When she was wet, he removed his fingers from her pussy to work the lubrication into her anus.

"Now, Hannah, I have let a lot of things slide with you after everything you've found out. I've given you time and space."

"I work for you. That's not exactly space, and I see you every single day."

"I am still your boss. Treating me with complete disrespect is not how I would advise you continue. Now, I know what your problem is, and don't you worry, I'm going to rectify that problem."

"Oh, yeah, and how do you think you know what is wrong with me? Do you now have a magic ball spying on me? Wanting to know my every waking thought and what I need."

He chuckled. She was just so cute when she was angry.

She'd be even more so before the end of the day, but he'd save that for when they were back at his home.

The danger to Hannah had lessened with Lawrence now out of the picture and the deal he'd struck with the cartels. His city was once again running smoothly, and he could function and think now.

"You need to be fucked, Hannah, and don't worry. I'm going to give you what you need." He ran his fingers across her ass, coating her anus in the lube. "I'm going to fuck this ass. I got you all nice and prepared for me, and now I'm going to take my reward."

"You're insane."

"You're not denying it. You don't want to want

me, do you?"

"You don't know what you're talking about."

"I know exactly what I'm talking about." He placed the tip of his cock to her slick anus, and he guided himself past the tight ring of muscles. She let out a gasp, but he didn't stop. He kept on pushing in until over half of his dick was deep within her. She let out a whimper, and he gripped her hips, pushing the last few inches deep into her ass.

She gripped him tightly, and he leaned over her, kissing her neck.

"I know what it's like to want, Hannah. To be so desperate you can't even think straight. To snap and want to kill anyone who steps in your way."

With his other hand, he slid his fingers between her thighs, stroking over her swollen clit. She let out a moan as he pinched the bud before soothing out the pain with his fingers.

"You hate me right now, and that's okay. You don't know me, but you will. Your body knows what it wants. It wants my cock, my mouth, my hands, and I'm not going to let it be punished because your head can't fucking think straight. You think I don't sit at home watching you touch yourself? Imagining my own hands giving you the pleasure that you fail to give yourself?"

"You're so wrong," she said.

He pulled out of her ass only to push back inside.

They both moaned, the sounds echoing off the walls.

He didn't give a shit who heard them.

She felt so good.

Another part of her body he now owned.

He fucking loved this woman.

Even as she spat and cursed, he couldn't help but love her.

She was his addiction, his everything, and he wouldn't let her go.

Not now.

Not ever.

Pushing back inside her, he took his time, taking her breath with each thrust as he owned her ass.

She thrust back against him, and he moved his hand from between her thighs, to spread her ass so he could watch.

Seeing his cock sliding in and out of her ass made him moan.

It was so perfect, so beautiful and sexy. He couldn't look away. With just the tip inside her, he watched as her ass opened up, sliding down his length before he pulled out.

Once again, he found her clit and began to tease her, bringing her closer and closer to orgasm. He held her just at the peak, not wanting to throw her over the edge. He had no idea how good being in her tight ass would be.

She was so perfect, every single part of her.

This was what he wanted.

Even with her hating him right now, she was like fire within his arms, and he didn't want to let her go. That was all he kept on thinking. Like a broken record.

Hannah was his.

He didn't want to let her go.

Mine.

Mine.

He'd never wanted anything with such desperation as he wanted Hannah.

"Please, West, please."

He'd give her the world, and he toppled her over the edge, relishing her screams of pleasure as they echoed around his office. Those sounds would stay with him forever. She came, and her ass tightened around him.

The pleasure was so intense from the pressure of her asshole that it set off his own orgasm. He held her hips, slamming all of his dick inside her as wave upon wave of his cum filled her tight, hot hole.

He was going to spend a lot of time fucking her ass. Collapsing over her, he kissed her neck, pushing her hair away from her face to suck on the pulse. They were both panting once again for breath.

"I don't hate you, West," she said. Her voice was so soft a whisper that at first, he wasn't sure he heard it. "I don't hate you, West." She spoke again.

Her words this time caught him off guard.

His cock was still balls-deep inside her ass. The buzz of his orgasm still very much there, but he knew this meant something. Her words were not because of the sex. This was something new for her.

"What do you feel then?"

She was silent for several seconds, and he heard her sniffle.

He didn't want her to cry or to feel upset.

If she hated him, he'd deal with it.

She wouldn't be the first woman that hated him. She'd be the first woman that he loved more than anything.

"I love you, West. I really do love you, and it scares me."

"Why does it scare you?"

"Because, it's not normal what you did. You shouldn't have to fill voids in my life. To make me believe what isn't. I don't know."

"Do you even care what I did?"

"Yes. No. I don't know. I don't like being lied to. You've got me all confused, and I feel so stupid. I don't even know how we met or what led to our meeting. I don't … what happened, West?"

"You want to know?"

"Yes."

"Okay, I'll tell you."

"The truth?"

"It's all I've got."

"I want to hear it."

"Let's get cleaned up." He pulled his cock from her ass and used some tissues from the dispenser to clean up his cum that leaked from her ass. Pulling her skirt down, and putting his cock back into place, he took her hand, pulling her down onto the sofa with him. Wrapping an arm around her waist, he locked their fingers together. He'd had no intention of ever telling her this, but he didn't see he had much of a choice.

She needed to know what happened that second time.

****

Five years ago

West wasn't happy. He really wasn't fucking happy. This piece of shit that he was gunning down had taken out ten of his girls, beating the shit out of them. It pissed him off. The brothels he kept were of a high standard, and so far, this man had been able to walk into three different ones over the past two weeks, flash his money around, spend some time with the girls, where he'd take one upstairs without anyone else seeing. From there, he'd beat them up, rape them, and leave them for dead.

Ten girls had died in the past two weeks because this fucker slit their throats before he left.

West was angry.

No, his rage was past that point.

He was going to hurt this man.

It was dark, and the library was about to close.

As the man ran toward the doors, he fired his gun,

and the man fell to the floor. Rome and Cage were not far behind him.

West always made sure to keep at the peak of health and fitness. The point of being king was to make sure no one could outrun or outfight him. He was the one that everyone feared.

The man went down, a growl erupting out of his lips as he grabbed his lap.

"Son of a bitch."

"My mother wasn't a bitch," West said, stepping up toward him.

The man wasn't done though as he got to his feet, limping. He fired his gun, causing West to collapse to the ground.

The piece of shit then charged to the doors just as a young woman was walking out.

Before West got a chance to fire off the weapon, the man running from him grabbed her and threw her against the wall.

Seconds later she collapsed to the floor.

West recognized her instantly.

It was the girl from the burger place.

Rome and Cage charged forward. They had the man knocked unconscious.

He was pissed off that he'd been distracted by the firing of the gun.

"Get him in the trunk. Tie him up, but I don't want him to come to until I've got him strung up."

"What do you want to do about her?" Cage asked.

"Just take care of him." He waited for Rome and Cage to be out of sight before he went to the young woman.

Her hair fell around her in waves, and he saw the bruise already forming on her head where she'd hit the wall.

Shit.

She needed to see a doctor.

Checking her pulse, he pulled out his cell phone and called the doctor.

She let out a moan as he finished the call.

"What happened?"

"It's okay. Go to sleep. It's okay." He pulled her into his arms just as Cage returned.

"You'll need this."

The needle had a tranquilizer, which would keep her knocked out for as long as they needed her.

He wasn't happy about using it but didn't see much of a choice.

Pressing the needle into her arm, he injected her.

Handing the needle back to Cage, who knew better than to throw it on the ground like trash, he picked the woman up in his arms and carried her to his car.

"Follow me to the warehouse," he said to Cage and Rome.

Without further instruction, he climbed behind the wheel and kept an eye on her as he drove across town.

He'd thought about the young woman at the burger place one too many times. He didn't understand why she'd gotten under his skin, only that she had, and it bugged him.

She was over eighteen now by a few months.

He wondered if anyone ever went to her party.

He doubted it.

What teenagers went to a burger party?

Shaking his head, he arrived at the warehouse in time to see his doctor.

Parking the car, he picked the girl up and carried her through the warehouse.

There was a small office in the back with a bed,

and he laid her out gently.

"She's out of it."

"To make sure she was safe, I put her out." He stood back.

"That's a nasty bump to the head. If she's got a concussion, tranquilizing her was the wrong thing to do."

"Just do your thing. Stop her from dying." He didn't even know why he felt this way about her.

Her breathing was really important to him.

He didn't get it.

Rubbing the back of his head, he left the office and made his way toward Cage and Rome, who were stringing up the man that was going to pay for all of his sins.

He'd thought about the girl often, and when Rome brought over her bag, he had no problem going through it.

Checking her purse, he saw her name was Hannah Ray. *Pretty name.* She had so many books, notebooks, and there was even a college acceptance letter along with a scholarship agreement inside. This woman clearly carried around her life in one backpack, and she was only eighteen years old.

The doctor was with her for over an hour, and after getting bored watching the fucker fall asleep and just drip blood down the drain, West decided to watch Hannah instead.

She was still out cold.

Her face was soft, and the doctor tutted.

"I'm going to need to come back when she's alert. Someone will have to sit with her. She's got no external injuries other than the bruised head, and I don't see any lump forming."

"Why do you need to come back?"

"To ask her questions. To make sure there's no

brain damage. Hitting your head can cause a lot of problems."

"I'll call you as soon as she's awake."

The doctor nodded and, without another word, left.

Sitting on the chair in the corner of the office, West watched her.

Her chest rose and fell with each of her indrawn breaths.

Her long, brown hair fanned out across the pillow, and she looked so peaceful.

So beautiful.

He'd remembered her these past few months.

When he was alone and sleep refused to claim him, he'd find his thoughts drifting off to this woman. Wondering if she was okay. If anyone went to her damn party. Who was taking care of her?

No woman had ever made him think about anything the way Hannah had.

The name suited her.

He didn't know how long he sat there, only that Rome and Cage came to ask him if he was going to deal with the problem outside.

Leaving the problem to them, he stared at Hannah, waiting, watching. Making sure she was okay. His cell phone was in his grip, the doctor on speed dial if he needed anything.

Time passed.

When she moved and let out a moan, he got up out of his chair, and moved toward her.

She lifted her hands up, and one went to her head. "Ouch."

"It's okay. You're okay."

Hannah opened her eyes, and he smiled down at her.

"I know you," she said, tilting her head to the side.

"Yeah, you do. You know me."

"Where am I?"

"You're safe. That's all that matters."

"I'm so confused. My head hurts."

"It's okay. I'll grab a doctor."

"You're going to have to tell my parents that I'm with you. I was … somewhere, and they are going to worry. They always worry."

"You've got nothing to worry about. I'll take care of everything."

He ran his fingers down her hair, calling the doctor. "She's awake." He hung up and watched.

"We're done," Rome said, drawing his attention to the door.

"You made him suffer?"

"Yes. You want to come and see?"

"Nah, I'll take your word for it. Let the doctor in when he comes."

"Do you need that drug that Reese has been working on? The one that will make her relax? Similar effects to the date rape drug but she's aware and you can talk to her. It makes her think she's in a dream."

The thought of drugging her didn't sit well with him.

"Yes." The word slipped out from his lips before he could stop it.

Over the next three hours, the doctor came and analyzed her.

She had a mild concussion and would need to be monitored over the next twenty-four hours.

So, he did just that. Following the doctor's orders, waking her up, taking care of her. Being sure that everything was okay for her and she wasn't hurting.

Rome and Cage would take turns staying with him.

After the twenty-four hours, he did something stupid. He injected her with the specially designed drug that he'd used to find out information about top businessmen. Knowledge meant power in his world, and that knowledge along with proof always came in handy.

When he pulled Hannah into his arms, she rested her head against his chest.

"This is nice. I like being hugged. I don't get hugged that much anymore. I got to go away to college soon. I'm going to miss my parents so much."

"You love your parents?"

"Yes. Of course. They mean the world to me."

"Did it upset you how they celebrated your eighteenth birthday party?"

"No, that was fun. I don't care about the people at school. They don't care about me." She sighed. "I feel funny."

"You'll be fine. I promise. You mentioned college. What are you studying?"

"Finance and business. I want to help people. No one was there to help my parents when they were advised about a wrong investment. No one cared, and I want to open a company that will help people like them and small businesses to make more money, not to lose every single cent they own and put their house at risk. If something happens to my parents." She stopped and sniffled. "They lose the house."

"Oh, honey."

"So many memories are there. People think because they were older that it wasn't fun to be with them, but they were all wrong. My parents are amazing. I love them so much. One day I hope I can find someone who'll make me feel special. When Dad looks at Mom, he looks at her and he loves her. That kind of love doesn't come around often, but they have it. They love each other so much, and I want to love someone so much."

"You want a family?"

"Yes, so many kids, so no one craves a sister or a brother. I feel weird right now. I shouldn't be talking about this with you. You smell so nice."

****

Present day

"So, for the next two days while your head recovered, I took care of you. I asked you questions and you gave me all the answers I needed. Your parents believed that you were away studying. They knew you took it seriously, and that's what I made them believe."

"I don't remember," she said. "They asked how my studies went, and I told them it went good."

"That's what the drug was designed to do." He ran his hand up and down her thigh.

"And we just talked?"

"I would never do anything to you, Hannah. You know that. All we did was talk, and I realized what an amazing, beautiful woman you were and your fate was sealed that day."

"It was?"

"Yeah. You see, I kept remembering you as the girl in the burger place. The one that didn't have any friends around her but you didn't let that worry you. You were your own person, and you had this amazing smile that seemed to light up your entire face and I wondered about you."

"So, it was after we talked and you took care of me that you decided I was yours?"

He cupped her cheek, tilting her head back. "There was no doubt in my mind that you needed someone to take care of you. Someone who was going to love you for you, and that person is me. It will always be me."

Tears glistened in her eyes, and he pressed his lips to hers.

"Also, you have to take this."

"Take what?"

West got to his feet and took her hand. Opening the drawer, he let her look.

He saw her tense.

"You may not like the outcome of that test, but you've got to take it and you're coming home with me tonight to do it."

Chapter Sixteen

There were a lot of things about West's story that Hannah knew deep down that she should hate. The fact he drugged her. That he kept her with him for several days. He'd been watching her closely for five years. He knew so much about her that he knew she'd missed her cycle and she was now sitting in the bathroom taking a pregnancy test that he'd purchased.

She didn't know why she wasn't hating him, only that she was so scared at that moment that hating him wouldn't help her.

Hannah *liked* that he'd done all those things for her.

He'd taken care of her rather than leave her for dead.

She wasn't so keen on the drugged part, but she could live with that.

West caught her hands where she was rubbing them together trying to warm them up.

"It's going to be okay."

"A baby is not in the cards." Even though he'd not been using a condom, and every chance he got, they'd been having sex, she clung onto this belief that she wouldn't get pregnant. By some miraculous design she wouldn't catch that easily.

The beep of his cell phone let them both know that it was ready.

"Do you want me to look and tell you the result?"

She shook her head. "No. We can look together."

West held out his hand and she took it, locking her fingers with his as she stood up. The test was on the counter near the sink, and as she stared down at the stick, she saw the results clearly.

"Pregnant. You're pregnant, Hannah."

He pulled her into his arms.

She was a little dazed.

Pregnant.

A little life grew inside her body.

Another human being for her to take care of.

She rested her head against his shoulder.

She thought about her mother. How she'd sit and look over the single photograph she had of Hannah from the ultrasound. She'd wanted so many children, but between life, work, and bad luck, they'd only ever had one child, her. She always wanted a brother or sister, but her mother couldn't have any more children after her.

Tears sprang to her eyes.

Her baby would never know how amazing her parents were.

"What's up, baby? I know this isn't what you asked for and that you hate me for everything that I've done…"

"It's not that."

"Then what is it?" he asked.

"They're never going to know their grandparents." She sniffled. "They would have been amazing grandparents for our baby." She put her hand on her stomach.

Pregnant.

"I don't have any family left," she said. "It's just me."

West put his hand over hers. He was so much bigger than she was in every single way. "This baby is going to want for nothing. He or she will have everyone it needs."

"But—"

"No buts. It'll have a killer aunt in Emily. I've decided she can keep breathing seeing as you and she are getting along much better now."

Hannah burst out laughing.

"She will have Emily's family as well."

"You made that family up."

"So? It doesn't mean I'm going to tear it apart just because you know the truth. Our baby needs a family, so we'll give it one. There's Rome and Cage as well. Our own little family, and they will make sure that our baby is loved."

"You can't make people fall in line, West. Or do something they really don't want to do."

"Of course I can. You're looking at the king of this city, babe. I started off in the streets, and I rule this town. Everything I've done, and everything I will do, was so that you and I could have this life." He pushed some of her hair back off her face. "Look at me. I'm not perfect. You and I both know I'm not perfect, not even close, but my love for you, that is pure when it comes to you. Tell me what to say, and I will say it for you."

"There's nothing else to say, West. I … I'm …what do we do?" she asked.

"First, you move in here with me."

She laughed.

"I'm being serious. I want to be here every single step of the way for our baby growing." His hand went to her stomach. "Then we're going to get married."

"Married?"

She couldn't believe what she was hearing. It wasn't possible, was it?

"Yes. I want you for my wife. I'm not letting either of you go."

"Marriage is a lot of change."

Did she *want* to marry him?

She knew the answer to that.

Yes. She wanted to marry him.

"All my life I've never wanted anything," she

said. "The friends or the popularity that a lot of people seemed to chase. I didn't care for it. You. Emily. All of this. I never thought I'd want something so badly, but I do. I love every single thing that you've done, and that scares me." She laughed. "You're a stalker, and rather than report you to the cops, I love it. How weird does that make me that I love you stalking me? That you've built a life around me that in some way keeps me safe? Emily, Rome, Cage, Emily's family. It is all there for me."

"Do you want to see?" he asked.

"What?"

"Everything?"

She nodded.

He took her hand, and she followed behind him, her curious nature getting the better of her as she did so. He walked down the long corridor and came to a locked door. She waited as he pulled his key out and the lock clicked open.

Entering the room, she saw a computer and lots of screens lit up.

"You have a computer room."

He let go of her hand, and she watched as he flicked on computer screens. The apartment where she lived came up on the screen.

Rome sat on one of the sofas, eating from a bowl.

The only two rooms that weren't on the screen before her were the bathroom and Emily's room.

She watched Emily come onto the screen, wrapping her hair up on top of her head. West switched the screen on.

"You don't have to sit with me. Hannah's not home."

"I'm also here to make sure you're okay."

"Ah, I've been stepped up in security for West?"

"Yep. Hannah loves you, and you know anything she loves will always be cared for."

"So sweet. I'd have not had a problem if you decided to stay here just to keep me company."

"You filmed everything?"

"I loved to watch you."

She stared at her bedroom, and her cheeks heated. "You watched me, didn't you?"

"I watched that you couldn't achieve real pleasure." His hand spread out across her stomach. "Yes, I saw that. I saw you read those dirty books and touch your pussy, but you were never able to get yourself off and it always pissed me off. Every time you didn't come hard, I knew you needed me and that I would be the only one who could give you what you needed." He ran his hand down her body, cupping her pussy.

"Don't you think Emily and Rome would be a good couple?"

"He's not the only one who wants her," West said.

"He's not?"

"No, not even close. Cage wants her as well, but I'm not going to interfere with that. The only person I care about is you." He sucked on her neck, and she gasped at the pleasure that rushed through her body.

This man was a monster. He hurt people, and in his world, he was on top.

Her own personal king.

And he wanted her.

No other woman.

"Marry me, Hannah. Let me give you the life you deserve."

One of his hands moved up to her breast, cupping the flesh. Her nipple was so hard, and she wanted him. His other hand stroked her between her thighs.

It wasn't enough.

"Please, West."

"What? Tell me what you need?"

"You. I need you. Nothing else, just you."

He bit her neck right over her pulse. Pleasure erupted around her body, and she cried out his name, not wanting him to stop. It felt so good being in his arms.

She didn't ever want to leave.

His cock pressed against her ass, and she turned so she could look at him.

Attacking his clothes, she started to pull on his shirt. Buttons sprayed everywhere as she got him naked.

West did the same, tugging on her clothes until they fell to the floor. His strength turned her on as the bite of the fabric dug into her skin as he pulled the clothes from her. When they were both naked, she kicked off her heels and he pressed her against the wall.

He grabbed her hands, holding them above her head. His lips trailed down her body, sucking on one nipple, going across to her other. He bit down on the red peaks, and she cried out, his name spilling from her lips as he soothed out the pain with the back of his tongue. He alternated between each breast, licking, sucking, biting, and lavishing her nipples with so much attention that she couldn't think straight.

The pleasure was out of this world.

He knelt down before her, and her hands dropped to her sides as he kissed her stomach.

"Hey, little baby. Daddy is right here. Right here for you." He kissed her stomach, and she closed her eyes.

They had created a life together. So beautiful.

"I'm going to take care of your momma and you when you come out. I don't care if you're a boy or a girl. I'm going to love you because you're part of me and my love." He nibbled her stomach, and she moaned once again.

Their baby.

Both she and their baby belonged to him.

Her nipples tightened, and as he lifted her leg up and his tongue stroked through her slit, she closed her eyes.

Sinking her fingers into his hair, she gasped as he bit down, seconds later stroking his tongue over the bite of pain. He slid down before plunging inside, making her cry out. He fucked her with his tongue, owning her once again. One of his hands stroked over her pussy, coating his fingers, and he drew them back to her puckered hole.

West had worked his way into her heart, and there was no way she could fight him, not that she wanted to.

She loved him more than anything else.

Marrying him, giving him a life, was what she wanted.

West had become her everything, and it may not be conventional but that didn't matter. He was hers, just as she belonged to him.

****

Sucking Hannah's clit, West nibbled on the swollen bud, using his teeth to bite down only to soothe out the pain. He was addicted to making her come, and before he took her to his room he wanted to feel her come in his mouth, to taste everything she had to give. Sliding his tongue down to her entrance, he plunged inside, feeling her tighten around his tongue. Stroking over her asshole, he felt her pussy get even wetter as he started to play with her anus.

His woman had a dirty side, and he loved that.

For the rest of their lives he was going to make every single one of her sexual fantasies come true, and he had plenty of his own.

This baby had given him the chance to bring his plan to completion. With her as his wife, he would own her in every single way.

Pushing a finger inside her ass, he started to flick his tongue back and forth over her swollen clit. With his other hand, he filled her tight pussy, adding a second finger as he started to stretch her cunt. He was a big man, and he wanted to fuck her hard without giving her time to get accustomed to his dick.

His name echoed around the room as she kept calling him. The pleasure from her mouth drove him crazy for more. He would never get tired of his name on her lips. It was perfect as far as he was concerned.

"I'm going to come," she said.

He knew as he felt her pussy squeezing his fingers, and he had no intention of stopping, not even for a second.

With a finger in her ass and two in her pussy, he drove her over the edge with an orgasm that had her screaming. If he'd not been holding her up, she'd have fallen. He would always hold her.

With his name spilling from her lips, he pulled his fingers from her body, picked her up, and carried her out toward his camera room.

"You're my crazy stalker," she said.

"I'm more than that, and you know it." Dropping her onto the bed, he followed her down. Spreading her legs wide, he reached down, gripping his cock. Running the tip over her pussy, getting himself nice and slick, he placed the head at the entrance and slammed in until his balls hit her ass.

She screamed, and he groaned as her tight cunt wrapped around him, squeezing him. He fucking loved it.

She was everything he'd ever wanted and more.

Staring down at her body, he pulled out of her

pussy until only the tip remained and slammed back inside her.

With every single thrust, her tits bounced from the action.

He loved watching her, especially as her cunt clenched his cock.

There was no denying what she wanted and needed, and he was it.

Pressing her tits together, he licked the beaded peaks, biting down on them, and she arched up.

Her legs wrapped around his waist as he drove inside her repeatedly until she couldn't think straight.

The pleasure was intense, and he knew he wasn't going to last long.

Lifting her leg up over his hip, he continued to fuck her, pounding inside her with every single thrust as she met him pushing onto his dick, driving herself closer to him. He wanted her so badly.

He was so close to orgasm, but he tried to hold off for as long as possible. That wasn't going to happen. She was everything, and he was diving headfirst into the abyss.

Slamming every single inch of his cock in deep, he closed his eyes and growled as his cum spilled out of his dick, flooding her pussy. Wave upon wave flooding her womb that was already full.

His woman.

His baby.

His future all wrapped up in one package.

Collapsing over her, he took possession of her lips, sliding his tongue into her mouth.

Hannah gripped the back of his head, kissing him back with a passion that took his breath away. She gave him everything, and he took it without any guilt.

"Tell me you'll marry me," he said.

"Yes, I'll marry you."

"You'll never be allowed a divorce, Hannah. You'll be mine."

She chuckled. "You're making it sound like I have a choice in the matter. Would you really let me leave and have another man raising your baby as his own?"

"No." He felt an overwhelming need to possess her once again.

"There's no one else I want, West. No one else that I could ever need. I love you. It scares me, and I don't think I'll ever not be afraid of the love I have for you, knowing what you're capable of."

"I won't ever hurt you. That I can promise you."

She cupped his cheek. "I know. I trust you." Her thumb stroked across his lips. He was still inside her. Cupping her face, he kissed her again.

"We're going to have to talk about the wedding. I want to get married on Sunday."

"Sunday? Are you crazy? That is two days away. There's no time to arrange anything."

"All we need is a couple of witnesses, a priest, and Vegas. We're done."

She sighed, shaking her head. "No."

"Hannah."

"No. You don't get to 'Hannah' me. You've controlled everything else about my life, and you're not going to have a say in how we get married."

"You do realize that I'm the one you're marrying."

"That may be, but we're going to get married the proper way. I was a virgin, and I want a white wedding like my parents."

"You want to get married in a church?"

"Scared you're going to set alight from all of your

sins?"

"Please, the church will love me. Three weeks."

"As long as it takes for me to organize a wedding that I want," she said. "Please, West. When we're together, I want it to be special, and I want to remember the day that you declare me as your wife to be something to remember, magical, forever."

"Is that what you want? What you really, really want?" To West, it didn't matter where he married her so long as he got his ring on her finger. His wife, the mother of his child.

"Yes."

"What about your pregnancy?"

"Then you won't have to wait too long, but I kind of like the thought of our baby seeing herself or himself at our wedding. What do you think?"

"I don't care. Just so long as you're there, forever, Hannah. I won't let you go."

He saw the smile that danced across her lips.

"I think we're going to need to negotiate."

West sighed. "How did I know that was coming?"

"Because it's not exactly right that you've been watching me for the past five years. How did you manage it?"

"A lot of strength. It was harder when your parents passed. Seeing you so upset and knowing I couldn't come and comfort you, that was tough. One of the hardest things I've ever had to do, and I've done a lot of things in my life. Sitting back, waiting, seeing you from afar, wanting to hold you. To let you know that I'm here and not being able to. That for me was torture. All I wanted to do was hold you. Love you. Tell you that you were never going to be alone." He stared into her eyes and saw the tears as they fell down her cheeks. "I don't want to make you cry."

"They're happy tears. Really happy tears." She sniffled. "I never thought it was possible to find a man that would love me the way you do. It's crazy and scary, and yet I wouldn't have it any other way." She cupped his cheek. "I love you, West Gallo. No matter how dangerous and scary it is. I will love you for the rest of my life."

"Good, because there's no way I'll ever be able to live without you. Not anymore. Not now. You own my heart, my body, and my soul. You are my greatest weakness because I love you so damn much."

He took possession of his lips.

No one else had ever made him say those words.

She was his entire world, and he would tear this place apart to make sure she had everything her heart desired. So long as he was there, he'd do everything he could to make her happy.

She'd taken his heart on her eighteenth birthday and shown him a kindness that he'd never known, and when they met again, she'd shattered his world, and now, she'd owned him, every single part of him, and he wasn't going to take it back.

Epilogue One

Five months later

Hannah held onto West's hand as the doctor placed the ultrasound device on her stomach. She was nearly six months along, but because of her honeymoon, she'd missed her last ultrasound. Now she was getting to see her baby again, and not only that, the doctor had told them they should be able to find out what the baby's sex was.

There was a knock on the door, and a nurse poked her head inside.

"Doctor Maine, you're needed in room one."

"Not now, Lucy."

"It's really important."

"Go," West said. "We can wait." He kissed her knuckles and smiled at the doctor.

She and West had been married for a month, but even before then, she saw his reputation preceded him. People from every profession were more than happy to go that extra mile for him.

"You nervous?" she asked.

"Not at all."

"You don't want it to be a boy or a girl?"

He kissed her knuckles. "I want it to be healthy. If it wants to make Daddy proud, then it'll be healthy and a happy baby, and not a cock-block."

"West." She burst out laughing. They were more than making up for lost time when it came to sex. He was always grabbing her, kissing her, fucking her, making love to her, and of course making her feel like the only woman in the world, and for him, she knew that to be true. He never looked in another woman's direction. He was always all over her, and she loved it.

When she agreed to marry him, she knew she

loved him, had no doubt about her feelings. Even as they'd been planning their wedding, she didn't realize how much she loved him. Those feelings just kept getting stronger.

Of course, she always got a little nervous when he came home late or if Cage or Rome were there. She could always tell when something was going down. West would come home in a different pair of clothes and a tension around him.

She wouldn't badger him about what was going on, but late at night, after he'd made love to her, and kissed her stomach, he'd tell her. He worked tirelessly to keep the streets clean, but she knew it came with its own set of problems. When he first started to tell her the truth, she didn't think she'd ever be able to handle it.

Now though, she found that she could. She liked that people were afraid of him because it meant that he'd be safe.

"I'm being serious. This kid in anyway stops me getting any, then they're going to be in for a rude awakening. Be it a boy, I will stop him at every turn, and a girl, please, she's staying locked up until she's fifty and can't date."

She burst out laughing. "Yeah, we'll see about that."

The doctor returned. "I'm sorry for the interruption."

"It's okay. We're just putting some things into perspective."

"Excellent."

The device was once again on her stomach, and she gripped West's hand. It wasn't painful, but she was so nervous.

She heard the sound of their baby's heartbeat. Her emotions were all over the place, and she couldn't stop the tears from running down her face.

"Well, your baby has a healthy heart, and is growing properly. A nice, big baby, that's for sure. Are you wanting to know the sex?"

"Yes." They both spoke at the same time, and she couldn't help but smile.

"Excellent."

After few seconds, he held the device over her stomach, and he turned the machine for them to look.

"Congratulations. You're going to be proud parents of a healthy, bouncing baby boy."

"A boy?"

"Yes."

"I'm going to be a dad?" West asked.

The doctor laughed. "Yes. You are."

He then pointed out the heart and other body parts. Her baby was right there in her stomach, and she fell in love. This was what she and West had made, and she loved him already.

"He's so beautiful," Hannah said.

"Just like his mother."

She cupped West's face, and she'd never thought she could be so happy in her life. He was going to be a great father, she had no doubt.

"I love you, baby. So damn much."

Her tears didn't stop. She was the luckiest woman alive. The doctor left them alone as West started to kiss her.

"You better shut your eyes, little one," West said as he lifted Hannah off the bed and got her to straddle him.

"We're in the hospital."

"Don't care. I pay a lot of money. They can let me have ten minutes."

Epilogue Two

Eighteen years later

West stared at his son, who was so much like him, it made him so proud.

"You're banning me from going out with my girlfriend."

Hannah chuckled behind him, and he glanced behind him to see her rolling out some cookies. Damn, she looked so fucking beautiful.

Their youngest daughter sat at the counter, pressing a cookie cutter into the dough as his other son placed the cut cookies onto a baking sheet.

The scent of freshly-baked cookies filled the air around them.

Ever since North had told him he was going out Friday night with one of the girls from school, West knew it wasn't going to happen. He made a vow on the one year that his son stopped him from getting his happy time with Hannah, that his time would come.

Staring at his son, he knew that time was today.

One day, North would understand.

Until then, he was going back up to his room to study.

"She's not your girlfriend. Give me your phone."

"You're being serious right now?"

"That I am. What's her name?"

"I'm not telling you."

"It's Annabeth," Thomas said.

"Tom!"

"This is what you get for spilling your secrets. You never know who is listening." He pulled up Annabeth's number and sent off a quick text. "There, all done. She knows you're not coming. Get back to your room and don't even think about giving me any lip. Off, now."

North glared at him but did as he was told.

West took great pride in being a father. All of his five children were spoiled, but he was determined for none of them to live the life he had growing up. One day soon, North would have to take his place, but when he did, he'd be ready. He wouldn't have to fight in the gutter, but he'd have the respect as West was making sure he was ready for the title.

"Off, you guys, head on upstairs. I want to kiss Mommy," he said.

His babies ran off upstairs screaming "Ewww."

"Was that really necessary?" Hannah asked, wiping her hands on a towel.

He gripped her full, rounded hips and slammed his lips down on hers. She tasted so good. Sliding one hand into her hair, he kept the other on her hip. "Yes."

"You do know he'll climb out his bedroom window, right? They have that thing on social media where they can arrange a meetup."

"If he knows what's good for him, he'll stay in his room," he said. "Cock-blocking little shit."

"He was one year old."

"And the pleasure of being a dad is being a royal pain in the ass." Running his hands down her back to her ass, he pulled her close. They'd been married over eighteen years, had five children, and he was so fucking obsessed with her still. No matter how many times he fucked her, made love to her, nothing could ever seem to the sate this need he had for her. He had cameras all over the house so that when he was out, he could watch her. She was amazing.

"You're going to stop him dating every single girl?"

"Nah, I'm going to head on upstairs and tell him to go and win his girl. I just want him to know what it's like to feel something taken from him."

She burst out laughing. "You are bad."

"I'm madly in love with you."

"Even after all this time?"

"My love doesn't have a use-by date, Hannah. I told you, from the moment we met, you were mine."

"I had no idea just how much." She cupped his face and groaned. "Go and tell your son he can date and I'll get these cookies out."

"Just so you know, your cookie is mine later, and I intend to eat you all up," he said.

He took possession of her lips as she moaned.

Be it eighteen years, ten years, fifty years, or more, the feelings he had for Hannah would never go away.

She owned him completely, just as he did her, and that kind of love never disappeared. It only got stronger.

The End

www.samcrescent.com

EVERNIGHT PUBLISHING ®

www.evernightpublishing.com

www.ingramcontent.com/pod-product-compliance
Lightning Source LLC
Chambersburg PA
CBHW030238200626
46816CB00002BA/423